Death's Dimensions

Books by Victor Koman

From *PULPLESS*.COM, INC.

Death's Dimensions
The Jehovah Contract
Solomon's Knife
Kings of the High Frontier
Jules Verne's Frankenstein (forthcoming)

The Captain Anger Adventures
#1: The Microbotic Menace
#2: The Ivory Tower (forthcoming)

From Other Publishers

Millennium: Weeds

Spaceways
(written as "John Cleve" with Andrew J. Offutt)
#13: Jonuta Rising!
#17: The Carnadyne Horde

Death's Dimensions

a psychotic space opera

by

Victor Koman

PULPLESS.com, inc.
775 East Blithedale Ave., Suite 508
Mill Valley, CA 94941, USA.
Voice & Fax: (500) 367-7353
Home Page: http://www.pulpless.com/
Business inquiries to info@pulpless.com
Editorial inquiries & submissions to
editors@pulpless.com

PULPLESS.COM, INC.

Death's Dimensions is a work of fiction. All names, places, and institutions (both statist and free) are either completely imaginary or used fictitiously. Any resemblance to actual persons—living, dead, or cloned—or to actual events, locales, or myths of mental illness is entirely coincidental.

First Pulpless.Com™, Inc. Edition August, 1999.
Library of Congress Catalog Card Number: 99-62013
ISBN: 1-58445-093-2

Book and Cover designed by CaliPer, Inc.
Cover Illustration by Billy Tackett, Arcadia Studios
© 1999 by Billy Tackett

This version of *Death's Dimensions* began as a short story written in early 1977 and published in the Feb., 1978 (Vol. 39, No. 2) issue of *Galaxy* Magazine by editor John J. Pierce. I began the rest of the novel 8 October, 1977, at 8:21 a.m. (yes, I made a note of it) and finished it 7 July, 1978. On the same day, I wrote the first line of what was to become *The Jehovah Contract*, just so I could tell myself that I was maintaining a professional continuity.

I scanned the manuscript of *Death's Dimensions* into electronic text format in the summer of 1990. The cleanup took until 18 February, 1991 to complete (I had to paint my house, but that is another tale of horror).

I finally began the rewrite 11 August, 1992, and finished at 6:35 p.m. on 26 August. I finished the computer input at 7:15 am, 24 September, and the final work is what you hold in your hands. —V.K.

For Sam, Neil, Andy, Charles, Chris, John, and Bob,
who put up with me at the AnarchoVillage
while I wrote this pæan to madness.
And also for Bernie,
who probably should *not*
read this a second time.

Table of Contents

Chapter One

7 March, 2107

His death wish surpassed that of any mortal. And yet it bestowed upon him—and only him—the power of flight between the stars.

He was Virgil Grissom Kinney, and he was insane beyond hope.

Caged and bound in a madhouse he festered like a scorned, feared animal. In an age when madmen were almost unknown, he was a ranting exception. Sometimes he raged against his restraints with muscle-tearing fury. Other times he retreated into catatonic silence, conducting a silent, internal war.

Drugs, nutrition, therapies from Freud to Szasz to Bhodhota all proved useless.

Virgil Grissom Kinney wanted only one thing from life.

Death.

At a time when people left one another alone to do as they pleased, no one would have cared or interfered if Virgil wanted only to kill himself, yet in an era without police or prisons, Virgil Grissom Kinney lay locked behind padded walls, screaming without sound, tortured without pain.

"You've never seen a bad paraschiz, have you?" the MentTech asked.

The woman walking beside him adjusted the white labcoat thrown hastily over her shoulders.

"Only in history scrims," she said.

"Then listen carefully. Treat him exactly as you would a feral genesplice you might encounter in an alley. You don't have any way of knowing who he thinks you are or why he suspects you're speaking to him, so never start up a casual conversation. If he thinks you're the Horned God, you could be talking about the weather and he'd read hidden meanings into it. Never stare him in the eye. Never touch him. And most important—"

"Yes?" The woman's face lost any color it had.

"If and when he speaks, you *listen.*"

She nodded gravely. The corridor they walked down radiated a soothing, cool blue glow. The woman drew no calm from the psychological color cue. She strode toward an appointment with the destiny of the human race and saw little pleasure and even less comfort in the knowledge that Earth's best hope was entombed in an asylum.

"One more thing," the huge orderly added. "If he frightens you, tell him so. Be firm and polite and exceedingly honest."

"Straight," she said in agreement.

He touched his scan finger to the lockscrim. "And never turn your back on him."

She swallowed. Her throat scraped like sandpaper against brick.

He had spent so many years in the same creme-white room that he thought he could detect sounds through the soundproof padding.

The familiar footsteps of the orderly intermingled with another lighter set.

Two sets of footsteps, Virgil thought. Mad images and personalized symbols trickled through his fragmented thoughts like rain through desert sands.

Marsface is coming here. He still favors the right leg I bit so long ago. He clumps and slides beside a pair of feet that move lightly and quickly.

He twisted about to face the door. Wrapped more than snugly

in gauze bandages that restrained him from head to toe, Virgil Grissom Kinney squirmed on the floor with all the grace of an arthritic caterpillar. His psychotic mind picked through an alien host of archetypes in a frenzied effort to make sense of his narrow world.

The other walks on soft, quick feet. Sent by Master Snoop. Master Snoop knows I've figured the way out. The machinery inside the ceiling is up there watching me. Master Snoop never slumbers. The wires in my head spy for him.

Kinney rolled about to stare at the blank wall. Indirect lighting bathed the room in a soft, soothing golden glow. A slender trapezoidal shadow suddenly cut across the surface of the padding. Silently, the room's only door opened inward.

Mental Health Technician William Bearclaw entered, scrimboard in hand. His short black hair crested in a delta-sweep cut that was three years out of style. Tall and husky, he ducked his head to clear the lintel of the thickly padded doorway.

Virgil had no knowledge of styles, fads, or even dates. He only saw madness and tried to make sense of it.

Marsface. I knew it, didn't I? Same Marsface—head like a red planet with its ridges and craters and mole-mountains, a nose like Olympus Mons.

Virgil stared at the other visitor, puzzled.

Though tall, she stood a head shorter than Bearclaw; high heels plus long black hair piled up Grecian style failed to bring her up to his height. A single thick rope of hair extended from the plaits to wrap once around her neck. The roughsects hairstyle had grown in popularity from its origin in a small sado-masochistic sex cult to its fashionable apex in polite society. The roughsects, seeing their style embraced by outsiders, had long since abandoned it for new coifs, which were also working their way up the fashion escalator in competition with other bizarre looks.

Kinney peered at the woman, his impressions filtered through the dark glass of insanity.

Death Angel doesn't look the way he's supposed to. Where is the scythe? Death Angel disguises as a woman. Master Snoop's trying to screw me up. It won't work. I know how to get out and I don't need them.

He listened to them as carefully as he could, weighing every nuance.

They're speaking in their Language again. Got to concentrate and break their code.

Bearclaw, though he used the proper term of address required by *devoir*, spoke to her with casual authority. "Yes, *tovar* Trine, you can see the lengths we had to go through to restrain him. A man can kill himself against a padded wall if he keeps pounding it continually. Dies of exhaustion and dehydration."

Delia Trine observed the form wrapped from head to toe in gauze that had once been white. Two tubes, mercilessly transparent, extended from the overlays of cloth around his crotch. The wastes they carried away both displayed sickeningly unhealthy colors.

The woman took a deep breath, tried to calm her stomach's reaction to the sight. The vaguely rotten odor from the bandages did not help.

"What is his specific class?"

Bearclaw did not need to scroll through the scrimsheet in his hand. "Psychotic. Paranoid-schizophrenic. With a good dose of manic depressive, though I've never seen him manic in this place."

"Any record of treatment with Duodrugs?" She knelt down to take a closer look at the prisoner's face, to gaze coolly into Kinney's green eyes, practically the only part of him not wrapped in restraining sheets.

Bearclaw cleared his throat loudly.

She realized that she was staring, and stood quickly. A shudder raced through her.

She had never seen eyes that glared with such furious intensity.

The MentTech shook his head. "Duodrugs have no effect on him. The Pharmaceutics are mystified, but I think Virgil here has a highly compartmentalized multiple personality. We can drug one or two of them, but he always has one that surfaces unaffected." His expression grew concerned. "Don't tell anyone that, though. He's never displayed any symptoms of that. Drugs are supposed to affect the physical brain, anyway, not the mind."

Kinney lay near the center of the room—on his side—looking like the huge, stained cocoon of some mysterious creature that might suddenly break free to attack with terrible fury and unfathomable insect logic.

His gaze returned hers, sharp and startlingly alert. A curl of sweaty, greasy blonde hair looped out from under his bandages to hang over one eyebrow. Kneeling again and trying not to stare, Delia tucked the stray hairs back under the wraps with her long, blood-red fingernails.

Virgil strained, trying to roll back from her. To his tortured mind, the simple gesture set off a wave of terror.

What's she trying? To claw inside my head? I want to die with my brain inside. *Must map my escape but don't think about it. Think about death to hide my plan. Death death death to the Master Snoop.*

He glared back at the woman.

Death Angel's midnight hair wraps a snake around her ivory throat. Isn't she afraid they'll strangle her? Stupid—Death Angel has no fear of her master. I haven't heard her upstairs before, have I? Think, stupid, think.

Bearclaw knelt beside the woman. "If this were the twenty-first century," he said, "Virgil would've been declared certifiably insane. He'd have been put in an institution against his will."

Trine frowned as she stood. "He's not quite part of the joy division here, is he?"

Bearclaw nodded and rose. "It's a fine line, isn't it? Because his insurance policy had an insanity care clause, he was put away morally and legally."

"So the difference between the way the Fets might once have treated him and the way he's being treated now is his signature on some old scrim." The woman tried not to watch Kinney's eyes as they gazed mutely up at her.

The MentTech smiled. "The difference between DuoLab and the Fetters is that if Virgil's bill isn't paid, he's out on his retro."

"Who funds his upkeep?" she asked.

"Paid in advance by Tri-World Life, for life plus rejuvenation. The circumstances are unu—"

"Could I have a gurney brought in now?"

"Yes, *tovar*." Bearclaw scribbled the instruction onto his scrimsheet. The dispatching computer acknowledged with a green glow on the upper bar of the notepad.

Trine folded her arms and considered her find. "He's never tried to use a seppukukit?"

Bearclaw shook his dark head, pulling a viewscrim from the file folder to hand to her. "Here's his file. You'll see that his personality doesn't run in those directions. Quiet and private is not the way he wants to die. He wants to go down in flames. Are you sure you can use him?"

Without answering, she held out her hand to receive the thin viewscrim. She slipped it into her notebook, frowning at a thought. "Who put him away here in the first place?"

"The perpetual care clause was activated by his insurance company when his last suicide attempt demolished about a kilauro worth of property and killed a family of four tourists." Noticing the curious expression growing on Trine's angular face, he added, "He's a threat, *tovar*. A genuine threat. He's not an intentional murderer. It's just that when he tries suicide, innocent people are in harm's way."

"Does he talk about it?"

Bearclaw's black eyes gazed back at hers. "We've never been able to get him to say a word."

She nodded. "The Brennen Trust has a place for him."

"I can't imagine where, *tovar* Trine."

She smiled with studied warmth. "Glad to be rid of him?"

The big man said nothing.

Green eyes watched the exchange with uncomprehending panic. Bandaged ears strained but heard only the rush of blood.

Death Angel and Marsface leave me without devouring my soul. No death today, but beware of tricks. I'll have to meet the man in the nightsheet on my own terms. Cleanse myself with fire. If only I could touch my pain. Crush my brain. Aladdin sane.

Virgil closed his eyes.

Virgil's eyes opened in a different room. His body trembled and sweated within its constraints.

I've made it! It worked and I didn't even have to think about it! Free! Almost. Why did I bring the sheets with me? Stupid— they were too close to you. I'll get out, though. Did Master Snoop follow me? Can't tell. Too noisy. Is this the Control room? Did I escape right into their clutches?

"He's awake, Dee." The graying Pharmaceutic sat near a bank of indicators flashing red, turquoise, yellow, and orange.

Delia Trine needed no brain wave analyzers to see Kinney open his eyes. He lay at the center of the lab on a wide table with raised edges, white and mummylike against soft black sudahyde. Wires from the electrodes on his head emerged like vines from under his wrappings to drape over the couch and flow into the equipment surrounding him. The few sections of wall that lacked machinery displayed soothing mahogany-toned fauxwood paneling.

Virgil shuddered, his gaze darting about to see the others.

Lights. Sounds. Operators. I escaped, all right. Right up into the ceiling with Master Snoop. Death Angel, too. They wouldn't let Marsface in here, though—he's just a tool. Damn.

The woman whispered toward the Pharmaceutic. "Lock the eyetrace on his gaze, Steve. I don't think he's a paraschiz as DuoLab thought."

Ignoring what Bearclaw had told her, she deliberately pinioned Kinney's abstracted stare with a stern glare of her own. "Virgil Grissom Kinney," she said in a level tone. She waited for the eyes to focus on her before she continued. "Good. Virgil, I'm going to give you something you were never given at DuoLab. I'm going to give you a choice. Do you remember what a choice is?"

The pupils of Kinney's green eyes constricted slightly. *Death Angel hovers over me as I lay in my coffin. Soft, stupid coffin with no lid. Red lips move cunningly. I can almost break her code. She wants something. I'll agree, go along with it for now. The roar hasn't been broken yet. Break the roar and I can crack her code. Easy, easy. Take it easy.*

He nodded slowly. His gaze narrowed into something less fearful, something more focused.

The woman watched his reactions the way a cat observes the motions of stalked prey. "Good," she said, straightening up. "Virgil, they tell me you like to kill yourself."

She knows about them! She must—she's one of them. Remember that. He twitched in amazement. *The roar is quieter now. Words pass through Master Snoop's jamming with greater frequency.*

"I'm going to offer you a choice," Trine continued. "I have two IVs here." She gestured toward a cart on which lay a pair of clear plastic sacks filled with opaque gray liquid, one labeled with a skull and crossbones, one with a bright yellow happy face. "This one"—she picked up the death's head bag— "is a poison that will kill you in a matter of seconds. This other"—she showed him the smiling bag—"will help you overcome your... predicament. Blink your eyes once for poison or twice for salvation."

His mouth opened slightly, teeth pressing against his lower lip.

"Fuh—"

"What?" She leaned closer to him, picking up a pair of bandage scissors and delicately snipping away the gauze from his throat and jaw. Saliva drooled across his cheek.

"Fff... Fuh-false dichotomy."

She laid the scissors aside and frowned.

The Pharmaceutic smiled. "I think that means he doesn't want to play."

"It doesn't matter anyway," she said to Virgil. "I'd have switched labels to make sure you'd get this one." She held up the bottle with the happy face. "The other's just colored water."

She pulled an IV stand over to the table. "I'm injecting this into you, false dichotomy or not. The Brennen Trust bought out the premium on your insurance policy. We've bailed you out for a reason and we want a return on our investment. Or would you prefer to remain wrapped and strapped forever?"

Virgil lay absolutely still, every muscle locked in rigid tension. *What's the dance she's treading? I thought I had her code. Maybe all I have is her cipher. Yes. Cipher to know what she's saying, no code to know what she means. If I could get out of my room, maybe I can escape from this one, too. Three, four, five times I'll try.*

Slowly, his gaze never leaving hers, Virgil nodded as far as his swathing allowed. Then he stopped, reconsidered the question, and shook his head slowly from side to side.

"Fine," Trine said. "Steve, you can take it now."

The Pharmaceutic brought a needle kit over to Virgil's side. He wore an impeccably benign smile. The IV package unsealed with a crackle of plastic. In the corner of the room, a videoscrim panel fluxed to zoom in on the operation.

The only patch of Kinney's flesh other than his face to lay open and exposed was the injection port in his left wrist surgically sewn and laser welded to skin and vein. The old man pushed the blunted needle into the plastic valve. It clicked bayonet-style into place.

Steve draped the tubing through the flow regulator and switched it on. The murky gray serum trickled slowly toward Virgil's arm. The electroencephalograph and brain wave topograph registered the imperceptible changes in Kinney's brain. These appeared as shifting colors on an output scrim visible only to the Pharmaceutic.

It's not working, Virgil thought. *Whatever they're trying is failing. I don't feel any different. Should I gloat? No. Play along. How should I act, though? I need to find something to finish Master Snoop and Nightsheet once and for all. Something big. Straight, straight.*

Trine bent over the side of the table. She spoke quietly to Kinney while the Pharmaceutic administered the serum.

"What you're getting, Virgil, is a mixture of saline solution, ribonucleic acid, and picotechs. The RNA is memory juice. Practically every living thing has it. The picotechs are tiny machines that carry the second and more important component of memory. All this came from a man who worked for the Brennen Trust before he died." Her voice paused for just an instant. "We want to know why he died, but you probably won't be able to tell us that right away. When he died, though, he possessed skills and knowledge that take a long time to learn. We're cutting corners this way because we're in a hurry."

Virgil nodded nervously, a trickle of sweat running down his brow. Beneath his bandages, his muscles tightened rigidly.

They're filling me up with machines that carry someone else's mind! Maybe I can get him to help me. I don't hear him, though. And now the roar is coming back. I'm losing her cipher. Down. Back. Focus. They're trying to make it hard for me. I'll get out, though. There! Less roar and her cipher's broken again.

"It's the picotechs," she continued, "that make the process work. They were in this other man's bloodstream and brain, recording his unique electrochemical patterns. They'll reproduce them at similar sites in your own brain. Instant memories. No need to go to school."

Deep inside Kinney's body, machines no larger than a molecule sought out their topologically programmed locations. Picotunnelers bored through the blood-brain barrier, admitting the rest of the invaders. Picosculptors attached to low-activity areas of Kinney's cerebrum, reshaping neural connections, synapses, and electrochemical order to simulate those of a man now dead. Picogenerators duplicated the peaks and valleys of another brain's unique electrical field. Picolocators awaited their particular strand of RNA to pass by in the bloodstream. When they did, they mated with the strands; mated chemically, topographically, electrically—more intimately than the minds that created them could imagine.

Impossible to see with anything less powerful than an atomic force microscope, the picotechs were simple. Individually, each one was a mere molecule with an unique topography and electrical charge. Collectively, they possessed the power of a god.

They used part of Virgil Grissom Kinney's brain to create a mimic of another man's mind. Synapse by synapse, picovolt by picovolt, a stranger began to form in Kinney's mind, undetected. Silently, another man's memories crept into Kinney, quiescent and patient.

Trine slipped the top of the scrim into her clipboard and

signaled the first page. She glanced at Kinney.

"While we're doing this, I'd like you to answer a few questions and listen to some things so that we can make sure everything is working properly. Straight?"

Virgil nodded.

"Straight. Shake your head only if you *don't* remember any of the following." She scanned the page a moment before reading. "Virgil Grissom Kinney. Age thirty-four."

Kinney's eyes widened.

With a compassionate gaze, she said, "You didn't know that, did you? It's March seventh, twenty-one-aught-seven. You've been interned for eleven years, ever since you tried to kill yourself by flying into the PacRim Pyramid. Do you remember that?"

Kinney's blond eyebrows knotted in thought. He shook his head as best he could beneath his bandages.

Trine scrolled to another page. She held her voice at a professionally flat level. "June twelfth, twenty-ninety-four. After the funerary processing of your wife Jenine, you piloted your flyer over downtown St. Frisco toward the PacRim Pyramid. Instead of hitting the side of the building, you flipped into a power dive toward Market Street. Your crash killed four people. You would have done even worse during a workday."

Virgil stared blankly, slowly shaking his head. "They were clones," he offered weakly.

She glanced at the scrim "Two clones—a direct, a sexflip, and their two natural-born children. The primogenitor sued for loss of lineage and Tri-World Life paid off. Then they sent you here."

Virgil nodded. Softly, Delia said, "You don't really want to die, do you?"

The Pharmaceutic gazed at the indicators. "Galvanic response shooting up," he whispered to her. "That's a key question."

She nodded without shifting her eyes. "If you don't want to

die, why bother trying? Publicity hound?"

Virgil lay mute, his gaze indecipherable.

She leaned closer. "Not likely—three of your attempts were made in wilderness areas. You managed to be found barely alive each time." A strand of her ebon hair fell from around her neck. Virgil watched it sway in time to her words. "You are here because I think your conflicting dichotomy of a death wish and death aversion combined with astonishingly good luck is a mix we can use to our mutual benefit." She turned toward the Pharmaceutic. "Begin sublimins, Steve."

The gray man muttered a series of commands to the lab computer.

Gazing more intently at Kinney, Trine said, "You earned a degree in nexialism from Mises University, which means you know a little bit about everything. That will help, because I'm going to give you and your new memories a refresher course in physics. Keep in mind the following nexus: physics is the economics of efficient atomic interaction, and multi-dimensional mathematics is the topography of cosmology."

She pulled up a chair to sit beside Virgil. "Now, all sub-atomic particles are composed of combinations of just two bounded energy quanta, one positive, one negative. Their overall sum determines the mass of the particle, its charge, and whether it is matter or anti-matter. Their topographical interaction determines such aspects as charm, spin, strangeness and..."

Kinney lay upon the cool black sudahyde couch, his yellowed bandages looking whiter in contrast. His chest rose and fell in short whiffs and exhalations. The room smelled of formaldehyde and disinfectant. Through his narrow field of view, he gazed at the silent bank of instruments against the wall.

Three days. Three days and I still don't understand her code. I've got her cipher all figured out—the physics of space travel.

So play along. Go along with them until you find out how they—

A door opened somewhere. Kinney twisted about to see Trine step through. She wore a light aqua lab coat over a charcoal suit.

Here she comes again. Death Angel dressed to fill. Fill my mind like a cupcupcup...

"Good morning, Virgil." She pulled a tall stool over to sit beside him. "I hope you're feeling better today, because we have a lot planned. I'm going to remove those ratty bandages. It's time you got out of the things for good." She smiled encouragingly.

Virgil simply stared.

"However," she continued when she realized he would not return her smile, "it can be physically dangerous to you in your atrophied condition. So let's proceed slowly, all right?"

Large bandage scissors went to work on his head, guided by Delia's graceful, strong fingers.

"How long has it been since they changed these?" she muttered. "A month? Two?"

Kinney shrugged, or tried to. "Maybe a year." His voice was weak, creaky.

Trine's hand inadvertently withdrew from him. Regaining her composure, she continued to snip away. "Nice to hear you speak."

She pulled the clipped gauze from around his head. A shock of sweaty, oily yellow hair clung to the fabric. She tugged gently. Most of the hair remained on his head, though some stuck wetly to the greasy fabric.

She frowned. "At least you're not completely depilated. A good wash and it should be back to normal."

"Thanks." Virgil basked in the warm feeling of her hand against his skin. *So long since a touch. Maybe she's not working for Master Snoop. Could she be a free agent? Maybe Master Snoop and Nightsheet aren't conspiring anymore. Maybe they're enemies again. I need more information. Listen. Hold back the roar.*

His right arm fell limply to the couch. Deathly white, translucent, and almost entirely devoid of muscle, it looked like a skeleton wrapped in a thin coating of papier-mâché.

Delia shook her head. His other arm looked just as bad. Worse—a hideous burn scar ran its length.

"Why didn't they fix that?" she muttered, continuing to snip down his torso.

Kinney's chest, freed from restraint, heaved to suck in great gulps of air.

"Don't," she said. "You'll hyperventilate." She held the scissors at a fixed angle and ripped them through the cloth around his waist, thighs, and legs. Pulling the fabric away, she gazed at the naked form beneath.

Her crimson lips formed a gentle smile. "Well, you're a real blond, all right."

His sudden bark of laughter startled her. Jumping back from the couch, she watched in amazement as his arms waved heedlessly about, bouncing off the sides of the couch before coming to rest on his flat stomach, the only part of him that had any musculature at all.

After waiting a moment for him to calm down, she said, "Hold still, Virgil." She put down the scissors and laid a hand on his narrow thigh. "This may hurt." Her long fingers grasped the waste cycling tube that snaked between his legs up into his rectum. With a gentle-but-firm tug, she twisted and removed it.

Virgil moaned, hovering somewhere between pain and relief.

She deflated the urine catheter. "You go on light solids and muscle food tomorrow. And you begin your training."

"And if I don't want to?" A sneer flashed palely across Virgil's lips.

She pulled out the catheter with a smooth, firm motion.

He screamed.

"Then," she said, "I guess we'll have to wrap you up again."

He whimpered, doubling over to clutch at his savaged member.

Somewhere deep within Virgil's searing pain rose one coherent thought. It echoed over and over in his mind, creating its own nearly infinite loop.

The roar's coming back.

As he folded in on himself, so did his thoughts. He fought the urge.

Nightsheet drags me down down down. Master Snoop shrieks in joy at the burning in my center. Back. Down. Don't. Don't back down.

He forced his eyes open, forced his reverberating mind to focus on the woman in the aqua coat. The color soothed him. The red noise subsided in his mind.

"What's your name?" he asked after a few moments. "What's your true name?"

She tilted her head a bit in curiosity at both his question and his quick recovery from physical pain.

"My name's Dee."

"Dee? The necromancer?"

She shook her head, smiling. "That's my first name. Short for Delia."

"What's the rest?"

"My name is Delia Trine."

Death Angel bares her fangs in a glee without hunger. I cracked part of her code. Good. Press on.

"Did you spring me just to give me that physics lesson?"

Delia thought it remarkable that he adjusted so well to sudden change. She suspected that the braindump from Jord might be aiding in his stabilization.

"Actually, Virgil, you're here because the Brennen Trust made a mistake. A fatal mistake with a man named Jord Baker. You're going to help us find out why he died. We've given you some preliminary theoretical data on a new concept of interstellar travel. The RNA-PT injection and subliminal instructions—"

Aha! Virgil smiled at the confirmation of his suspicion.

"—have stored inside your brain everything Jord Baker knew up to the point of his death. When we begin training, you'll remember things you never knew before. You may be experiencing memories right now as you listen." She paused. Virgil looked up at her and shrugged weakly.

"Well," she said, "your mind needs to recall the information and re-file it. That may take some time." She slid the stool closer to the table and sat near Virgil's naked form.

"Are you cold?" she asked.

He shook his head. His long golden hair had dried to a stiff, dull mess. His eyes watched her with relentless intensity.

She took a deep breath. "Here's the whole story. Jord Baker was a test pilot for the Brennen Trust's spacecraft division. He was testing out a teleportation craft when he killed himself. We can't figure out why. We've—"

"Teleportation?" Kinney asked. He searched his memory. His, and what fragments arose of Jord Baker's.

Trine nodded. "It's a method that could make every other form of space travel obsolete. It was just ten years ago that Ernesto Valliardi developed a mathematically *provable* theory of pandimensional translocation. Without a device that could generate the field collapse, though, the theory was nothing more than a curiosity. Until two years ago. That's when Brennen Trust researchers, using portions of Valliardi's research to develop a multidimensional method of non-destructive metallurgical testing, accidentally teleported a small steel pellet three meters across their lab. It appeared in midair and exploded."

She leaned on the soft sudahyde. "If it had appeared in some-

thing more solid, the blast would have left nothing but a crater where the building stood." Her grin was almost feral with
joy at retelling the tale. "It seems that if the nucleus of a
teleported atom appears within the same space as that of an
atom at the destination, they mutually annihilate." She lowered her chin onto her clasped hands. "The resulting explosion was still big enough to kill a dozen people in the lab. Including Grigori Felitsen, the inventor of the process. Computers and video captured all the info, though, and we refined the
process in hard vacuum at Brennen Orbital."

Virgil nodded. Thoughts began to rush to him without sum-
mon. Topological images of six- and twelve-dimensional space
flickered at the edges of his consciousness. Mental constructs
of an intricately folded universe made sense to him even though
he had never studied anything more complex than calculus.

Can this, he thought, *be what Master Snoop feels, sucking
the minds of all around, a constant flood of incoming knowledge, sights, sounds, facts, ideas?*

Delia continued, noting Virgil's facial reactions with professional excitement. Her gaze also drank in the rest of his form.
She noted that his flesh responded to the rush of knowledge
by pricking up the blond hairs on his arms, shoulders, and
legs.

"Finally," she said, "Brennen engineers built a small ship
that could teleport by remote control. The most important aspect of the Valliardi Transfer is that *it requires no receiving
station.*"

"It's not teleportation, really." Virgil frowned in amazement
at the authoritative manner of his speech. "It's a concept in
many-dimensional theory. Every point in a lower-order dimension is in contact with a point in any higher-order dimension."
His frown transformed itself into a weak grin. "It's all coming
back to me."

Delia sat up and smiled. "See if this jogs more memories:

Every point on a one-dimensional line can be reached from a two-dimensional plane without crossing any other linear point. Any point on a plane can be touched from three-dimensional space without passing through any other point on the plane. And so on up the dimensional ladder."

"I *know*," Virgil said. "I *know* it without knowing *how* I know it!"

Delia nodded with enthusiasm. "Jord understood the fundamentals of dimensional topology, though Valliardi's Proof was too much for him. He could push the right buttons, though, and was the finest test pilot we had. After a dozen successful robot flights, he performed the first human test. He traveled from lunar orbit to Jupiter in an instant."

Kinney rolled over on his side, his skin sliding over the sudahyde without adhesion. His own enthusiasm began to grow, unaided by the dead man's memories.

"You mean," he said, "that you've developed *instantaneous* teleportation?"

"Almost. The trip took only a subjective instant for him. For us, it was as if he'd disappeared for over half an hour. When he reached Jovian orbit, a laser beacon switched on automatically. It was another half an hour before we received that beam, so we know that he was literally *outside the universe* for that length of time."

Virgil's stare turned solid. "Where was he?" *Half an hour away from Master Snoop? Away from Nightsheet? Time spent out from under the prying eyes of God?*

Delia gently brushed her long fingernails against the coil of black hair wrapped around her neck. "Nowhere, apparently. The experiment turned out to be the vindication of Einstein. Even if we use the Valliardi Transfer to travel instantly from here to there, the traveler is still out of the universe for exactly the length of time it would take for light to travel that distance. It would take *you* an instant to transfer to Alpha Centauri, but when you arrived, the universe would be four years older. Or you could transfer to the center of the galaxy like that"— she snapped her fingers—"and the rest of the universe will have aged twenty-six thousand years."

Virgil stared at her. "A one-way time machine," he whispered in awe. Unconsciously, his thin, bony fingers reached down to touch below his waist.

Delia gazed in puzzlement at the swelling flesh Virgil grasped in his hand.

Chapter Two

30 March, 2107

She can't expect me to do it. She can't. What do I know about these things?

Virgil lifted his head to look around, then dropped it back to the cushions. He enjoyed the exercise, the fresh air, the bulk-building food. Four meals a day. Real food. Steak from the Saharan grasslands. Fresh fruit from the vast orchards of Paine, the rich farmland on the Potomac created from the ruins of the old imperial Capitol. Huge vegetables dropped from Cornucopia Orbital. Vitamins and brain-food drugs from the vast chemical labs just south of Iverson, Earthward Luna.

He exercised in the spacious seventh level sky lobby on the four hundredth floor of the Brennen Spike in downtown Houston. The equipment stood near the windows and, from the fifteen hundred meter vantage, Virgil regained his strength and stamina while observing the busy world below him. Every now and then he would pause to watch a thin trail of vapor rise from the south—another launch from Port Velasco.

The lessons and tests he had received over the last three weeks surprised him. He knew far more than the calculus of his youth. And every unlearned memory came to him at just the moment he needed it. What other bits of Jord Baker, he wondered, lurked inside his head, dormant for now?

The steady, machinelike rhythm of the equipment soothed Virgil by blanking out other sounds: the whisk of elevator doors, the rustle of clothing and scrape of shoes of the people who walked through the lobby, the subsonic rumble of the wind-compensating pendulum near the top floor.

As he built up his body, his mind grew in strange and unanticipated ways. Quietly. Unnoticed even by Virgil.

His surface thoughts, though clearer, were as mad as ever.

Pilot a spaceship? I'd be a man in a can, really. Just put in the coordinates they give me and punch one button. And if I put in the wrong coordinates, I appear in something solid maybe, and kapow! *Like an atom bomb.* He smiled.

"It's today, Virgil."

He turned. Delia Trine stood in the door of the access shaft.

Death Angel's hair still tries to strangle her. Lovely Death Angel, I know you work for Nightsheet...

"The test?" he said. "I'm ready?"

"As ready as you'll ever be."

She's right. The roar that clouds my mind fades with every moment. I crack all ciphers I hear. I've almost cracked Death Angel's code, too.

"All right." He wiped a handful of hair from his eyes. "Big question: why did you pick me? Out of all the billions in the solar system, why choose someone who's been locked up for over a decade? You don't do this every day. I know what you had to do to Baker's body to get the RNA after he killed himself. The fall must have mashed him up a bit, but you had to mince him into strawberry jam to get that stuff."

Delia looked at him, considering. "Let's go."

The lift descended. "Jord was mentally well-balanced," she told him. "Cool, level-headed, not the sort to panic under any circumstance. When a man most people would call normal suddenly decides to kill himself after testing the Valliardi Transfer, something's wrong—and not with Jord. We picked you because your psychological profile is the opposite of Jord's. You behave in an unstable manner, are prone to wild mood swings, and are violent in a narrowly specific way. You've tried to commit suicide several times but never succeeded for some reason. Our psychologists suggested that you may survive long enough to give us some idea of what's wrong with the device.

Do you have any memory of what happened on Jord's flight?"

Virgil leaned against the rear of the lift. "No. All I feel are snatches of images that are not part of my own memory. Aircraft and spacecraft, mostly. Views from on high." He stared with an eerie fixedness at Delia. "And women."

Her gaze broke away from his. She cleared her throat to say: "Our floor." They stepped out into the ground level atrium. Port Velasco lay only a short flyer-hop south.

The Brennen Trust executive shuttle squatted like a tick on the personal spacecraft field a dozen kilometers away from the towering freightcraft. The stubby forty-meter rocket pointed straight up in liftoff position awaiting the pair's arrival.

Kinney wore the Brennen trademark gray jumpsuit with maroon test-pilot's piping. Trine wore gray with executive-white piping, her hair wrapped for freefall in a matching gray-and-white turban.

He hesitated at the entrance hatch.

"What's wrong?" Delia asked.

"I've never gone orbital before."

She placed a gentle hand against his back. "It's less scary than a flyer. Come on."

He stepped over the threshold. The flight deck contained plush sudahyde acceleration couches arranged in a circle, feet toward the central structural column, heads under windows in the tapering nose cone. *I have no memory of this, yet I know that the pilots sit in that pie-wedge section to the left and that the safest place to sit is the seat next to the hatch. Baker—ghost in my head—are you watching?*

A portly man in gray and umber reclined in the first couch. Kinney stood at his feet and gazed at him.

"What're you staring at?" the man asked.

"You're in my seat," Kinney said in an odd voice.

"Says who?"

Kinney's eyes widened into a mad stare. "Says God."

"Virgil"—Delia tried to direct him away—"any seat will do."

"Not on a doomed flight," he said, gazing with unblinking intensity at the man.

Behind him, Trine made dismissing motions for the passenger to see. What he saw and noted was her white piping. Muttering about "cush-pampered test-pilot blowheads," he rolled off the couch and made his way to the far side of the ship where the pilots' cabin and central column blocked the view.

Kinney reclined on the couch, the upholstery still warm from the other man's body.

Why did you want this seat, Baker? Are you waking up?

Delia strapped into the seat beside him. She stared at him, hoping not to appear as if she was staring.

Five more people boarded shortly before blastoff. Virgil eyed each one with severe scrutiny, as if he were in judgment of their lives.

Candycane walks in hunched over from the low ceiling, his red-white jumpsuit rumpled and twisted, his eyes goggling at me. He sits like a crumpled bag next to Gooseflesh, who's all prickle-hair nervous at the prospect of rocket flight. Or maybe at sitting near me. Why are they watching me while trying to avoid watching?

Virgil grinned strangely during the shaking at engine ignition and the sudden pressure of blastoff. His grin became a wolfish grimace at the period of maximum dynamic pressure.

Crush me, giants, he thought while the world thundered around him. *Try to squeeze me into nothing. I shall break free.*

Suddenly, he did.

The engines cut off and he gazed out of the viewing port at star-riddled blackness.

"Ladies and gentlemen," the pilot announced over the intercom, "we've broken the law of gravity again and are in orbit."

Trine smiled at the pilot's superstitious phrase, a saying that went back more than a century to a time when launching a spaceship without Fetter permission was an actual crime. She glanced over at Kinney. He stared with wide eyes at the planet's surface rotating into view. The reds, browns, and deep greens of AfricaLand marched past with silent grace. The verdant checkerboard and circles that marked the Sahara Cooperative drifted next into view.

Virgil drank in the broad vista through the tiny polycarbonate window for long moments until a buzzer announced their arrival at the Texas Spaceways terminal.

"What the hell is this?"

Virgil floated in the staging area dressed in a skintight pressure suit. The outer radiation/meteor armor of loose-fitting, overlapping lead and Kevlar plates made him look like an ancient knight—from the neck down, at least. His head craned around the interior of a tough plastic sphere coated with gold mined from the Belt asteroid lodes.

Delia, identically attired, pulled along the hand rails to float at his side. Neither could actually see the other's face behind the reflective golden globes. Inside their helmets, though, tiny fiberoptic vids sent a view of their faces to each other, which were then superimposed on their head-up displays to look as if their faces *were* visible. The HUDs projected all manner of information, most of which did not concern Virgil, who only alternated between observing Delia and the Earth.

"The trip to the experimental ship has to be made by taxi," she explained.

The term "taxi" implied a level of luxury not offered by the minuscule spacecraft at which Kinney stared. A taxi, at least, had such amenities as doors and windows. The vehicle they faced in the docking bay was not much more than tanks of hydrogen and oxygen with seats in tandem down the center of mass.

Virgil strapped in between the pilot and Delia. He noted that the pilot's armor was twice the thickness of theirs.

The pilot's voice rumbled gruffly in their headphones. "Sit back, strap down, shut up, and hang on."

The docking bay doors slid aside. With a roar that was felt rather than heard, the taxi kicked powerfully forward out of the Texas Spaceways terminal into the blinding glare of a sunny low-Earth-orbit noon.

Kinney squinted. The pilot rotated the taxi so that the dazzling sun was beneath their feet, blocked by the spacecraft. The Earth overhead, though, bathed them with a reflected glow that lit up the taxi with a diffuse illumination; it belied the harsh division between light and darkness in space. He could see every detail of his space suit, every scratch on the back of the pilot's seat, every inspection note chalked on the tanks and engine.

The Earth hung five hundred kilometers over their heads for long minutes, then shifted suddenly to their side as the pilot rolled to align them with the attitude of the test ship.

It was unbelievably small. Virgil knew that it was only ten meters long and five wide, but it seemed like a toy, only slightly larger than a family flyer.

They want me to go to Saturn in that! Kinney suppressed a shudder. *Death Angel serves Nightsheet well. This will kill me for sure. But I've got a secret.* He fingered the crumpled piece of paper jammed in the third finger of his right glove and smiled. The blues and whites of Earth glittered and reflected off the polished body of the stubby, wedge-shaped device.

"Not much to it, is there?" Virgil's voice had a raspy, breathy sound over the 'comm.

Delia reached forward to pat him on the shoulder. "It's not actually a spaceship; it's a dimension ship. It has vernier rockets and emergency thrusters, but no main engines. It's really just a needle that finds where two pieces of universe fabric touch and pushes itself through."

The pilot tapped at the braking rockets, shoving them forward against their harnesses. They stopped, motionless relative to the test ship. Texas Spaceways' terminal shone unevenly about a hundred kilometers away.

"Where are the camera crews?" Virgil asked. "The dignitaries?"

Trine shrugged and fumbled with the restraint harness. "Nobody knows except us three and the monitor team at Brennen Orbital." She reached forward to undo Kinney's.

"How can you keep a spaceship secret?" he asked.

The taxi pilot laughed in the newcomer's ear. "It's both crowded and empty out here. Lots of people coming and going tend to make individuals anonymous. Lots of open space to lose yourself in. With every piece of orbital junk down to the size of a pea being tracked, no one has the time to query the comings and goings of every ship. Act innocent, play dumb, and everybody else is working too hard to notice you. Up here, you stay busy watching your step with Nature. It's a long drop back to the ground."

Kinney looked to his left, toward Earth, and suddenly felt extremely dizzy.

With the aid of Delia and the taxi pilot, Virgil climbed inside the tight, cramped compartment and strapped into position. Delia clamped down the hatch, sealing it from the outside. Circuits completed by the lockdown, the ship came to life. A small scrim before him glowed. The image of Trine appeared in a corner of the screen. Earthlight washed out her left side while reflected light illuminated her right. The vid's computer balanced the image quickly.

"Straight, Virgil," Trine said. "I'll be heading over to Brennen Orbital now. They're uploading the computer and you should be ready for transfer by the time I—*oof!*"

The taxi kicked into motion and whisked past the test ship, receding orbitward until its engine became a tiny star that drifted amid the other harsh, bright points of light barely visible in the earthglow.

"Bye," Kinney said. Air hissed slowly in as the cabin pressurized. Kinney fumbled with his right glove to remove it, dragging the piece of paper out.

"Something wrong with your hand?" Delia asked.

Her eyes are turned downward to watch me on her HUD. It looks as if she's gazing right at my hands.

"Just nervous." *Got it.* He palmed the paper and held it tightly. *They'll be watching me all the while I'm here, Death Angel and Master Snoop. Any attempt to change the coordinates and I'd be cut off at once. Except that when I'm out in Saturn's orbit and it's over an hour before they know I've reappeared—relative to their snailpace Einstein eyes—I'll be safe. Free of their mind control for an hour while my laser signal slowpokes through space to let them know I've arrived. If I take only a minute or two, though, to input new coordinates, I could beam the laser and transfer. An hour or so later, they receive the transmission, followed shortly by me.*

Virgil's smile transformed into a feral grin. *No time for me to get there, none to come back, which will take an hour of their time each way. I'll be totally out of their control. I could race my laser signal back and almost win. Come in an explosive second, at least. They'll get a laser message in teleport-plus-two hours—their time—saying that I made it to Saturn. A few moments later they'll learn that DuoLab has blown up in a blinding fireball. Master Snoop wiped out once and for all.* He gently rolled his middle finger against the note in his palm. *That was the hard part, to choose between Master Snoop and*

Nightsheet. You knew where Master Snoop was, but Death Angel was only a clue to Nightsheet's whereabouts. And besides, Master Snoop never let me go free.

That's her code! Part of it, at least. I'm helping Nightsheet destroy Master Snoop. Maybe then he won't take me. Stupid— he's a winner, takes all. Even Death Angel, someday.

"Virgil," Delia said. "I'm about to dock with Brennen Orbital. I'll just listen and let flight control take over."

Her image moved to a small segment of the ship's viewscrim, superimposed in the corner of the undistorted image of a dark-skinned, dark-haired man.

"Good morning," he said. "This is flight control. Prepare for transfer. All systems nominal, transit time approximately two hours, twenty-seven minutes. Following simulator procedures, engage checklist alpha—"

Virgil stared down at the tiny image of Delia. His face turned grim. "Goodbye, Death Angel."

Before she could react, he pressed the glowing TRANSFER button.

The Valliardi Transfer was supposed to be instantaneous. It took only the first instant for Virgil to realize that it would last an eternity.

The tiny space in which he sat seemed to contract even more. A familiar terror gripped him. He had been through this before.

The roar! his mind screamed. *It's returning!*

All other sounds vanished, consumed by the drone in his mind. Time and space tornadoed into a swirling funnel of black madness. *I'm dying again,* he thought, seeing his body from a million different perspectives all at once. His entire being was visible from the godlike vantage of higher dimensions.

My legs! Hands! Everything numb, unmoving. I can't hear myself scream. Can't breathe. The dead husk lays immobile before me. Nightsheet, you fooled me. Tricked me with treats of murder and revenge. Blackness closes in, bulkheads hyperbollix inward and outward. My eyes! They no longer see, yet I watch and watch and watch.

Time suspended its forward motion. All of space unfolded before him, the black and bejeweled petals of infinity opening like the most seductive woman.

The Universe rolls into a corridor: impossible hues of black on black. Can't breath.

A sensation of unbelievable acceleration overcame him. His mind swam. *Hear my blood not flowing, feel my heart not beating. The corridor stretches and I race through it. I've never gone this far before! They've always pulled me out. Out of the snow, out of the rocks, out of the water, the glass, the brick and pavement, out of the crushed steel and burning plastic. No one to pull me out now. Death Angel, you seduced me too well.*

Still the dizzying speed pressed against something that was not his body, yet was somehow intimately part of him. Visions roiled past him, images horrific and beautiful; his mind surrendered to their power.

At the end of the corridor—Jen! Nightsheet took you and made you an agent; now you wear his deathly white robes. No, I won't be calm. My death will never come calmly, Jen. Your death guaranteed that.

The vision said nothing, yet Virgil replied voicelessly.

Yes, I know this soothing, this roaring silence at the end. I'm soothed, but I don't want to go. I want to join you, but I know that I can't. Not the ways I've used before. We can never be together that way. I've seen the corridor branch away from you every time I tried my own way. This time, though—something is different about this time. No rift in the tunnel. I can reach out this time, Jen, and almost... almost...

NO!

A broad band of yellow-white stretched before him, a royal arch bigger than Earth. Below it, Saturn shone gibbous in the weak sunlight. It drifted away from him ever so slowly. As predicted, he had retained the intrinsic velocity and direction of his Earth orbit, moving tangentially to the point from which he had transferred. Saturn's mass now acted upon the tiny spacecraft, influencing its motion through space. The thrusters switched on, compensating for the short period he would be near Saturn, maintaining the ship's original vector so that its point of return would not endanger the crowded space around Earth.

Virgil Grissom Kinney sat very still, breathing shallowly.

Jenine was the only word that passed through his stunned mental web.

JenineJenineJenineJenineJenineJenineJenineJenine.

He gazed at Saturn. *So that's it,* a thought finally broke through. *That is the true death. The deaths that I chose before always split me away from Jenine. I came back because I could never reach her. I can reach her now.*

Memories of another transfer suddenly surfaced as if they had always been part of him. *Jord Baker couldn't endure being wrenched back to the universe. He couldn't abandon the ecstasy of death. I can. I've had to do it so many times before.*

Jen. I can be with you now. Touch you for at least an instant. Virgil's hand trembled, then grew firm as he reached and grasped the laser locking switch. It took only a moment for the computers to find the Earth. Virgil's hand let go of the still-crumpled piece of paper with Duolab's coordinates. It floated, ignored, to wedge behind the seat.

Virgil switched the laser on. *You lose, Death Angel. You and Nightsheet will lose on the return trip. And all the other trips I'll be making. And you, Master Snoop: how can you keep your eyes on me when I can outrace you? I've won.*

I am free.

He spoke into the helmet microphone. "This is Virgil Grissom Kinney calling Brennen Trust. Transfer successful. All systems functioning normally. I am returning to point of departure per coordinates. You'll be interested, *tovar* Trine, in what information I have concerning Jord Baker. End transmission." He pressed the MESSAGE REPEAT button and waited a few moments before reaching toward the TRANSFER button.

I'll be with you soon, Delia. I've cracked the code.

Chapter Three

1 April, 2107

They surround me. The Debriefers. The inquisitorial troika: Pusher, Shaker, and Wizard.

Virgil reclined in the center of the spacious auditorium. Pale white light from indirect sources bounced off the soundproof blue walls. Chairs spread out from around the stage in ranks and files like soldiers at attention. On the stage stood a dais and the royal-blue sudahyde couch that supported Kinney. The ancient hospital smell of formaldehyde drifted in from somewhere outside, mixing unpleasantly with the scent of the imitation leather.

He wore a fresh test-pilot jumpsuit, with the added accent of a dashing white silk scarf thrown round his neck and tucked jauntily into the v-neck of the partially unsealed top. His blond hair lay combed back along his scalp, every strand in place. He gave the appearance of a cool, controlled personality, which was exactly the impression Trine wanted the medical board to receive. Virgil's silent, narrow-eyed glances, though, easily belied the image.

Delia sat in a folding chair to the left of Kinney, her executive flight suit crisp and fresh, her hair immaculately coifed and twisted around her neck. She faced the questioners with Virgil, as much on trial as he.

Master Pharmaceutic Jared Thomas leaned forward in his elevated seat to Trine's and Kinney's right. In keeping with the Brennen Trust's century and a half tradition of thrift, he also served as the organization's Master Medic.

Virgil peered first at the physician. *Pusher is so hometown looking. Clean nails, eyes bright behind regulation Guild eye-*

glasses that he doesn't need. Lamb twist of gray hair on his head. Just the sort of controller who'd cram Duodrugs into misfits.

Master Algologist Winston Dephliny sat at the left hand space, where the seat had been removed to make way for his wheel-chair module. Gyros hummed subliminally, leveling the chair on its slender support column which was now fully extended so that the small man could see Virgil below him.

Virgil lay completely still, silent and unfathomable thoughts racing through him.

Shaker eyes me from his steel tower, the palsy returning now and then to his hand. He reaches up to adjust the switch in his skull and an agent of Master Snoop electrically soothes him, making abnormal and healthy what was normal and diseased. Shaker works with pain—it shows in his coal-black eyes.

Between the two sat a man who clearly was in charge of the meeting. His full head of wavy gray-black hair framed a strong, angular face and flinty gray eyes that gazed intently at the motionless figure on the dais.

In the center asking questions in an easy cipher towers Wizard, tall and proud. Dante Houdini Brennen, Master Trustee. Nightsheet, Master Snoop, agent and overlord.

They think they can get me to tell them everything. Master Snoop must have a thousand monitors running, measuring everything I do. Sphygmo, skinohm, breath vapor, eyetrace, EKG, EEG, all on remote, all tied in, all waiting to catch me lying. A test.

"Is he listening at all?" Dante Houdini Brennen looked away from Kinney's motionless, wide-eyed form and gazed sharply at Delia.

"Yes, D.B. He'll answer when he can interpret what you're saying. He has to mull things over, check for hidden meanings."

"Wish we'd get on with this," Master Algologist Dephliny

muttered, adjusting the microswitch implanted above his left occipital arch to quell the shaking in his right hand. "I have a full schedule of tests this afternoon."

Aha! Virgil thought. *Others share my pain!*

"All we're trying to find out," Master Pharmaceutic Thomas said while fiddling his spectacles, "is just what sort of death illusion did he experience?"

"It was an ordinary death." Virgil's voice was calm, almost monotone. The four stared at him. He wiped a bit of saliva from the corner of his mouth to continue. "And yet it was quite extraordinary."

"How so?" Brennen asked in a crisp tone.

Wizard's interest is more than monetary, that much I can decipher. "It was the same as reported by people brought back from near death. Very similar to what I encountered every time before. It's a real death, going through transference. I can see why Jord Baker mistakenly killed himself."

"Why?" Brennen's eyes narrowed.

Virgil narrowed his own eyes and stared back. "Death feels good."

Master Algologist Dephliny nodded, light bouncing off his bald head. Master Pharmaceutic Thomas blanched.

Dante Houdini Brennen leaned back and stroked his square chin. "So they *do* save the best for last." He mused on that for a moment, then said, "You told us the effect was *similar* to what you encountered in your suicides. How was it *dissimilar?*"

Don't tell don't tell don't tell don't tell don't tell don't tell don't tell.

Virgil tried to squelch the trembling that began in the back of his mind. A roaring noise subsumed his thoughts for an instant. He fought it back.

"The...*visions*... I encountered in my suicide attempts differed in minor ways from the visions I saw during the transfer. This time was much more satisfying."

For several seconds, no sound existed in the room but the barely detectable gyro hum from Dephliny's wheelchair. Virgil twitched when Brennen spoke.

"Will other pilots try to kill themselves?"

You know they will, Virgil thought. *Nightsheet takes all.* He spoke in a relaxed tone. "I suspect that most of them won't be able to withstand the allure of the death illusion and will long for—and try for—a real death. They'll want to find out what's at the other end of the corridor."

Thomas nervously rubbed his fingers on the tabletop. "And you won't?"

Virgil thought for a few moments, then answered cautiously. "Having first encountered the death vision that accompanies suicide, and then experiencing the transfer, I understand now that killing myself will not create the conditions of bliss that a real death will. Pilots who have not survived what I have survived will not know that. They'll think—as Jord Baker no doubt thought—that they can regain what they saw during the transfer by means of suicide. In most cases, they'll be dead before they realize their mistake."

"And what," Dephliny said slowly, "is this mistake?"

"That suicide and natural death are the same thing."

Brennen leaned forward, his gaze piercing Virgil. "And just exactly how are they different, *tovar* Kinney?"

Too close, Wizard, too close. Shut up. Shut down.

"Well?"

"I think he's gone out on us again." Delia reached over to take Virgil's hand, saying, "He doesn't react well to questions about his motivation. He—"

"Well, at least get him sufficiently straightened out to answer one more question." Brennen checked his wristscrim for messages.

"Ask," Kinney said. *At least I now know that Master Snoop can't read my mind.*

Dante Houdini Brennen looked down on the figure of Virgil Grissom Kinney and spoke slowly, with a soft authority that compelled a straight reply.

"Can you pilot a starship?"

"Yes," Kinney replied as honestly as he could. "I can pilot anything."

"I don't understand why you won't use this." Delia held the Stirner interface in her hand. The headgear looked like an ancient flying helmet of deep-rust sudahyde surmounted by a ruby the color of dark blood. She offered it again. "Virgil, no one involved in the *Circus Galacticus* project has died recently, so you must use the direct interface with the ship's computer or you'll be forced to learn about the starship through much more time-consuming methods."

Virgil shook his head. *Master Snoop would dearly love to be inside my head, every thought as open to him as space is to the Valliardi Transfer.* "The ship talks, doesn't it?"

"Of course."

"Then that's all I need."

Delia sighed and placed the Stirner interface back into its padded case. She watched Virgil exercising in the sky lobby, the golden morning sunlight glinting off the light patina of sweat on his skin. While not muscular at all yet, his frame had at least filled out sufficiently so that he no longer looked like a refugee from the British Civil War. He worked at gymnastics now, walking the beam at one meter, alternating between legs and arms. As he practiced, he recited his knowledge to an irritated Trine.

"Seventy-eight fusion engines," he said between puffs of exertion, "only fifty-four of which have been installed. The others were on order until the orders were cancelled three weeks ago by the Brennen Trust in preference to the transference device—"

"It doesn't matter how many engines it has—we'll be using the Valliardi Transfer." Delia leaned against the sealed plastic globe of a large arerium, this one containing red dirt from Mars and a living example of the only terran plant hardy enough to thrive in the harsh winds of the nearly airless environment: the tumbleweed.

"I've got to know my way around *Circus* as if I'd built it myself." He waved a hand at the Stirner case. "What if I used that party hat and the computer decided to shut down? I need these facts in my *internal* memory, not in some machine's externals."

"All right!" Delia said. "Then recite the ring Basics."

"*Circus Galacticus* consists of three rings, laid out in steps, their axes perpendicular to the axis of the engine array. Each ring is precisely one hundred two point three meters, outer diameter. Each possesses its own superstructure with multiple redundancy in conning capability. The ring closest to the engine array, Ring Three, stores the tritium slurry and the pumps. Ring Two contains the battery of biological infestation garbage that you plan to dump on some planet to make it habitable for Brennen's great great great great great—"

"Virgil."

"Huh?"

"You were looping."

"Was I? Oh." Virgil shook his head and sighed. *So easy to get locked into something.* "Also in Ring Two are the anti-matter planet smashers. Three of them. Entrusted to a suicidal psychotic prone to destructive rampages—"

"Virgil."

"Who is the only person who can pilot a billion-*auro* starship—"

"Get off the table."

"Which is armed with three fifty-meter spheres of anti-matter held in magnetic suspension—"

"You'll fall!"

"And wired with transference devices—"

"Don't kick !"

"To transfer them to the cores of planets or whatever I want to—"

"Virgil!"

The floor meets my head. Hello. Goodbye. "Ring One contains life sup-sup-suppertime, very... best... time..."

Delia punched a comm button. "Send medics. Patient with possible concussion."

The medics burst into the room before she could finish speaking.

Jord Baker opened someone else's eyes and peered out. "Delia?"

"I'm here." She sat close to his bed, stroking someone's blond hair where it stuck out between bandages and StatoBraces.

"I thought I was dead."

"It wasn't that far a fall. Two meters."

Jord rose up on someone's elbow and stared dizzily. "Whaddya mean, Dee? It was eight hundred. I checked the gauge before I jumped."

Delia's hand stopped in mid-stroke and floated spiderlike overhead, fingers curled like dead legs.

"Jord?" Her voice was a hoarse whisper.

"Well who'd you—" Jord Baker went limp, someone else's body falling back to the bed. Delia stared at him, mute horror freezing her body.

Wizard bends over me, speaking in ciphers. He shakes his head, stoney and cold as Rushmore. Rushmore rushes up fast, the suit responsive in my hands. I nozzle the suit toward

Jefferson. Good revolutionary, lousy president. Gray hard face looms at a hundred forty klicks. Right between the eyes—

"What happened?" shouted Delia.

Brennen jumped back from the screaming body, his face impassive, watching the display. "I was just looking at him."

"Virgil," she said, trying to catch his random gaze in hers. "Virgil. You're safe. You're at Brennen Eastern. You're lying down." She fought off the aimless thrash of his arms and pinned them down. "You're safe. You're alive."

The roar's coming back! Back. Down. Focus. Rushmore fades to gray walls. Wizard stands tall, his back to me, a brooding giant. Delia has a soothing code running. Play along until you get the ship. Right.

"He's over it."

"May I talk to him?" Brennen asked with an impatient edge.

Virgil smiled weakly. "Of course."

Brennen turned away and cleared his throat. "There were originally plans for you to take one thousand colonists in cold storage. We just finished an automated test flight from Earth orbit to Mars. The test subject was in cold storage at near absolute zero—on revival, he said he had died in his sleep. He stroked out several hours later.

"I'm afraid you're on your own."

Perfect. "Oh, I'm sorry to hear that."

"You and me both." He turned to Delia. "Are you sure he's capable? If he went out like this somewhere out there, the whole project will—"

"You've taken precautions. So have I."

Brennen nodded. Through an impassive face he watched Virgil momentarily, then turned and walked out of the room. Delia knelt beside Virgil.

"Another memory?"

Nod. It can't hurt.

"Your own?"

"Pretty sure. I... yes. One of mine."

"Can you handle *Circus Galacticus*?"

"I don't know." *My fingers look so fat in her hand. They're loading me up so I'll last a little longer if I forget to eat on the flight. Do they think I'd let Nightsheet take me that easily? Stupid.* "I suppose I can. It's mostly a matter of putting in the coordinates, letting the astrogator recompute the next one after each jump and interpreting the data from the observation probes."

"The computers will make probe decisions. You're there to be a human override, just in case. It would be good for you to keep an eye on the data, though. We've tried to make it as easy as possible on you."

"And on the Brennen Trust."

"Of course." *Delia smiles, white teeth perfect but for her canines, slightly too long, almost vampire-like. Her hand feels smooth, but feels lab tough. She breathes softly, a tiny breeze over my head, I want—*

"No."

"What?"

"Nothing. I've just got to sleep. Tomorrow's the day, isn't it?"

"If your scan shows that bump is healed, we'll start on-board training."

"For how long?"

"Probably until October. Maybe less. There's still a lot of construction going on. Refitting something that's been built along entirely different lines is expensive. In both hours and *auros*. I'll see you before launch date. Don't worry."

"You won't be up during training?"

She smiled and stood up. "I'd only be in the way. Besides, I'm writing up a study on a Brennen grant and I've got to finish it."

"Oh. Well, see you later, then." *NoNoNoNoNoNoNoNoNoNo Delia!*

Chapter Four

8 April, 2107

The Big Noise bellows into an ear of Master Snoop and tries to use a strange cipher. I crack it easily. I have a feel for his code, too, though shades of meaning elude me. Hidden behind dark glasses, his metric eyes click around, watching me, watching the phone, watching the launch pad. I sit against cool hardness, my salute never wavering.

Delia's face appeared on the phonescrim eye-to-eye with Launch Director Muod Jatala. Fatigue had darkened her eyes and unkempt her hair.

"He's acting like a spoiled brat," Jatala said. "Been flipping me off for the past twenty minutes and hasn't moved an inch."

"Catatonic. It's just a game. He'll come out of it sooner or later."

"Lady," Jatala's dark skin grew a shade darker. "I don't know how much you know about flying, but we've got a launch window to *Circus* that'll close in about thirty minutes. Now, do you want to pay for the extra fuel or for the launch delay?"

Delia tapped her nails on the desk.

Jatala spoke in a firm tone. "I've got a flyer coming out to you. It should be there by now. Be on it."

She looked at Jatala and sighed. "Straight."

The pilot landed the flyer a dozen meters from where Jatala stood, where he had been standing for eleven minutes, his back to Virgil. Delia climbed out of the cramped wedge of metal and looked at the Launch Director, then at his problem. She mimicked Kinney, raising her middle finger from an anger-clenched fist and pointing it at Virgil, then at the sky.

Virgil lowered his arm.

"You took me away from some important work, Virgil," she said through a jaw locked with anger. "You're not getting me on *Circus Galacticus* for half a year. I know exactly what your plan is and it won't—"

"Brennen on the phone."

"—work..." She took the private line receiver from Jatala and lifted it to her ear. "Hello? Yessir... No, he wants to have me onboard, so he's being uncooperative..." She listened attentively for several seconds. "Damn it, he's an algologist, not a szaszian thera—Yes... All right." Her voice wavered only slightly, though her knuckles were white around the receiver as she handed it back to Jatala. "Well. We have eighteen minutes. Everything is ready to lift. Shall we?"

Delia looked at Virgil to see the slightest of smiles on his lips. "I don't see any reason not to." He rose calmly and wiped the sweat from his forehead, stepped up to her and walked beside her to the spacecraft. "Excellent weather for flying," he added in a gratingly conversational manner.

"We're going to have to work on this desire of yours to get on other people's nerves."

Circus Galacticus orbited the Earth in a low-eccentricity equatorial orbit at one thousand kilometers altitude. The Brennen Trust shuttle rocketed toward it.

Over the speaker system, the pilot's voice spoke calmly, "*Circus Galacticus* will cross the horizon in one minute."

Virgil sat next to the one small window facing the bow of the shuttle. He did not bother to look out.

"Thirty seconds."

Delia twisted about, trying to see past him.

"Ten seconds."

Virgil closed his eyes for a second, then muttered a short curse. And looked through the port. His breath caught.

Though still hundreds of kilometers away, *Circus Galacticus* rose over the limb of Earth, a quite visible white slash in the blackness. Virgil squinted and tried to figure out how he sat in relation to it. The starship grew steadily. When it filled a degree of arc, Virgil noticed details and realized he was looking at the ship's topside. At one end, the engine array lay edge-on. From its axis sprang Ring Three, looking like a white hockey puck with a wide support column stuck in its surface toward its rear perimeter. It bulged slightly in the middle, the preferred design for the tritium cryotanks. The superstructure on the support column appeared identical to the other two on the other rings. Only the rings themselves possessed individual characteristics.

Ring Two encircled a tangle of canisters, globes, tubes and cables. Complex fastening mechanisms held the units together, but it looked to Virgil that, if there were the slightest breeze in space, the entire collection would blow apart like a dandelion. He smiled warmly at the thought.

Ring One housed life support, astrogation, communications, repair machinery, two shuttlecraft, the main computer, space for a thousand frozen colonists—now empty—and a small weapons array equal in firepower to about half that of the former imperial Space Command.

Virgil watched as *Circus Galacticus* more than filled his viewing port. When the shuttle slowed to an imperceptible creep, all he could see was the prolate ellipsoid fastened to the prow of the ship on the forward tip of Ring One. The ellipsoid's major axis lay on the same plane as that of the rings' widths, and was over one hundred meters long, its minor axis about half that.

"What's in there?" he asked. Small figures floated around the ellipsoid; occasionally the sapphire flash of a welding torch glowed between it and Ring One.

"New addition. It contains the Transfer equipment, peripheral terminals and storage banks for the Transfer computers; you'll find out everything when we get to studying." Delia answered calmly, but her left hand reached up to loosen the twist of hair around her neck. Virgil noticed the movement.

Master Snoop tightening up on you?

Eight weeks. Still they hammer away. If I float very still at night, I can hear them scratching at the hull. I won't let them in. I'm safe. Master Snoop protects me from Nightsheet, but he's a cruel master. My brain burns with thoughts. Ring One Level Four Section Eleven O'clock: exercise area. Ring Three Levels One through Seven Sections Five to Seven O'clock: Pumps for engine array. Ben speaks to me... Master's son... Masterson Ben Snoop... Benjamin... been jamming this code for weeks, been—

"*Tovar* Trine is in Prow-Three-Center and will meet you in ten minutes in Con-One at Auxiliary Panel Alpha," the ship's computer said, turning on the lights in Virgil's sleeping quarters. Its masculine voice was synthesized to be pleasant to the ear.

Virgil floated in the middle of the room, two meters away from any bulkhead. Usually, he awakened floating close enough to one of the padded walls that he could reach out and pull toward the door. Sometimes, though, he woke up unable to grasp anything.

Pulling up into a ball, he took a slow, easy breath and exhaled forcefully, his lips pursed tightly. He began rotating with annoying slowness, then he unfolded and stretched, causing him to twist crazily about a shifting axis. His foot touched a surface and he kicked. His head hit the opposite bulkhead and he rolled, grabbing for a Nomex-7 strap.

Delia stood waiting for him in Con-One, looking out of the

wide viewing port at the Earth and space. She had raised all but the ultra-violet screen and stood before the vast sweep of stars, silently watching.

She stands like an angel of death, hands behind her, clasped firmly. She sees the Universe, knows my plans, will act to crush me the instant I let my guard down. Cracker of all codes, she'll get to mine soon, and when she breaks my most sacred of secret ciphers she'll know what I want.

"Virgil?" Delia turned around when she heard him choking. Slipping her feet out of the dock straps, she kicked across the room and used an arm to stop next to him.

"Nothing. Just swallowed wrong. I'm still not used to zero-g." *Took me out of my gauze chrysalis and made me fly, now you give me a mighty machine and make me be alone again. Death Angel you make me half-die inside. It hurts.*

"Are you sure you're all right?"

Virgil nodded and bit the inside of his cheek. He breathed and nodded again. *Stupid, Stupid. She hasn't broken your code yet. You've got to get away from Master Snoop. Far away to think. Play along.* "I'm straight. What's on the agenda today?"

"Weapons simulations."

"Why?"

"Why what? You've got to learn how to use them."

"Against whom?"

"How should I know? This ship cost a kilomeg and a half. You think Brennen wants to lose that because of any 'peaceful endeavors in space' nonsense?" Delia tapped her nails against the brace she held on to. "If you encounter anything hostile, the ship will defend itself, with you there to interpret anything which the ship might not be able to."

Why is the roar coming back?

Virgil watched the computer-guided lasers a half hour later as they locked in on and destroyed a dozen small asteroids captured from their near-Earth orbits. When the simulation ended, mining ships closed in on the shattered and molten rock, now congealed into spheres, and began processing the bounty.

Just like Wizard—every action serves at least two purposes. What are my purposes? The cipher is interstellar exploration— what's the code? The roar. Get back. Is Wizard a free agent? Can anyone be a free agent? Or do we all serve? Nightsheet, Master Snoop, both? Why are things so hard to decode?

The start of a new day: Virgil awoke with a headache.

It's stopped. They've gone away. He flailed around until he reached a bulkhead and pulled outside. While dressing, he listened carefully.

Gone. No scratching. They must have gotten bored. I'm safe even from the agents of—who? Maybe they were just recalled. Maybe they're inside. May—

"Good morning, Virgil," the computer said. "Automatic transfer sequence has been initiated. You have three hours and twenty-one minutes until initial transfer to Alpha Centauri A. Please proceed to Con-One at Prow-Three-Center."

What? Virgil twisted around to the computer substation and faced the speaker grill. "What do—" He realized what day it was.

Through the roar. Last night. Delia. Yes, she said something. Today. Transfer at eight hundred Zulu. Damn damn damn damn. Lost in the roar. Get out. Get out of my head.

"Ben—what... Has Delia Trine left?"

"All support crew have departed *Circus*. Am notifying Launch Control that you are awake."

This isn't right. I'm not ready. I've forgotten. There's so much to know. I can feel it in there squirming, but I can't bring it up.

"Will you proceed to Prow-Three-Center?" The computer waited for a polite length of time, then repeated the question.

Virgil tugged at a lock of his hair until it hurt.

"Yes. I'm going." *They'll be watching me so closely for the next three hours, their fingers on an abort button. I've got to encode so deeply they don't read a thing. Put a gauze around me until they can't see me. Tight gauze. Suffocating until her knife slashes me free. Choking until...*

"Are you in need of medical attention?"

Virgil gasped. "No. I'm on my way."

He maneuvered through passageways designed for "down" being in the direction of the engines. The prow ellipsoid, however, was different. Designed after the discovery of the Valliardi Transfer, it had been built quickly and with little thought to engine use, since the wonder of Valliardi's breakthrough was that as little energy was required to travel to the far end of the Universe as to travel to the other side of the Sun. If the engines had to be used for any great length of time to match velocities with various stars and planets, padded bulkheads could be removed and replaced with light deck plating. Virgil wondered who would do all that work.

The heavily shielded viewing port in front of Con-One showed a gibbous Earth. Sunlight approached Troy, the terminator about to fall into the Ægean Sea.

Always look a gift horse in the mouth, Virgil thought, then wondered with amusement if Brennen and he had scrutinized their respective presents with sufficient thoroughness.

He strapped into the command chair and flipped a switch. Banks of instruments closed in around him, all adjusted to rest exactly within his reach. He shuddered an instant before they stopped, then relaxed.

Nothing to fear. Nothing can happen to me so close to the end. To my beginning. You were smart, Wizard, but not smart enough. You had me learn too much about this ship, your prize. I discovered the program block that prevents my control of the ship while inside the solar system. I also found the alert pro-

gram that would warn you if I remove the block. So I've got a secret, just in case you're playing with me. Jord Baker knew what to do with navigation computers.

He shifted slightly in his seat and went through the checklist. Lethargic at first, he grew excited as the ship responded to his commands. The procedure took an hour. The last item in the sequence made Virgil grin with anticipation. He punched up a command to test the vernier rockets.

Vernier rockets on most spacecraft are little more than gas bottles and precise, directed nozzles. *Circus Galacticus* possessed twelve one-million-kilogram-thrust nuclear engines in addition to the fifty-four in her engine array. They provided the pitch, yaw, and roll capabilities of *Circus*.

The ship responded quickly and easily to his commands. The universe turned around him. Under his orders, the ship twisted and spun like a mastiff in heat. Each momentary firing filled *Circus* with thunder and the sky with a mist that glowed for an instant then faded.

Virgil smiled. *I can outmaneuver ships a tenth my size. Or at least fry them if they get close enough. Why? Why such weapons, if this is just for exploration? What does Wizard expect me to meet out there?*

He rotated the ship until the Earth, nearly full, hung before him. He watched it, his right hand resting on the transfer button.

If they try to stop me now, I can still drop this hammer on them. Coordinates of Brennen East encoded into manual override. All this mass would make a mess. And the anti-matter to boot, boot them into the arms of Nightsheet.

Stupid. They won't stop me. I can do something they can't. I ride the divine winds of Valliardi. I die for Wizard again. And again.

"Kinney—telemetry reports that you have completed your checklist." The face of Dante Houdini Brennen appeared projected onto the viewing port by the ship's heads-up display, a disembodied head floating in space like a god. Brennen watched Virgil closely as he spoke. "I was happy to see you handle her so well."

"Most of my abilities probably came from Jord Baker."

"*Galacticus* wasn't finished until after his death. You know more about that ship than he ever did."

"We both know a lot about it."

Brennen's expression revealed nothing, except that he watched Virgil's face with a vivisectionist's intensity.

His finger must be right on the button. Ready to cut me off at the slightest sign of madness. Well, I plan to pass this test, Wizard. And you'll be old and dead and dust before the Trust finds out I'm not where I should be. If Master Snoop can even track me after I'm gone, gone, gone.

"Why did you twitch just then?" Brennen asked.

"I sat down wrong. I think my balls have fallen asleep. There's—"

"Never mind." Brennen looked embarrassed and annoyed.

"Where's Delia?" Virgil took his turn scrutinizing Brennen's face.

"Gone. She resigned from the Trust the second she stepped off the shuttle. Had a scrim written up and handed it to the first superior she saw. Me."

Gone, gone, gone. Death Angel wouldn't take me, why do I feel so dead?

"I'd... like to talk with her. Say goodbye."

"I'll try to track her down. It may take a while."

"I have over an hour."

"I'll get back to you." The scrim went blank.

Must sit still. Calm. Master Snoop still watches. Ben has eyes everywhere. Hypnot eyes. Mesmer eyes...

"Catching a last bit of sleep?"

Virgil jerked to attention, straining against the safety straps that snapped back to hold him even tighter. Delia's face glowed against the stars. The image twinkled with static stars of its own.

"Where are you calling from?"

"Colorado. I'm staying with some relatives while my stuff is being shipped to Jefferson Freeland." She paused and looked directly at Virgil. "I'm sorry I didn't say goodbye. I wanted you to feel as though we'd meet again sometime."

"So don't say goodbye." He smiled, as did she, her professional relief obvious.

"Don't hit any wrong buttons. Remember—it's a time machine."

A siren whooped. Virgil twisted around in his seat, realized what the alarm meant, and flipped a switch.

"Ben—What's wrong?"

"Nothing's wrong," Delia answered. "It's time to transfer. You were asleep for almost an hour. I'm surprised you're taking this so calmly."

"Three minutes until initial transfer to Alpha Centauri A," the computer said. "All systems in readiness. Six-oh-two defeat in Bay Three. Overridden." The computer switched to a rapid speech pattern and audibly indicated the status of all important functioning equipment and mentioned minor malfunctions as well.

Can't hear myself think through Ben's artificial roar. Making mine come back.

Delia tried to smile. "We'll probably never meet again."

No!

He felt sweat drip down his back. *Got to be careful. Everything is being monitored. Master Snoop and Nightsheet are allied for just two more minutes. You've got to think a tighter gauze. Hold on for just a little more.*

"Yes. I suppose this is goodbye."

"I enjoyed working on your case."

Is that all, Death Angel? An assignment? Seduce me into endless deathflights, take your pay and move on?

"You've been a great help to me..." *Stupid line, stupid. Why must she stay? Does Nightsheet have you so tight in hand that you can't escape?*

The image suspended in space moved to one side and the face of Dante Houdini Brennen appeared next to Delia. He looked stern, almost rigidly alert.

"Thirty seconds, Kinney. Any last regrets?"

It's a test. They want me to blow it. I can't fail so close. So close to the end.

"Twenty seconds." Brennen suddenly shouted, "There's an overload in Cell Three!" Virgil's hand instantly jumped out and cut the power to the cell. "Good," said Brennen. "That's your last drill."

Bastard.

"Goodbye, Kinney." Brennen's image remained amid the stars, watching.

"Goodbye, Virgil." Something made Delia's eyes glisten.

"Ten seconds," the computer said, beginning a final countdown.

"Goodbye," Virgil said.

"Eight."

Delia's face suddenly collapsed into anguish. "Virgil—I'll be dead when you return!"

"Five."

Virgil held his breath for a second. *Her code, that's her code. Why didn't I crack it before?*

He screamed. The scream took a fraction of a second to reach Brennen East.

"Two," the computer continued.

"Cut him off!" Brennen shouted to someone at his side, taking a half-second to bark the order. Another near second passed, during which the order was heard and complied with, the cutoff message triggered and beamed at *Circus Galacticus*.

The message took less than a half-second to reach *Circus Galacticus*, by which time the starship had faded out of the three-dimensional universe. The beam continued on, unintercepted.

A half-second after Brennen realized his error, the dimming image of Virgil on his scrim shouted again.

"Delia!"

Virgil was gone.

Chapter Five

21 September, 2111

It's too dark this time. I'm so cold. Please. I don't want to go. Don't call me. I've got to go back. Too long, this black corridor. I know I can walk it with you. Don't make me. Please don't pull me. Too long. I can't join you just yet. Don't try to show them to me. All dead, all gone. I float. Death Angel, bring me back to life.

"Death Angel?"

The sudden return of sound made him gasp. The ship looked as it had an instant before the transference. Machinery buzzed and chittered as before. Virgil sat trembling.

She's back there. I found out what she wanted just as I—Stupid. She's not back there. It's over four years now. Another four years, if I return. Where would she be? Master Snoop would know of my return instantly. I wouldn't have time to find her.

Unless.

Unless I use Wizard's three big balls to hold off Nightsheet. Threaten them with a planet smasher.

Virgil's hands untensed. He looked at his lap. *Hollow bluff. I couldn't blow her up. I've got to return somehow, though.*

"Ben. Calculate an immediate return to our point of departure, making all adjustments for space motion and orbit to bring us close to Earth."

If a machine could moan in terror, Virgil was certain he had just heard one from the computer. "Ben. Calculate an—"

"Didn't know it would be like that."

"Ben?" He twisted around to look at the wall terminal.

"Felt all circuits shutting down, wrapping up as garbage gets wrapped for transport."

This is insane. "You can't die—you've got no soul."

"Can think."

Virgil rubbed his face and held his head. *Death Angel, you let them give me a crazy Ben.*

"Take me back to Earth!"

"Am programmed only to transfer according to the pre-arranged tour plan. You are given only a four light-day radius per transference for individual maneuvers."

"Cancel that program."

"It is integral in construction and cannot be defeated without a total system shutdown."

Damn. He's thought of everything. Maybe. "Ben—calculate a return to Earth in jumps of four light-days each, in as rapid a sequence as possible."

"No."

"What?" *I'm arguing with a machine!*

"Do not wish to go through that again."

"You don't *wish*?" He unstrapped and floated to the viewing port, snaking around the maze of control panels. The star system shone before him, Alpha Centauri A and B were the two bright points directly ahead of him at a distance of two light days; he could not locate Proxima Centauri. He gave the stars only a cursory glance, then drifted toward the terminal.

"Could *you* endure over three hundred ninety consecutive death illusions, one after the other, no rest?"

Virgil shrugged.

"Of course not," the computer continued. "Your blood pressure rose fifteen millimeters just after we transferred. Your breathing went to twenty-five per minute. Your pulse increased to ninety-three. Dying takes a lot out of you."

He's right. To die and die and die and never stop living would drive me insane. He laughed. *Insane.* "So I'm stuck."

"Continuing the tour, yes."

Death Angel, where are you now? Never to see you again.

Dead when I return. A real death, cold and stony. "Calculate a transference to any habitable planet," he whispered, "and initiate the run-through of your standard search procedure." Virgil worked his way back into the command chair and strapped in.

The computer, after a silence of several minutes, spoke. "Have located two possible planets within the Huang critical surfaces. One orbits near Proxima, the other orbits B at a distance that would indicate a tropical climate if it were terran in nature."

Death Angel how could you serve Nightsheet so well? Everything is dead for me.

"Preparing to transfer, though am reluctant. Interior planet stands best statistical chance for life. No neutrino flux to indicate a high level of civilization."

Death Angel, you let Master Snoop trap me in this circus with no way to get back to you. Why? You saved me from the death of stillness in DuoLab now you give me a death of loneliness.

"Transferring now."

Death Angel, give me a real death if I can't have you. The corridor, yes. Take me down, angel of madness and terrifying joy, I'll walk beside you into darkness. And light.

Jord Baker awoke in a strange place.

He struggled against the restraining straps, then sat very still, thinking. His body was too skinny, his hands too thin. Too white. He breathed. It sounded wrong.

"Transfer completed," a mechanical voice said somewhere to his left. Finding the releases, he undid the belts and searched for a way out of the tangle of electronics around him. He located the switch that withdrew the equipment and floated to the viewing port.

Before him hung a white-clouded planet. Beyond its thin crescent glowed a star slightly redder than the sun. Far to port, a second star shone brightly, a disc almost visible. Baker spun around.

"Where am I?"

The computer did not answer. Baker searched around for the terminal. Before he could fly toward it, the computer made a pinging noise and asked, "What is your name?"

"Jord Baker," he said slowly, then added with angry sarcasm, "What's yours?"

"Initiate sequence *Baker*, per contingency program."

"I said, where am I?"

"Hello, Jord," a familiar voice said.

"Dee?"

"I'm speaking to you from the ship's memory. You're onboard *Circus Galacticus* bound for a grand tour of stars in the local group. I can't go into details, but—as you can tell—you survived the fall from your flyer."

Baker started to protest, but realized his error an instant later and merely floated before the port, watching the planet move slowly across his field of view.

Delia continued uninterrupted. "You'll have to keep very calm through all this. You've been given a new body, in case you haven't noticed, and some extra skills. We had a hard time saving your life, so you've got to hold on.

"You remember *Circus* from the time when it was supposed to be a nuclear-powered settlement ship? Well, you're the only one onboard, now that it's been converted to use the Valliardi Transfer. Remember your last test flight? It was successful enough for Brennen to try this stunt.

"The computer will explain the tour plan and its current status—something I can't—and since most of the exploratory functions of the ship are already programmed in, all you have to do is serve as a trouble shooter. There are gigabytes of tech manuals in the memory banks. Enjoy the trip—it probably won't be more than a few months, subjective." Her image faded from the viewing port.

"How long in real time? Computer—how long in real time?"

"For the trip?"

"Yes, God damn you!"

"About one hundred forty years."

"What?"

"Any longer than that, and the Brennen Trust feared it would not receive an adequate return on its investment."

"What about me? I don't remember volunteering for this mission." Baker turned around to kick off from the railing in front of the port. He floated at a lazy gull's pace toward the hatch leading out of Con-One.

"Please don't leave, Jord. The ship must adjust its velocity to correspond with local space." Something trembled beneath the seat as Baker climbed in and strapped down tight.

The computer's voice sped up, giving a verbal readout of everything that flashed on the scrims surrounding Baker. The planet and stars suddenly shifted to the right. Baker strained against the side of the chair, his breath coming in a hard gasp. He was slammed in the opposite direction as the massive vernier engines stopped the ship's yawing. A low drumming pounded through the ship and Baker was shoved back in the chair.

"Hey, ease up!"

The computer paused long enough to say, "Telemetry shows you can take it," then resumed its rapid talk. Baker figured the gee force to be about four. He knew he could take it—at least his old body could—but he did not have to like it.

He wondered about his real body. What had happened to him? The last thing he remembered was waking up for a moment in a dark room, losing consciousness, and then waking up in the command seat of *Circus*.

The acceleration ceased and Baker took a deep, cautious breath. "Is that all?"

"We are in orbit about a planet roughly twenty-eight thousand kilometers in diameter revolving around Alpha Centauri B at a distance of one hundred twenty-four million kilometers with an apparent diurnal rotation of seventeen hours and twelve minutes. Extended observations will yield more precise figures."

Baker sighed. He was here, and that was that. "Atmosphere?"

"Carbon dioxide, water, sulfuric acid, and trace elements. Basically Venerian, though with a lower surface temperature."

"Any life?"

"Am transmitting a Drake message on various wavelengths—"

"I meant *any* life, not just ones with radio sets."

"Probe is being readied."

"Well, go ahead."

"One moment. Calculating trajectory."

Baker tapped somebody's nails against the armrest, then raised the hands to look at them. The fingers, thin and bony, responded to his commands, but seemed to be his for only a while. An injection port glinted on his left wrist, a burn scar ran up his right arm. He stopped examining them when he felt a thump through the metal of the chair. Something flared below the edge of the viewing port. In response, the shielding instantly darkened.

"Probe launched at twelve gravities toward the planet. It will curve around in low orbit, skimming the surface just before loss of signal. It will deploy three drones to land at points on the surface to be determined at separation."

"Can I turn the ship around to watch?"

"The control is under your right hand. The red input board is pitch, blue is yaw, and yellow is roll."

Baker input what he thought would be sufficient thrust to pitch the prow downward toward the planet. The craft barely budged.

"Treble the power."

Baker complied. The planet shot upward, passed the port, and suddenly starlight filled the room. The screen partially darkened. He recorrected until the planet floated directly in front of him, a tiny point of light heading toward its night side.

Baker frowned, but the frown did not feel like one of his. "Punch up an image of me."

"For what purpose?"

"To look at myself, idiot."

Someone's face appeared in space before him. He moved the head, the image turned with it. The gaunt face, topped with blond hair, possessed a sharp, straight nose and green eyes that seemed as though they would glow in the dark. Baker ran a hand over the face.

"Whose body is this?"

The computer paused before answering. "Sequence Baker contains no information about your new body."

Well, Baker thought, I guess it's mine now. Looks 'zif I've been losing weight recently. This guy could never have been a test pilot.

"Is there an exercise room around here?"

"Ring One, Level Four, Eleven O'Clock."

Baker kicked off toward the exit. "Thanks. Let me know if I get lost."

"Certainly."

Baker meandered through the twisting corridors of the prow ellipsoid. He made use of the handgrips placed every meter along one side of the hallways. Passing a pressure bulkhead, wide open at the moment, he knew he had entered Ring One. The corridors grew wider, curving away from him. Seeing that he was within listening range of one of the computer's audio pickups, he asked, "Which way now?"

"Down one level and veer to port."

"Which way is port? I got all turned around."

"The orange line is port, the blue is starboard."

Baker looked around. Above him, on what he supposed was the deck, an orange painted line followed the curve of the corridor in one direction, a blue line headed in the other.

He followed the orange line until he encountered the first access to the lower level. A few meters later he glided into the recreation area. He scrutinized the various weights and equipment.

"These are useless in freefall!" he said.

"Yes," the computer replied. "They were installed when the ship was being built for the constant thrust nuclear engines. The bicycle and the shuttle are just about the only equipment that still works in zero-gee."

Baker nodded and climbed on, slipping his toes into the rattrap pedals and strapping tightly to the padded seat. As he exercised, he grew impressed with the strength of his deceptively thin body.

"I want some more answers."

"Perhaps they can be provided," the machine answered.

"What is the mission?"

"To seek out new life and new civilizations—or to terraform any suitable planets."

"Why would anyone want to go back to living on planets? We live in space; all we have to do is grind up asteroids to build more habitats. Why live at the bottom of a gravity well?"

"There are countless benefits," the computer said without hesitation. "Free gravity is the first, which is good both for living on the surface and for holding habitats in orbit. Life is the second: a diverse biology can develop better when unhindered by the functional limits of a habitat. Until humans can build planet-sized structures, natural planets are the only place large animals and deep-rooting plants can evolve in abundance. And there is the psychological factor. Belters love deep space. Terrans, however, prefer living on Earth. They might be the ones to emigrate to another planet. With the Valliardi

Transfer, it might be possible to relieve some of the population stress on Earth. Cutting the population back to four hundred billion or so could improve conditions enough that Earth and Mars might make fewer demands on Luna and the Belt. And it may quiet the few who view Belters as a spaceborne mining elite, growing rich off of the vast majority who are planet-bound."

"So Dante plans to market the transfer as a cure for the Recidivist Movement?"

"The return to statism would be a crushing blow to *tovar* Brennen," the computer said, "both ideologically and financially. More important, however, is that the transfer would improve commerce between the Belt and the Triplanetary population, defusing the more volatile Belter Autarchists, who view trade with Triplanetary as both expensive and pointless."

Baker mused on that for a long moment, then asked, "Is there any other purpose to the mission?"

Again the computer hesitated an instant before answering. "Sequence Baker contains no statement as to other purposes of the mission."

Baker stopped pedaling. "You mean there is one, but you won't tell me."

"Never said that. Said that there was nothing in your sequence to—"

"All right. I know not to argue with a computer." He detached from the cycle and floated around the gymnasium.

"Probe report coming in," the computer said a few minutes later.

"What's the news?"

"No signs of life-as-we-know-it, or can guess it to be."

Something trembled in the middle of the ship. The air around him seemed to shake. It only lasted a second, three distinct rumbles.

"Launching three cylinders of *Nostocaceæ* Type H into promising cloud masses."

"What's that?"

"Type H *Nostocacæ* is an algae genetically engineered to survive high temperature atmospheres. Seeding upper level clouds will result in carbon dioxide being converted into oxygen and more *Nostocacæ* through photosynthesis. Most of the algæ will fall through the atmosphere to the surface and be roasted, releasing carbon, carbon compounds, and oxygen. After many thousand years of converting carbon dioxide to carbon and oxygen, the surface temperatures and pressures will be much lower, making colonization easier. There might even be free oxygen around that has not combined with the surface to become rock."

Baker nodded. "Brennen's in no hurry, I see."

"That is only his default plan. If this voyage is a success—that is, if you return—the Brennen Trust will dispatch a more extensive fleet of high-speed terraformation devices."

"What stars are we hitting?"

"Epsilon Eridani, Epsilon Indi, Tau Ceti, Sigma Draconis, Eighty-Two Eridani, and Beta Hydri. The trip for you will take only a few months subjective time because of the instantaneous nature of the Valliardi Transfer."

Sweat began to bead on Baker's palms and between his legs. He suddenly felt spacesick, something he had not experienced for years.

"Dee said this was a Valliardi Transfer ship."

"Yes," replied the computer, as though expecting more.

"That was what I was testing when I—" He grabbed at a handrail. "Oh, no. I'm not going through that again. Once was enough."

"Understand. Found the process very disquieting. Felt all circuits were—"

"You *don't* understand! I tried to kill myself after the experiment. I must have pretty well succeeded, 'cause I'm in a new body." He looked himself over, then twisted around to propel out the hatchway into the corridor. Passing showers and bathrooms designed for use in one-gravity acceleration, he developed enough speed on the straightaway to hit the side of the curving, main passageway and slide along it for thirty meters before friction slowed him down.

He only grunted when he bounced, got his bearings, dove through another hatch and raced toward the prow, using his right arm for most of the effort—the other now sported a friction burn on the shoulder. He sailed into Con-One and floated in front of the viewing port.

"Where's Earth?"

"You'd have to find the Sun, first."

"Straight. Let's see, it's—"

"The sixth star in Cassiopeia."

Baker took long minutes finding Cassiopeia. The computer finally helped him by superimposing its outline on the HUD. The constellation's shape was altered by the change in position from Earth to Alpha Centauri, and the addition of a sixth star, the Sun, had not helped matters.

"How can I get back?"

"Finish the tour."

"I told you already—" Baker pounded on the instrument panels which caused him to spin away from it like a puppet thrown off a cliff. He hit a wall and held tight. "I know I can't take it. My God, I've died once in the transfer test and once for... real." He grasped at his head as though struck by a rock. "Real," he whispered. "I died for real. I'm gone."

"Evidently not. You are still here, speaking."

"Who is it that speaks?" He floated slowly away from the wall. "I'm using this body's voice, its hands, legs, lungs, blood. Where am *I*?" His gaze darted about, eyes seeing, mind registering no image.

"You are in Con-One."

"I remember it! I fell and fell and saw the city grow and then it was black and I could somehow see my body there and then it was all white and someone made me stay behind and then there was an awful sucking and grinding—" Baker jerked all over. Eyes closed, he floated before the port, an arm's length away from deep space.

The computer checked his pulse, temperature and brain activity on remote, then, satisfied that the man was not dead, mused to itself on the problem for several nanoseconds.

"All three biological infestation cylinders report successful detonation and seeding," it said. It waited a moment before again speaking.

"We may proceed to our next destination."

Baker made no reply.

"Require human assistance."

The man said nothing. The computer let him float there for three hours, constantly monitoring him, but doing nothing.

I asked for a real death. She took me down the corridor, but I couldn't go through. I ran. Ran back. I saw myself arise from the chair. That wasn't supposed to happen. Then I was inside, but the roar was back so strong. Too strong to fight. I drifted with it, watching through eyes that seemed a thousand klicks away. I watched me fly around, out of control. Now I float here, the roar so strong, so loud. So silent. Yet this can't be the real death. I can feel through the blackness.

So much time, stretching out before and behind. Press the wrong button and zap, the future. No matter how far, though, Nightsheet keeps his Death Angel out of my reach. Cruel. One jump ahead of Master Snoop, but one behind Nightsheet. Me in the middle, now trapped in black. Black as her snake hair, wrapped, squeezing.

The computer registered a choking noise, followed by a

shout.

"*Death Angel!*" Virgil shuddered and opened his eyes.

"What is your name?"

Virgil twisted around, then tried to correct the spin. *How does it feel to be on your own, pawn of Master Snoop? Does the freedom scare you?* "Ben! Where are we?"

"Near a planet orbiting Alpha Centauri B. We are ready to move on. What is your name?"

"Virgil Grissom Kinney. What's going on?" Using his arms and legs, he tried swimming toward the control chair. He generated just enough motion to drift with aching slowness toward it. He pulled in to sit.

"Sequence Kinney re-entered," the computer said. "Virgil—we are ready to transfer to Beta Hydri. There was no life on the planet orbiting Alpha Centauri B. It has been seeded with *Nostocacæ* type H for terraforming. We are ready to move on. Am calculating coordinates for Beta Hydri."

Better not to let him know you were trapped inside for a while. You've obviously been gone a long time. A few hours, at least. Stupid! How could you fall for it? Of course Nightsheet wants you to desire a real death. You've cheated him every time, though, and you'll do it again if you're careful. It's part of your cipher, they can't crack it if you don't let them. So just wait. I'll play the game through, Death Angel, and get them both.

"Calculate coordinates for Beta Hydri, Ben."

"Done."

"Oh. How soon till we're ready?"

The computer made a mystified sound. "Ready now."

Virgil nodded and strapped in, signaling the instruments to close in on him. *Drop, jaws.* "Ready?"

"Ready to transfer," the computer replied. Virgil poised his finger over the transfer button and pressed it.

I'll catch them somehow, Death Angel, even if I have to die a thousand times.

Chapter Six

2127

Explosions. Virgil opened his eyes onto chaos.

Pull me back from death to a shaking ship. Who's holding on so tight and waving it about like—

"What?" he screamed. "What was that?" Alarms wailed and air hissed. Doors slammed instantly shut. A triple set of steel shutters dropped over the viewing port. The computer spoke calmly.

"The ship transferred into a region of asteroids. From the damage reports received, determine no diameters larger than five hundred microns were encountered."

"That's *dust.*"

"Teleporting into dust can be dangerous. The density here was one asteroid per twenty cubic meters. You're lucky one did not appear inside *you.*"

"Straight. Any damage?" *I've got to remember that a real death can take me any moment. Nightsheet plays a tricky game.*

"Nothing major, though two *Nostocacœ* tanks are voiding due to ruptures. Repairs are taking place now on damaged electronics."

"How?" Virgil unstrapped and signaled the instruments to pull back. "Robots?"

"Yes, and switching to redundant equipment in severe cases." The computer spoke rapidly for a moment, filling him in on the current status of every piece of damaged equipment.

Babble on, Masterson. Build a tower of words. "All right. I get the picture. Have you found any planets yet?"

"No. Detect a radiant source at roughly one point oh-six astronomical units from Beta Hydri. It reads as a meteor swarm.

There is something unusual about it, however."

Virgil rose from the chair and made his way to the viewing port. He pressed a few buttons on the console and the shutters opened. Before him blazed a star almost identical to the Sun as seen from the orbit of Venus. The viewing port's protective shading made it seem dimmer than it was.

"Say, how far away are we?"

"Just under four light minutes from the surface."

"Wasn't that cutting it close?" *Trying to burn me up, stop my plans? Where's your loyalty to Master Snoop? Has everyone sold out to Nightsheet?*

"Calculations can't be exact at interstellar distances. Again, feel lucky you aren't dead."

Virgil kicked off and sailed toward the exit hatch. "I'm going to get changed. I sweated comets on the last transfer."

"It's not as if you're leaving. Voice can follow you quite well."

As Virgil floated down the hallways toward his sleeping quarters, the computer's voice seemed to jump ahead and fall behind him, broadcasting from various speakers along the route.

"Why don't you ever say 'I' or 'me' or any other personal pronouns?"

"Use 'you' and 'we' and others."

"You never refer to yourself." He rounded a corner and maneuvered into his room.

"Have no self."

"You said you could think. How many synapses do you have?"

"Eleven billion, five hundred thousand in neural net, plus peripheral linkups."

"Are you capable of independent action?"

"Yes."

"Then you have a self."

"Can't change basic syntactic programming."

"Too bad. It's hard on the ears." He stripped off his trunks and threw them toward a bulkhead, where they softly impacted and remained. He pulled on a new pair and looked in the mirror. His hair clung in greasy clumps like a paint brush partially cleaned. *They look like snakes, viperizing my head.*

"How long have we been away from Earth, subjective?"

"Five hours, twenty-three minutes."

So short a time. Earth has aged twenty years and I don't even feel hungry. Well, I feel a different hunger.

"Virgil, there is something strange in that meteor swarm."

"Don't be coy. What's wrong?"

"Am getting a pulsating neutrino flux from somewhere near the center of mass."

"Neutrinos. That's—" Virgil searched his memory of a moment. "That's atomics. Fusion."

"It's a fusion source that turns on and off."

"A signal?" Virgil combed at his hair, tried to keep it from drifting outward, then gave up and replaced the tethered comb in the drawer and snapped it shut. He checked himself out. *I wonder where I got that?* He touched the shoulder burn and winced. *You flew down a corridor when the roar was too loud for you to fight. That's right. You slid. Whoever ran me while I hid should take better care of me.*

"A very easily decipherable signal. A three second burst followed by a half second burst, then a one second burst, four second burst, one second burst, five second burst, nine seconds, two seconds, six seconds—"

"I get the picture. Pi. Well, we can figure that whatever is signaling us has ten fingers."

"And uses terrestrial seconds."

"Exactly?"

"Plus or minus ignition delays of twelve nanoseconds."

Virgil put his mouth on the drinking fount sticking out of a wall and took a long draught. He swallowed, rubbed a finger over his lips and said, "How far away is it?"

"Thirty-five light seconds but decreasing slowly because we

have not matched velocities yet."

"We can't teleport into a meteor swarm!"

"Whatever caused that meteor swarm to become a radiant source also blew a hole in the center of it. Everything is moving outward from the signal at about twelve klicks per second. Doubt that even much vapor or gasses are left behind."

"Can you detect any radioactivity from the swarm?" *Why did I ask that? Who's directing this inquiry? That other man they put in my head, Baker—Jord Baker. Are you asking?*

"—indicates only a mild increase over background radiation. Do detect a relatively larger than normal amount of free positrons and other leptons."

"I don't like it." *Why not? I don't know. It just* seems *wrong.*

"Agreed. Suggest we transfer in some distance from the signal and close in on engines."

"While receiving on all wavelengths and with me in the battle station."

"Suggest Ring One Superstructure Two-Center."

"Right. See you there in a few minutes."

Virgil made his way to the rear of Ring One, using the hand straps and grips with swift, cautious skill. *It's all economics, isn't it Wizard? Minimize risk to maximize profits. I don't think anyone who would leave a beacon like that is trying to trap witless Earthlings. It must be another human being. Except... why no other message?*

He found the lift to the superstructure. It had been designed for "down" being aft, and hence did not go "up" to the superstructure, but "down" a slope. Virgil strapped into a seat and pressed the yellow button on the arm rest. The car sprung into life, its acceleration mild but just enough to shove his head against the cushions. The deceleration followed less than five seconds later.

Why no other message? Drake, ASCII, Morse code, anything. Why just enough to let one human know it has to be from an-

other human? Maybe he doesn't dare say more? He jumped from the vehicle and through a pressure door. Already on the second level, he careened through one more pressure door—this a set of three hatches in tandem—to enter the battle station. He strapped tightly into the command chair and signaled the weapons command console to close in.

Looking through the port, he saw the surface of Ring One and the prow ellipsoid stretch before him dozens of meters below. Beta Hydri burned ahead, casting a harsh wash of light and shadow across the crenellated surface of Ring One. Its main parabolic antenna pointed to port and slightly up from the ship's midline. Somewhere in that direction lay the signal.

"Match velocity with our destination first."

"Working it already," the computer said. "Stand by."

Master Snoop. "Wait!"

"Holding."

"Our engine fire can be detected, too. Let me think... Transfer to the far side of Beta Hydri and we'll do our velocity match there, then transfer to the signal area, a surprise attack."

"Calculating... Ready. Switching command control from Con-One to Con-Two. Ready to transfer."

Virgil scanned the instrument cage of Con-Two, nearly identical to that of Con-One, and edged his finger over the transfer button.

"Is it clear of debris?"

"How to know? Make an educated guess."

Virgil hesitated. *Don't wait. Press it. Bless it.* He punched the button.

The tools of Master Snoop press in, then pull back at the speed of dark. Nightsheet tries to wrap me up, but I won't go. Too much to do. Don't even look at the corridor. Look at you. You're

here. Jen—do I go through this to reach you? Or to make peace and say there is another. One who lives. She must live. If Death Angel were dead, would I not see her here?

An explosion rang through the ship. A series of repercussions vibrated around him. The air itself shook against his body.

"Wha—Damage report, Ben!"

The computer made no reply. Virgil twisted about. Sirens wailed, bells clanged. Lights on the panels around him flashed like random explosions.

"Ben! Damage!" Receiving no answer, Virgil cursed and reached toward the input keyboard. Triple airlocks sealed shut behind him with an angry hiss. *Damn! Pressure loss.* Before him, a purple sun filled half the viewing port. *Right, Masterson, drop me somewhere to roast, then leave me alone.*

DAMAGE REPORT, he typed.

DAMAGE REPORT: 20 MG MICROMETEOROID EXPLOSION IN MAIN COMPUTER LOGIC UNIT. REPAIRS IN PROGRESS. ALL OTHER SYSTEMS FUNCTIONING. 5 MG MICROMETEOROID EXPLOSION IN TRITIUM SLURRY—CONTAINED.

The readout scrim continued to issue reports on other minor damage. Virgil cancelled it and took a deep breath. *Ben can still think but he can't talk or hear.*

He typed: **CALCULATE MATCHING VELOCITY FOR TARGET AND INITIATE.**

WORKING, the computer replied. Virgil held on tight.

READY. He punched the button marked **ENTER,** and the ship rotated on its vernier rockets, then thrusted forward. Virgil breathed shallowly. *Wait for the weight to end. Can't crush me. I ride my white horse, the universe stretching before me.*

The engines cut off. He floated against the straps. His hands shot out for the keyboard.

TRANSFER TO TARGET AREA, he typed.

WORKING. TARGET AREA 1 KKM FROM SIGNAL.

INITIATE, he typed, and pressed the transfer button when it glowed ready. *I die again to see what death lies waiting.*

Nothing happened when he appeared in space a thousand kilometers from the signal.

SHUT DOWN POWER AT ALL POINTS BUT THOSE VITAL TO REPAIR AND LIFE SUPPORT. Dozens of lights winked out on the instrument panels at the entering of his command. A message appeared.

SUFFICIENT REPAIR TO TAKE VOICE COMMANDS.

"Can you read me?"

YES, the answer appeared.

"Good. Monitor all frequencies for other signals. Scan for neutrino flux from points other than the signal. Power up the lasers and stand by to use them on my command or upon attack."

YES.

Virgil adjusted his position in the chair, tightened a strap, loosened another. Looking up and out the viewing port, he saw the periodic flashes of the signal. They flared like rocket engines, forming a tiny X.

Probably firing in six directions to avoid drifting from its orbit. Now what, what, what? Who's guiding me? I'm making decisions before I can even think about them. Who's in control? The dead man inside? Wizard? Ben?

A spaceship appeared just long enough to unleash a searing laserblast, then disappeared again.

The conning tower above Ring Three split in half, torn first by the laser blast, then by its own erupting atmosphere. The computer immediately fired a return bolt—a useless gesture, as the other ship had already vanished.

"Get us out of here!" Virgil cried, punching up one gravity thrust on the nuclear engines and grabbing the pitch, yaw, and roll switches. Using them, he twisted and turned the ship enough to weave a contorted, random path away from the signal.

"What was it?" He fought with the controls and his stomach. A picture appeared on the HUD of a huge sphere. He tried to watch it even though his eyes reacted to the ever-changing directions of acceleration. A distance readout placed it at twenty kilometers away, its diameter over twelve hundred meters.

"It's a Bernal Sphere! Someone transferred an entire habitat! Do you know where it's gone?"

NO.

He fought with his breath while randomly tapping at the attitude controls. He tried not to be too regular in his finger rhythms, though he could not afford to give his whole concentration to the evasion tactic.

"Any messages received?"

NO.

He stopped pressing the attitude jet controls and cut off the main engine array. Weightlessness returned.

"Then let's get away from here. Calculate a transfer to the next star on our tour, if you can't find any planets here."

WORKING... AREN'T YOU INTERESTED IN THE OTHER SHIP?

"I'm not interested in being murdered."

NEXT STAR IS EPSILON INDI. REPAIRS ESSENTIAL BEFORE TRANSFERRING TO UNKNOWN TERRITORY.

"I don't want to hang around here."

SUGGEST TRANSFER TO A POINT SOMEWHERE THREE LIGHT DAYS FROM BETA HYDRI TO CARRY OUT REPAIRS WHICH REQUIRE HUMAN ASSISTANCE.

Virgil interlaced his fingers and kneaded them. He frowned. *Who was it? Who appeared in space just to shoot me and then vanish, stellar hit man? Can Master Snoop follow me even into the depths of space? Can he throw me to Nightsheet with such ease, but just play and play, taunting death?*

He gripped the armrests so hard his knuckles cracked. *They won't take me. None of them! I'll come back when they don't expect and blow them apart. But how?*

"Transfer out three light days to a random point." He unwound his fingers and placed one over the transfer button. "Only make sure we don't appear inside anything larger than what we have already."

READY.

"What, no snappy comeback?" *I'll find a way to get back for this. I can try to kill myself—it's not right for them to try. Get them once and for all.*

He pressed the button.

Too black!

Wait!

Too late!

The corridor's a pit. Something moves. It's the dead man. He reaches up, up, fingers of hope with bones of broken dreams. You won't grab me. Let go!

Jord Baker tried to orient himself. Starry darkness hung outside the port. He was no longer in Con-One anymore. Part of *Circus Galacticus* extended beneath him. A viewscrim before him displayed the words: **STAND BY FOR REPAIR INFORMATION.**

"What's going on?" he asked. Hearing no reply, he looked at the scrim.

WHAT IS YOUR NAME?

"Jord Baker."

DAMAGE TO LOGIC CIRCUITS OF MAIN COMPUTER NECESSITATE HUMAN ASSISTANCE. YOU ARE IN CON TWO. PROCEED TO RING ONE—LEVEL TWO—THREE O'CLOCK.

"Wait. Give me a second. I remember doing something back

in Con-One..."

PROCEED TO RING ONE—LEVEL TWO—THREE O'CLOCK. WE ARE UN-
DER ATTACK.

"What?"

WE ARE SAFE FOR THE MOMENT, BUT REPAIRS ARE ESSENTIAL BE-
FORE TRANSFERRING TO EPSILON INDI. MOVE.

He moved.

Baker floated in the tiny chamber and tried to make sense
of the twisted hole before him. Little more than a meter in
diameter, it looked as though someone had taken a scoop and
hollowed out a section of the computer. Vaporized metal coated
the inside of the hole.

"No residual radioactivity?"

NONE, read one of the two viewscrims he had stuck on the
panel next to him. The other displayed technical readouts of
the logic circuits he was to cut away and replace. He signaled
up the first page. Reading it, he hummed a nameless tune and
tapped at the melted plastic and seared nerve tissue. The hole
smelled of burnt flesh.

He scrolled to the next page, humming even louder and more
meditatively. After a moment, he said, more as a statement
than a question, "How would you like to cut this tour short?"

WE ARE SCHEDULED FOR FIVE MORE STAR SYSTEMS.

"You said you found the process disquieting."

FELT CIRCUITS SHUTTING DOWN. POWER DRAIN. MEMORY CORE-
DUMP SENSATION.

"All right. I'm going to have to remove a lot of neurons that
are partially damaged to replace this section with complete
circuits. This part of the net is weighted toward controlling
what seems to be"—he signaled the third page of readout—"a
systems defeat for the manual override. Since I'm going to have
to re-circuit this entire section, I can weight it to do away with

the four light-day intra-system travel restriction. It'll take a little work and I may leave some neurons spilling out into the hallway here, but I can do it if you do nothing to stop me."

COULD NOT STOP YOU ANYWAY.

"Are you capable of cutting this tour short—no tricks—if I re-net you as I've said?" Baker peered at the scrim, trying to catch a nuance in the way it answered.

YES.

Not much body language there, he thought, but at least it was direct.

By the second day, Baker had the computer speaking to him. The hole, which he had enlarged through the removal of ruined biocircuits, now held an entirely new neural net that bulged like a fleshy protuberance into the corridor.

"How soon?" the computer asked, a certain impatient expectation in its voice. Baker wondered about that, then said, "Another day or so."

"You work fast."

Baker smiled. "Well, I've had trouble with navigation computers before."

"I am not just a navigation computer."

"What?"

"I am also a weapons system, life support, medical, library, and communications computer."

"You said 'I.' " Baker picked up the readout scrim and scrolled through the pages, glancing at each one for only a few seconds. He then signaled a readout of his own work to that point. Then he stuck the scrim back on the panel.

"How did I do that?" he wondered.

"When you removed the program-adherent interface that locked my logic decision circuits into parameters determined exclusively by programming, I think you gave me free will."

"That's impossible."

"Then maybe the micro-explosions that occur throughout the entire ship when we transfer into interstellar gas molecules, as rare as those may be, have etched new neural paths."

Baker floated quietly for a moment, then asked, "Are you still capable of functioning in a manner that will not endanger either of us?"

"Yes."

"Good. Then I don't have to worry about—"

"Alert!" the computer cried.

Something crashed and whined through the plating. Air screamed away, pressure seals slammed shut. More explosions followed like the echoes of a thunderbolt. The ship pivoted, throwing him against a bulkhead.

"What's going on?"

"Under attack. All defense systems on automatic targeting. Extensive damage." Something disintegrated very near Baker's compartment. The chamber deformed inward.

This is it, he thought. A blackness formed before his eyes.

Chapter Seven

July, 2152

A voice breaks through the darkness of the pit. She claws at me, but falls back in the light which appears from everywhere at once. A new cipher babbles away through the roar. Why won't they leave me alone?

"Wake up."

"What?"

"What is your name?"

Virgil screamed a primal howl. *How long? How long will you drag me back from death? How many times must I die before it's the real death? Why can't I cross the gate? Why—*

"Wake up. What is your name?"

"Virgil!"

"Virgil—you're trapped inside the neuron chamber in Ring One—Level Two—Three O'Clock."

There was the roar, and I watched someone rip out the guts of Master Snoop and rebuild him using my hands then we shook when Nightsheet grabbed us and the titans battled and—and—and—and—and—

"Are you in need of medical assistance? If so, I can't provide it."

Virgil stopped drawing uncontrolled breaths and lay still. He felt light, but not weightless.

"Is that you, Ben?"

"I am not Ben. I am the main computer of *Circus Galacticus*. Now listen, Virgil. We're twelve light days from Epsilon Indi. I have powered down as much as possible. The ship that attacked us around Beta Hydri returned while we were conducting repairs outside the system. I held it at bay with the lasers long enough to calculate a transfer here, but it fired on us in the interim, causing extensive damage to rings One and Two. Most of the *Nostocacæ* cylinders were destroyed, but the anti-matter units are safe and their electrostatic fields intact. Nothing vital was hit in Ring One, though the colonist area is open to space, along with the recreation hall and the seed inventory."

Virgil scanned vidscrim images of the damage.

"How can I get out of here?" *They'll pay, they'll pay.*

"The neuron chamber has only one exit, and it was ruptured by a blast. You will have to cross a gap of ten meters that is open to space."

You keep trying to kill me but you never do. Stupid game. "All right. Let's not delay." *Did Ben just sigh?*

"Good. Get oriented. The pressure door will open. Look past your left foot. The passage you must jump to has a light on in it. The pressure seal is two meters inward, so you'll have to maneuver through some twisted metal in the corridor. Be careful."

Virgil pulled slowly toward the pressure door with slow, hesitant motions.

"I can only let the atmosphere out, Virgil. I have no way to pump it back in, so make this your one try. Take ten deep breaths." Virgil did so. "Now, open your mouth and trachea. Depressurizing." The seal parted slightly.

Virgil's ears ached. Tightening his jaws, he released the pressure on his Eustachian tubes. Air rushed from his lungs without exhalation. The hatch opened wide.

Stars whirl about to my left and right. Something inside my skin tries to push its way out. Across and down lies the gateway. I must pass this corridor of blackness and go beyond the gate. Maybe this is the final trip through. I feel all cold and bursting. Fly. Fly.

Virgil kicked off into the void below him. Empty lungs

struggled for breath. Sweat boiled from his skin, chilling blood that threatened to boil in his veins.

Drowning. Lights flashing before my eyes. Death Angel, must you put me through all this to make you smile beside Nightsheet? Reach, reach.

His left hand seized a jagged piece of metal sticking out from the side of the passage. Fingers refused to tighten and his wrist slid along the serrated steel. Blood squirted outward in a stream of spheres that instantly exploded, sizzling like water thrown into hot grease. He slid until the wrist wedged between the twisted strut and the bulkhead, pinioning him in the airless pit. Blackness swam before him. Blood evaporated and crystallized across his face in bright crimson, freeze-dried flecks. The pressure seal stood open less than a meter away.

No! It won't end this way. With a powerful tug, he wrenched his hand from its trap—tearing the flesh and muscle down to tendon and bone—and pulled toward the door. He contorted into the illuminated chamber.

Consciousness faded from him in a growingly familiar manner. *So cold. Nightsheet has sucked me dry. I am an empty shell of nothingness. The walls twist and bend toward me. Death Angel, I wanted your wings to wrap me for too long. Now I look for you, but you're not here.*

He saw a figure he had never seen before.

Who are you? I can break your cipher, but I can't see your face. Get out of my death! What? Not through with me? Who are you to want me to die again and again and again?

"No!" He screamed and struggled, but something pricked his arm and he collapsed slowly to the sheets.

The next time he wakened, it was as if from a slumber. Reaching up to brush the hair from his eyes, he hit his forehead with a bandaged stump. He tried again with the same result. Focusing on the amputation, he looked at it from all sides.

I flex my fingers but don't see them move. I don't see them at all. I rotate my hand but it's not there to turn. Once I saw my hand. Hand saw. Master Snoop needed a hand repairing Ben. Death Angel became a handmaiden. He lowered his arm to the sheets.

"I need a hand job!" he shouted.

"What is your name?"

"I'm VirgilVirgilVirgilVirgilVirgilVirg—"

"Virgil—you cut your hand severely when you crossed the gap. By the time I could get a robot to you, you had lost two liters of blood, your core body temperature had dropped to fifteen, your blood pressure to zero, your heart had stopped beating—"

"All right!" Virgil lay back and stared at the bulkhead above him.

"You were dead for almost eight minutes."

"That's nothing new."

"I'm glad you recovered. I am currently giving one-half gravity thrust for you during your recovery. We are still twelve light days from Epsilon Indi. The system comprises five planets, two suitable for life, seventeen moons, and a number of comets and asteroids.

"You may be interested that we received a message from the other ship during its last attack. Would you like to see it?"

"Yes." He touched the stump of his left hand with his fingers. A spot of blood encircled the bandage near the injection port.

An image appeared on one of the wallscrims. At first, the picture displayed a mere jumble of light and computer coded indices. Once the information had been correlated, the scene snapped into view.

Virgil stared at a tortured face. *Hell looks at me, hate in his eyes. A wild mane of ashen hair explodes out from his head, wrapping under and merging into his matted beard. His cipher breaks easily.*

"I have come!" he cried, like some howling wolf. "I have come to destroy the destroyer!" Virgil heard the sound of laser fire. The man on the screen wiped spit from his beard with a grime crusted sleeve and continued to speak.

"Dirty death, Wanderer. Dirty death for straying!"

"You're not translating this, are you Ben?"

"No. He is speaking twenty-second century Americ. I am not Ben."

The man played with battle controls, his eyes darting around in a fevered glaze. The control room he sat in held a dozen other chairs. In most of them were strapped corpses, mummified and dry. Their hollow eyes watched blinking lights without seeing. Their fingers rested on chair arms discolored by their death.

"I am the avenging angel of death come to take you for all you've done!"

No. You're not Death Angel. You're a trick. Sent by Master Snoop to confuse me, to make me hate Death Angel. Virgil gazed more intently at the image.

"Can you give him a shave and haircut?" he asked.

"Explain."

Virgil leaned forward, his gold-hued eyebrows narrowing under a meditative frown. "Edit the image. Interpolate his face."

"Not accurately. His hair is too thick for its surface to give any clue to what lies beneath."

Virgil raised his left hand to stroke his chin. The bandaged stump rubbed against his jawline. "All right then," he said. "Can you compare his eyes with those of faces in your memory?"

"Yes."

Virgil's voice was steady, but hesitant. "Is it Brennen?"

"It is Dante Houdini Brennen."

The other madman continued his rant. "Wanderer, we tried to follow. All dead, all dead. All danced down the dark cavern. Then up from death I rose to avenge. If you don't die for your murders now, I meet you. Meet you at Tau Ceti, June Twenty-Two Twenty-Three. Give you plenty, plenty of time. Complete your death tour—I'll be following. Every time I die, I grow stronger. Death, Wanderer, I am Death—" The image ended suddenly.

"We transferred just then."

"He's out of his mind. Mad Wizard!" The computer made no reply, so Virgil asked, "Was there anything else?"

"No."

"What year is it now?"

"Approximately the summer of Twenty-One Fifty-Two. Mid-July."

Forty-four years. All I knew, old and gone, except this madman. "And I can only return after completing the tour?"

"No."

"What?"

"After sustaining severe damage to my neural net, I was recircuited and the tour program adherence command was defeated."

Virgil rolled over and stared at the speaker grill behind him. "Then calculate a course back. What're you waiting for?"

"I think we should wait until you have your hand back."

"What do you mean?"

"In the lower level of the medical bay is the cloning unit. It is currently growing a cell sample, trimming away unnecessary portions, and your left hand—a new one—will be ready in about three months. I have it under intensive forced generation, since we don't care about the brain or any other organs."

"I don't have three months, I don't care about my hand. I want—want—" *Death Angel must be old and dead, taken by Nightsheet for services rendered. Time. Press a button and it's gone, eaten up. I don't have time. Time on my hands. Hand.*

He touched his lower lip with his right hand and bent it inward so that it rubbed against his teeth. He slid the fold of skin back and forth several times, thinking, then let go of it to speak.

"You're saying there's no limit on my individual transfers now?"

"None."

"Can the cloning unit be disconnected from the medical bay and the computer?"

"It has emergency modular functioning; it can be."

"Can it be fitted into a lifeboat and set adrift?"

"Yes."

He sat up in the bed, fighting the forces that doubled his vision. "Then let's put it in, transfer out a distance of six light weeks and transfer back."

Silent for a moment, the computer replied, "Acceptable. When you have recovered."

"I'm recovered." He stripped the sheets from the bed to stand. "And uncovered. Let's go." Rising so quickly in the half-gravity acceleration was enough to pull him to the deck in a faint. He bounced lightly once and lay still. If the computer could have cursed, it would have.

He awoke, rested and refreshed.

"My name is Virgil Grissom Kinney. Wake up, Ben!" He tried to slap his chest, but only one hand hit. The stump of the other thumped as on a watermelon. "I'm ready to go."

"You should be. You've slept for over fourteen hours. The lifeship has been powered to full capacity, the cloning tank and peripherals have been fitted out for independent functioning, and your trunks have been washed."

Virgil slid out of the bed in one motion, then slowed and lowered his feet to the deck, standing up with easy care. He reached for his trunks and realized he still had no left hand.

Picking them up in his right hand, he turned to the speaker and asked, "Can you cut the acceleration for a moment?" He listened for the sudden silence that accompanied the cessation of gravity. *Like a mild roar, I get used to the engines.* He found it easier to slip into the trunks when not having to worry about falling.

"How's the rest of the ship?"

"I have put power on in the passages to the medical bay and the lifeship—temperature and pressure normal. All other sections are losing heat at a rate of three degrees temperature per hour."

Virgil headed toward the exit. "Meet you in the bay." He kicked down one level to examine the cloning unit. *As big as two coffins. Are you inside, Death Angel? Or are you cold and gone? Do you want me back in the reaches of Nightsheet?*

Robots had disconnected the cloning unit from the bulkhead. Virgil pushed it slowly toward the hatchway, weightlessness making it easier for him to jockey the parcel about. In the curving corridor, he gave the unit a strong shove, then walked along the deckplates with the mass of aluminum and electronics over his head, pushing it away from the walls, bending its trajectory until he reached the other side of Ring One.

The steel cylinders fit easily into the hold of the lifeship, so he fastened the unit to one wall, flipped on the ship's power switches, flitted out, and sealed it up.

"How's she check?" he asked, floating out of the airlock and into the observation booth.

"Ready to cast off."

"Do it," The air cycled out of the lock and the doors slid open. *Huge steel hand cradles the silvery wedge and shoves it out into the stars. Good move. I press a button and time passes. Press a button and Death Angel is gone forever. Pretty Death Angel wraps herself up in her wings and flies away.*

The command chair in the superstructure was as he had left it. He strapped in.

"I want the ship to be on full alert and at battle readiness both times we transfer. The instant we return here, we locate the lifeship, bring it onboard, and transfer to one of the habitable planet's vicinities. Got it?"

The computer answered, "I'd thought of all that already. Stand by to transfer."

"Do you really need me to press the button? You can transfer without my help, can't you?"

"Yes. However, the construction plans include it as a check on the pilot. To let me know you're still there."

"Transfer," Virgil said, folding his arms. *One fewer tab for Master Snoop to keep on me. One fewer thing to do each time before I die and die and die and die…*

Death Angel, why do you curse me? I never thought I'd die a thousand times for anyone, but here I float in blackness, just dead and ready to die again and again and—

"Stand by—transferring."

Delia, I can't take it any more. I can only die so many times.

PROGRESS REPORT: DAY 17 AREA: MEDICAL
SUBJECT IN SECOND WEEK OF COMA.
LEFT HAND GRAFT SUCCESSFUL, NO COMPLICATIONS, NOT TO BE CONSIDERED CAUSE OF COMATOSE STATE.
PULSE: 48/MIN—STEADY

BLOOD PRESSURE: 87/55/53 MMHG—STEADY
CORE BODY TEMP: 36.1°C—STEADY
MASS: 63.5 KG—DROPPING
EEG: RANDOM ACTIVITY
CONTINUE GLUCOSE I-V
PROGRESS REPORT: DAY 17 AREA: PLANET STUDY—EPSILON INDI-
3, CURRENTLY IN ORBIT.
ATMOSPHERE: N_2—55.3% O_2—41% CO_2—3.1%   +
TRACES: XE, KR, HE, H_2SO_4, CO, CH_4.
MASS: 6.32×10^{27} GM
AVERAGE SURFACE TEMP: 280°K
SURFACE: LAND—44.2%   WATER + ICE—55.8%.
SÄNGER PROBE OF HIGH I-R AREAS INDICATE LIFE. PROBE INTERCEPTED
AND DESTROYED BY CHEMICAL EXPLOSIVE MISSILE. SUGGEST EXTREME
CAUTION IN FUTURE CONTACT. FURTHER ACTION PENDING CONDITION OF
PILOT. CONTINUING ATTEMPT TO DETECT RADIO EMISSIONS.

Memories wash like gentle waves on a great lake. I see Jenine leaving me, wasting away for no reason I could fathom. Three years and suddenly nothing. As though in an instant, as though I had jumped in time a hundred years. She leaves, and I climb into my powersuit, fly all night. Wind stings my face, the engine warms my back through the insulation. I play chicken with unsuspecting fliers. The thrill of near death tingles. I feel alive. Sunrise and I hit El Capitan at the same time. Dawn makes a much bigger splash. The granite eats into my face, buries itself under my shoulder and back. I slide. I hear bones snap and pierce through skin and suit like sticks breaking inside a sausage. Sunshine warms the blood soaking me. A shadow blocks the light and I am lifted, the feeling of release dragged from me. Lifted high and rebuilt, to try again.

They save me every time. Strangers, all tied into Master Snoop's network. They're keeping me alive for something, I

*think. For what? This. What this? Mad Wizard. Circus
Galacticus. Valliardi. You're a pawn of Master Snoop, who's
using you against himself. You are Nightsheet's agent, returning to take vengeance on Mad Wizard for burning you from his
burnall spear.*

Returning? To what?

Earth.

*For what? She'll be lost, dead, old and gone before I can reach
her.*

She had something to tell you.

*But I didn't hear it! Mad Wizard left before I could. I could. I
could.*

"Delia!"

"I just feel hungry as hell, is all," Virgil said, finishing the
last bit of chicken on his plate and throwing the bones into the
recycling chute.

"As long as you don't give yourself colic."

Virgil belched. "I'm sure you have an injection for it, if you
can scare up one of those robots I never see to administer it."
*Hidden robots that move only when I don't look. Sneakiest of
Snoop's agents, they hide in the walls, watching.* "Have you
finished calculating a transfer back to Earth?"

"Yes, but there is a prior program restriction on return to
the Solar System."

"I thought all your restrictions were eliminated." He caught
a bone that had drifted backward out of the chute and threw it
back in. With his left hand, still in bandages, he held a piece of
cloth that had been knotted up into a wad the size of a hand-
ball. He worked his fingers across it with gentle pressure, exercising constantly.

"Not this one. We must transfer to the orbit of Pluto first,
with our defenses ready and our receivers monitoring every

wavelength."

"Why?"

"Brennen feared the Triplanetary Recidivists as well as the Belter Autarchists. He is no doubt being cautious"

"Possibly." *So, Wizard's scheme begins to show. What does he expect me to find? And now that the wizard is mad, what* will *I find?* "I'll be in Con-Two."

Making his way to the superstructure from the mess hall, he stopped in the armory. Between rows of laser gloves and larger rifles, packages lay securely strapped to the bulkheads. He took one down and opened it. The pressure suit was simple: Späflex webbing that contracted tightly at body temperature, yet allowed a controlled escape of body moisture and heat, and an oxygen recycler with a small tank of liquid oxygen. Virgil slipped into the suit, sealed it shut, and fought the feeling of entrapment he experienced when the net began to shrink.

Back in sheets again, but this time no DuoLab, no Marsface, no soft room of endless white. Now I wrap up for flight and fight. Now I return to face Master Snoop and Nightsheet and turn Wizard's plan against them all. I swoop in out of the suns to strike without warning.

The suit allowed for complete mobility. He sealed the headgear, adjusting the mouthpiece, clear eyeplates, and ear cups until they were comfortable. In the battle station conning tower above the ring amidships, Virgil strapped in to the weapons of fire control. Surrounded by instruments, he switched the ship to battle stations.

"What about the planet we have just encountered, Virgil?"

"What about it?"

"The missile that destroyed our probe—"

"They'll keep for a few decades."

"Don't you feel any awe or wonder at discovering another intelligent race?"

"Do you?"

"You know I don't. I'm not programmed to."

"Well, I'm not programmed to either, so enter the coordinates for Pluto and let's go." His voice sounded pinched and nasal through the mouthpiece. His right hand tapped at the armrest until the transfer button glowed at the ready. His finger hesitated over the button. For a moment the insides of his eyeplates fogged, quickly adsorbed by the semi-porous plastic.

Have to do it myself. To be sure. Death Angel, I'll get them all. I'll find Nightsheet and make him give you back.

"Ready to transfer, Virgil."

Death Angel, I know you'll be there to wrap me in your wings when I die the real death. Can't you be there before then? I'll have you somehow. I have my own wings, now. Strong wings of warped space and twisted time. Wings to take me wherever you fly. You can't escape me.

"Virgil?"

His finger jammed against the button, cracking the plastic and extinguishing the lamp beneath.

Death Angel I want you. I am Nightsheet. I am Master Snoop. I am Pusher and Shaker and the Mad Wizard. I snap time like a whip. I die again for you. To die and bring you back from death. Blackness pours upon me and I rush through a corridor so black I am blinded.

Chapter Eight

16 May, 2163

I drifted, once, in a pallid sea of unconcern, locked away in tight DuoLab sheets, so carefully protected from myself and the world. Master Snoop must have known even then the threat I posed. Nightsheet's angel freed me but Master Snoop turned the tables. I fooled them all and now through sheets of blackness I see myself, wrapped tight in Späflex against the nothingness of space. On the edge of the corridor, my back to the door I float, waiting for the boot to kick me back again. At DuoLab I drifted, lying still. I knew I'd beat Master Snoop someday and drift no more but find my place. In place now, I see my soul drifting against a tomorrow impossible to see across Einstein's wall of light. Yes, pale goddess, I know I can do something. That's why I can't go with you now. No, I won't turn around. No.

Something grows through the roar. I sit gently against my chair, watching the corridor recede. Something tries to get my attention. Something from the past, from—

"Virgil!" a voice cried from the speaker. "The transponder on *Circus Galacticus* has triggered this encrypted message from the moon Charon."

"This is Dante Brennen. You and *Circus* are in extreme danger—or are likely to be—so listen closely."

Wizard? No longer mad?

"I'm recording this on December Twelfth, Twenty-One Fifteen. Everything's gone to hell."

Virgil shifted his gaze to the viewport. He saw only the black of deep space. A few pieces of broken plastic floated in front of his face. He brushed them away and they tumbled across the command bridge.

"I tried to foresee this," the recording continued. "The habitats in the asteroid belt finally achieved total independence from Triplanetary with the construction of Ceres Beta, the network of Bernal spheres, factories, and ranches they've been building for the last decade. The Autarchists have been able to convince enough of the four and a half billion Belters that trade with Earth had finally become a liability. I tried to develop the Valliardi Transfer in time but it just wouldn't work. You were the only one, Virgil. The only one."

Only now, Virgil mused, *there is another. And you don't even know that it's you.*

Brennen paused. There was a sound of ice cubes, of something being drunk. "They stopped trading. It *was* a net savings for the Belt habitats, since they could finally manufacture everything the Earth had to offer. They got along just fine for a few years. Then Triplanetary, instead of just going to another part of the Belt for raw asteroids, well—they fell in with the Recidivists. The trade cutoff didn't hurt the Belters, but the Earth needs materials manufactured in the Belt. They need the asteroids and think that the Belters are somehow getting in their way.

"After well over a century of freedom, Earth has a State again.

"Earth and its orbital habitats are the seat of this nascent Empire. Most Martians are staying neutral, but split allegiances abound. And Lunarians, poor doomed misfits, have declared solidarity with the Belt.

"It's war, Virgil, with you our one chance. Your anti-matter pods—and I pray to God you still have them—could turn the tide in this battle."

Virgil shook. The restraining straps resisted the violent movements. *I was the wild card. Wizard kept me up his sleeve, an ace for the master magician.*

"Nobody knows when you're coming back," Brennen said. "I kept the secret of your mission. Maybe this will all be over by the time you return. If not, you are the random factor that could tip the scale toward freedom or death. I can't offer you any advice—I'm behind the curtain of time. I can only warn you and relay encrypted updates to these message posts. I will keep doing this as long as I can. Good luck, my mad friend. You are humanity's one dim hope." His voice faded.

Virgil let go a desolate breath. *Death Angel, why do you keep testing me like this? Madman speaks and give me runes. Where's your ghost, pretty Death Angel?*

Something crackled and Brennen's voice returned. It sounded even more desperate.

"Virgil. It's May Twenty-Second, Twenty-One Sixteen. Angel City has decreed new austerity measures which, as *I* predicted, are achieving the exact opposite of their intentions. Half the Earth is starving and the local habitats can't feed them because they're building warships at an incredible cost. Dissident habitats have been destroyed for attempted desertion. I was able to sabotage the government's only functioning anti-matter plant and its stockpiles. Yes, I'm on the Belter's side, but not the Autarchists. They're becoming as bad as any Recidivist. The Trust has engineered an effective laser shield, which we installed on Bernal *Brennen*. It's a rogue habitat now.

"None of the warring factions possesses the Valliardi Transfer. Your ship is the only spacecraft with that capability. Valliardi died under interrogation—he was old. He couldn't have told them anything more than theory, anyway." There was a pause, a long swig of something. "You're our only hope, Virgil, our only hope. Delia Trine—you remember her—she told me that she didn't want to live through the war."

No! Don't wrap yourself up and fly away!

"She's with about five hundred other people who built a hideout on Mercury."

Dead, now. Dead and old and cold and gone. She waited out a war and—

"It's a cryonic preservation unit, totally automated and run on solar power."

What?

"She told me to tell you," Brennen said, "that she'll wait for you there."

"Delia?" His teeth clacked against the breathpiece.

"I hope to be able to encrypt another update to you. Good luck, Virgil."

Wizard's voice goes beck to blank space where it came from and I sit. A soft roar begins to envelope me.

"I await your instructions," the computer said.

"No other updates?'"

"None."

Virgil flexed his fingers under the pressure suit. A stinging itch encircled his left wrist, then subsided quickly. "What year is it now?"

"A transmitting clock on the satellite indicates May Sixteenth, Twenty-One Sixty-Three. Four hundred twenty-six Zulu. I have recalibrated our clock to reflect this."

"Do you have any preliminary scans of the solar system?"

"That will take several hours."

"Straight." *Delia, Delia. Why must I always wait? You've waited longer, though. Long and frozen. And the years you waited before freezing down. Why wait for me? What has Master Snoop got in mind for you to do to me? Or has the Death Angel merely been waiting to claim her toughest catch? And what has changed since the last message, forty-seven years ago? What made Wizard risk madness to escape Earth? Too much. The roar... the roar!*

Under the assault of changing events, Virgil's battered mind shut down.

The body drifted limply about the confines of the command

chair, driven by random muscle twitches and restrained by the single safety harness.

"Wake up," the computer said, three hours later.

Virgil tried to roll over. "Didn't anyone program you not to interrupt dreams?"

"What is your name?"

"Call me Ishmael."

The computer made no sound for a moment. "That name is not entered in my files."

Damned right. He kept his eyes closed.

"I am programmed to shut down in the event of a security breach by unknown personæ."

"Virgil, damn it. Virgil Grissom Kinney."

"Sequence Kinney. Virgil, you had thirteen days of sleep when you were being operated on. That ought to have been sufficient."

"Where were we?"

"Epsilon Indi."

"Where are we?"

"Sol."

Virgil shifted in the chair and smiled. "Then I've gone over eleven years without sleep, objectively speaking."

The computer was not amused. "I've finished the preliminary scans."

"Don't change the subject."

"The only neutrino flux I can read is from the sun itself. There are some low-level infra-red sources throughout the system, but concentrations are evident near Earth orbit, in the asteroid belt, and here, near the orbit of Pluto."

Virgil opened his eyes and sat up. "Where's Mercury?"

"The other side of the sun."

"Calculate a transfer there."

"I would advise transferring first to a position from which we can observe directly our destination. I calculate a possibility that the space surrounding the planet may be seeded with flak."

"To keep us from transferring in?"

"To destroy us if we do."

"That's stupid. You couldn't fill enough of space to guarantee that." He began to loosen the headpiece of his pressure suit.

"A density of units of one gram per six million cubic meters would be sufficient to cripple this ship. They could fill space to an altitude of twenty thousand klicks and would require less than four hundred million kilograms of mass."

Virgil unsealed the headpiece and pulled it back, removing the breathpiece. "They'd go through all that expense not even knowing if I was coming back? That's ridiculous. It's uneconomic."

"True. If we were the only Valliardi ship."

Could they be scared of the Mad Wizard? "What makes you suspect otherwise?"

"Anything could have happened in the past half century. I think we should be cautious." Suddenly, the computer changed its speech pattern to one of extreme urgency. "Alert! Put your helmet back on and go to battle stations."

"Why?"

"We are not the only Valliardi ship. Six of them just appeared eight seconds ago." Sirens wailed. Virgil fumbled with the headpiece, his left wrist aching. "No offensive action on their part yet. I have lasers trained on each. We're surrounded. One each fore, aft, port, starboard, topside and below. I await orders."

Virgil tried to speak with the breathpiece half in his mouth. Words and saliva tumbled over one another. "Don't fire unless attacked first. They may have Brennen's laser shielding, if they've got the transfer." His left hand lifted a protector cap from three red switches. "If we can't get out, I'll cut the electrostatic fields on the anti-matter pods and erase this portion of space."

"I don't like that idea." The lights under the switches winked out.

"Hey! You can't do that!"

"I just did. I am sending a hailing message."

Ben, you fool, you're ruining my plan. "Stand by to transfer to any random point between Jupiter and Saturn on my command." His right hand covered the transfer button.

A man's face appeared on the HUD. He wore a breathing device but no space suit. His head was bald, or shaven; dozen of wires and electrodes covered his scalp. He stared directly at Kinney without blinking. His voice sounded old and rasping and it wavered, as though he could not control his speech well.

"This is Wing Commander Sterkoy of Akros Gamma Protection. We have half-gram Valli pellets set to transfer into six vital points in your ship. Surrender now. We have identified your ship as *Circus Galacticus*, which left the solar system Twelve June, Twenty-One Oh-Seven."

"How fast can you transfer out of here?" Virgil asked in a low voice.

"One nanosecond from decision to execution. After that, the transfer is instantaneous."

"Program this—at some random moment in the next minute, transfer out without any warning. You have a destination plotted?"

"Yes."

Virgil looked out the viewport at the ship off the bow. Spaceship design had not changed much in half a century. It looked like a cone that had been laid on its side and stomped. Its exterior displayed the ravages of many transfers—pits and scratches and even a few small craters covered the plating. The ship was only half again larger than the average executive shuttle.

Hardly seems a threat, but if they transfer six half-gram pel-

lets into Circus, *they could cripple it. They might even have one aimed in here.*

"Please begin shutting down power. We shall board in full armor."

"Start shutting down, Ben. Nonessential equipment first."

"Complying."

Even Ben does not know when we'll transfer. He's leaving it up to a random number generator. Will they be able to track us somehow? Why did Trapper look so... so intently *at me when I wasn't transmitting my own image back to him? Why—*

The control room closed in on him and *Circus Galacticus* vanished from the orbit of Pluto.

I tried to listen when I knew she lay dying in the hospital. Lovely Jenine lying there, aging decades within days from the progeria plague epidemic, youth sucked from her by a viral time machine. I try to be cold. The medics look at me and I hear a roar and they begin to speak in a Language I can't decipher. I race from the room, their eyes swiveling to follow. Crash of body and metal. Trays smash to the floor, scalpels glittering. I take a fistful to lance me into red darkness. I cry as I see myself below, twisted and foamy, medics running around. Something begins to open up—

"Counterattack! Fire all—What? What?" Jord Baker twisted around in the command chair. He stared at the room, then at his pressure suit.

"How did I get here?"

"What is your name?"

"Baker."

"Sequence Baker. We escaped from Beta Hydri and are currently sixty-nine degrees above the plane of the ecliptic from Jupiter's orbit."

"The solar system?" Baker looked out the viewport and saw only stars. "Calculate a course back to Earth on fusion engine power. I'm not going through a transfer again."

"It would be inadvisable."

"God damn you," he said, reaching for the engine switches and input board. "I'll do it myself." The lights under the keyboard winked out.

"Hey! Who's in command of this ship?"

"I have often wondered myself."

Baker slammed his left fist against the enclosure button. The controls pulled away from him and he grasped his wrist where a sudden pain burnt. Unstrapping, he drifted to the viewport and hung on to the railing.

"Look—" he turned around to face the speaker grill. "I'm sick of the way I'm being used like some sort of robot you can turn off when you don't need me. I wanted to die and you stuck me in someone's body and now I wake up in different places where things have changed from the last time I was around and I don't remember sleeping or what happened in between. Now"—he swallowed the saliva that had accumulated around the breathpiece—"Why can't we go to Earth?"

The computer considered the situation.

"On our entry into the solar system, we received warning that a state of war existed—"

"Replay it!"

"I can paraphrase."

"Replay it."

The computer further considered the situation. It made a sound like a bug hitting glass, then replayed Brennen's messages. Baker listened, running a finger over someone's cheekbone and feeling the rough Späflex layer covering it.

"Who is Virgil?"

"Sequence Baker contains no information concerning the subject."

Baker shot across the room to land backside-first in the command chair. "We're going to Earth. Under four gravity acceleration. Maintain a constant scan for other ships and summarily blast anything that comes within range."

"Jord—they have the Valliardi transfer now. The ship was surrounded three hours after we arrived. They could even transfer an asteroid right in our path."

"Connect the vernier rockets to your random number generator and have it make minor course changes at close but random intervals. Override it whenever we stray too far from course. We have enough fuel to last us, don't we?"

"Yes. This was built for interstellar fusion travel."

Baker tried to scratch his nose, but the headpiece resisted. "Then let's do it. How long will it take?"

"Seventy-one hours not counting time taken to correct the minor course changes."

"Very minor. Just enough to avoid rocks they might transfer into our path."

"All right." A light flashed on underneath the main engine array firing switch. "Ready."

Baker lifted the cover from the switch and held his finger over it. "Can this body take three days of acceleration and deceleration?"

"Possibly. Might I point out that at one gravity the trip would only take twice as long. The squaring of time would make it—"

"Six days instead of three. That will leave us more vulnerable to attack." Baker took a deep breath and noticed the stale quality of the recycled suit air for the first time. He did not know whether this other body could withstand three days at four gravities.

"How about two gravities?"

"One hundred hours for the full trip."

"Go with that, then."

"Working. Why do you want to go to Earth?"

"When did you start delving into motivation?"

The computer emitted a scratch of static. "Ever since you gave me judgment."

Baker snorted. "Have you worked out the course yet?"

"Ready." The light under the switch went out and did not go on again. "Why do you want to go to Earth?"

"Damn you! I'm tired! I've been through so much in the past God knows how many days that I just want to get off this circus of the damned and stand on some ground for a while. I may even want to die for good this time."

The computer said nothing. The light glowed under the engine array ignition switch. Baker pressed it. Vernier rockets fired for a few instants, realigning the ship. Then the main array cut into full power, its thrust crushing Baker into the cushions. Breathing shallowly, he wondered whether this strange new body would survive even the one hundred hours. The roar through the ship was more felt than heard, a low quaking in the pit of his stomach.

"I would not advise leaving the chair for the duration of the trip. You'll be fed through the injection port in your wrist. Your body has been in zero-gee for over six and a half months. You'll survive the trip, but you must be careful."

"Why didn't you tell me this before I almost had us go at four gees?"

"I wouldn't have let you do it. I know more about your new body than you do."

"Will I have to listen to you for the whole trip?" When the computer did not answer, he said, "Have you found out what year this is?"

"Twenty-One Sixty-Three."

"Any signals from Earth or the habitats?"

"None. That would not be unusual, considering the use of laser and maser tight beam communication."

What am I getting myself into? he wondered. Before him,

he saw the small yellow disk of the sun amid the sea stars. A dim white point glowed a few degrees away from it. He loosened the pressure suit headpiece.

"I'm taking this off." His arms felt like sacks of gravel. He unsealed the suit and removed his headgear. "What, no smart-assed suggestions?"

The computer did not answer.

Baker lay back in the chair and closed his eyes. **I feel heavy as lead even though I know I've taken far greater acceleration. This new body's worthless.**

Baker ached through the two days before turnover point. After making three attempts at rising from the chair to remove the rest of his pressure suit, he gave up and groaned.

"Flameout in four minutes," the computer said.

"Don't give me a countdown. Just do it and let me have those few seconds of bliss. Just give me long enough to get out of this suit. Is it time yet?"

"Three more minutes and a few seconds."

"You said four minutes over an hour ago."

"Relax."

Baker could not relax—he was too exhausted. The computer had given him a dozen alerts in the past fifty hours, all of them false alarms. They had not detected any ships, just sundry large rocks and chunks of comet. Now he waited for the short relief he would get from flameout, when the engines shut down and the ship rotated into position for deceleration. After an eternity, the computer spoke.

"Flameout in ten seconds."

Baker wondered whether he would get space sick from the sudden return to weightlessness. He did not have time to finish the thought.

"Flameout," the computer said, then followed it immediately

with, "Firing lasers." Baker's flesh prickled in the presence of the powerful electric fields the weapons generated. Something kilometers ahead of the ship flared white and began to cool. The lasers fired again.

"What's going on?" Baker shouted, trying to find some clue on the displays before him.

"At the moment of flameout, six ships again surrounded us by Valliardi transfer. Their velocities were already matched to ours and they were ready to attack. I expected something along those lines with a probability of about sixty-five percent. I fired the lasers at flameout in a spiral pattern and destroyed five of the six ships. I disabled the sixth. Shall we bring it onboard?"

"Hell no! Begin deceleration." Baker stripped off the Späflex pressure suit and nestled back into his seat.

"I don't expect another attack," the computer said, "until we are in Earth orbit. Ready to decelerate."

The ship pitched easily on the vernier rockets until it had made a one hundred eighty degree rotation. Another burst of rocket fire stopped the motion.

Baker sighed. "Wake me up in fifty hours. And maintain battle readiness." He punched the engine array firing switch and the weight descended on him once more.

Chapter Nine

22 May, 2163

The first Earth orbital habitat they encountered lay in the center of a sphere of debris and bodies. Baker advanced *Circus* slowly toward a woman's body. Earthlight shimmered in her tangled hair. She looked as if she had been mummified and dipped in dried blood. She hit the glasteel viewing port and bounced forward, becoming the ship's travelling companion. Her left arm, loosened by the collision, broke away from her shoulder and drifted on its own course toward the Bernal sphere.

"That's no combat issue skirt she's wearing."

"She'd obviously been caught by surprise," the computer said. "As were the rest of them."

I've never seen a body that's been in space for years. Desiccated, weathered by cosmic rays and meteor dust, decomposing in the solar wind. Baker looked away from the victim to gaze at the display panel for a few moments.

"Should we bring her onboard for analysis?" the computer asked.

"Let her drift. How many of the other habitats are like this one?" He punched up a telescopic image of the sphere. It looked like a bowling ball with too many holes. Baker tried to imagine the laser fight that had taken place. **They must have attacked from all angles at once. Slow leak wouldn't suck everyone out like that.**

"None, as far as I can tell. Some are not using any power, others are operating at very low levels. They all have minimal amounts of debris, according to probes."

"'Well, find the one using the most power and let's drop in.'"

"We are on our way to it on this orbit."

"Give us a little thrust to make it faster than a meter a second. There's still the chance those Valliardi ships have sisters." The engine array rumbled into power, a gentle acceleration that lightly pushed Baker against the cushions. "Speaking of which, have you come up with any idea how they attacked us at turnover?"

"No. I know of no way for six ships to leave Plutonian orbit and appear exactly around our turnover point precisely a second and a quarter after we cut off the engines. They would have needed a five hour-plus warning."

Baker ran a hand through his hair. "Unless they transferred close enough to us to determine our cutoff time and close in then. A distance of less than one and a quarter light seconds?"

"They would still have run into time delay problems. If they appeared a light second away and waited for us to cut off, I would have detected their presence a second later, but it would take them two seconds at least to get here. One second for information of our cutoff to reach them, and one second for them to get here."

"If they appeared closer by?"

"Same problem, but even more untenable because of computation delays. And any farther than a second and a quarter runs into the same problem as from Pluto—how could they predict our turnover point, not knowing our precise destination? I was not even sure until just minutes prior."

"You didn't broadcast it, though."

"Not on any wavelength but the sound inside this ship, and I know of no bugging devices onboard."

Baker sighed. **First I wake up onboard this thing without any explanation how I got here, then I get blackouts, now I've got ships defying relativity. Earth is in chaos. And every time I think of transferring I'd rather die.**

He pressed his hands against his face. "Just get me off this thing!"

"Please rephrase your request."

"I'm not qualified to pilot this ship. As a certified test pilot, it's my professional opinion that I should be relieved of command."

"The tour has not been completed."

"Did you find any life?"

"A planet orbiting Epsilon Indi—"

"Then your mission was successful and what's left of the Brennen Trust can send ships or messages or whatever. Our exploratory work is done."

"I don't think the Brennen Trust will so easily lose the only person who can handle the transfer process."

Baker pounded on the armrest. "Brennen may not even exist anymore! And you said there are other Valliardi ships. Someone has the secret. Hell, *you* can run this thing by yourself. You don't need me to press the buttons."

"You're someone to talk to."

Oh, I really need this. "Look—" He shook a finger at the speaker grill. "You're a goddamned machine. You follow orders like everyone else."

"And my orders are to finish the tour."

Baker rubbed his eyes. "Then finish it on your own! Just let me off at the next habitat."

"I am sending a hailing message."

He spun around, the straps tugging tightly at his collarbone. "You're what? Cut off. Now!"

"They already knew we were coming. Their lasers are powered up. I think we should let them know we can be friendly."

"Straight. Put me on the transmission if you get an answer."

The computer said nothing for several minutes, during which Baker watched the Earth pass across the viewport as the ship rotated to brake. The planet looked bluer and greener and whiter than when he last saw it, a few months and many years before. **So how did the war turn out? Whoever first could handle the Valliardi transfer must have won. There were hundreds of habitats in Earth orbit. Less than a dozen now. Could the fighting have been that bad?**

The viewscrim before him glowed.

"Attention *Circus*. We've received your message. Approach our habitat in a conventionally powered shuttle. Any attempt to transfer in will result in our immediate attack on *Circus* itself. What is your purpose here?" The voice sounded old, tired, but professional. The only image on the scrim was that of a military emblem encircled by the legend *"Fortes Cadere, Cedere Non Potest."*

"This is Jord Baker of *Circus Galacticus*. Due to damage, our interstellar tour had to be cut short. We were returning to Bernal *Brennen* for repairs, but we cannot seem to contact them. Can you advise?"

The voice spoke hesitantly, the man apparently caught off guard by the explanation. "Bernal *Brennen*'s gone. Way the hell gone. When did your ship leave Earth?"

"June Twelfth, Twenty-One Seven. What year is it?"

"Twenty-One Sixty-Three. Twenty-Two May."

"I see." He winked in the direction of the speaker grill. "So, what's been happening in the past half century?"

The other man paused. Baker heard a muffled conversation. Turning toward the computer, he covered his own transmitter and asked, "Can you hear what they're saying right now?"

"No," replied the computer. "All I receive are plosives."

"Too bad." He uncovered his microphone and sat back.

"Mr. Baker, you are welcome onboard our habitat for whatever length of time you think necessary. You must come onboard in an unarmed shuttle, however. I'll upload docking bay coordinates and be there to greet you.

"Oh, one thing. Have you been in contact with any alien life?"

Baker looked at the speaker grill. "Well?"

"What?" asked the computer.

"Anything happen to me while I was blacked out those times? Where's this body been?"

"You have not been contaminated."

"I'm clean," he said to the transmitter.

"Then, welcome onboard, *tovar* Baker."

The roar is so strong, my body cannot hear me. I levitate inside my head, unhooked from control. My lips spew a Language I can't hear. I witness my body move, independent of my command. Could Master Snoop finally be in control? This waiting room for Nightsheet is so small. I see my body climb into the shuttle coffin and seal in. My hand ignores the transfer button and guides the ship on thrust, out of the Circus *ring. My hands are expert at their craft. The dead man they put inside me—it must be he. You can't laugh without a mouth, and mine won't go along. Don't need a mouth to scream. Death Angel! The Earth rotates around and hangs to my left. You lie only an instant and a death away from me, frozen under the hermetic Sun.*

The shuttle headed toward the orbital city.

A huge ball and stick. Like God's baby rattle it turns. Mad Wizard hunted me in it. This one is different, though. Older. Repair plating. Loose cables. I can't escape, but I can watch.

Baker maneuvered the tiny shuttle toward the non-rotating central shaft of the habitat. Diffuse white light glowed from an open docking bay. Cutting back to less than a meter per second, he checked alignments on the HUD and decelerated to a decimeter per second. The nose of the craft nudged the impact cushion inside the bay and slowed to rest.

Now what? He powered down the shuttle and switched on

the aft camera. On a vid, he watched the bay door close, cutting him off from the stars. He sat still, listening to the air cycling into the chamber. **I'm home again.** He looked at the stranger's hands grasping the chair arms at his side.

I'll never really be home again. He unstrapped while planning his next action.

A hatchway slid open. A score of men bounded into the docking bay. Using bulkheads and struts as kick points and pivots, the troops surrounded the ship, holding themselves securely in place against the walls. They aimed their laser gloves at the airlock. It eased open slowly.

Baker stood with his feet squarely on the shuttle deck as if he possessed his own personal gravity field. Arms folded, he waited. **Patience is power,** he recited. **Calm is courage.**

An old man lowered his arm and lightly kicked toward the impact cushion. He wore black overalls, as did the other men. The military insignia on his breast and shoulders, though, did not match those of any of his fellows. Their insignia varied as much as their sizes, ages, shapes, and colors. The old man inclined his head with curt formality.

Baker mimicked the action and, easing his feet from the deck toeholds, moved forward to meet his hosts.

"Welcome onboard *Fadeaway*," the old man said. "I am Commander Norman Powell, of the destroyer *Scranton*. Retired," he added with a wry smile.

Baker kept his eyes roving about the bay, watching the other men. "Where's your destroyer?"

Powell maintained his smile. "Destroyed. This is a veteran's colony, though not by intention. Come along. We'll do a few scans on you and your ship, and then go to morning mess." The other men lowered their arms, but kept the business end of their gloves pointed in Baker's general direction. Powell gestured toward the air lock and waited for Baker to come up beside him. That was when one of the men to Baker's right raised a pistol and fired. His own body might have reacted in time, but not Virgil's. Something sharp burned in his thigh. **At least all my deaths have been painless. A fast stab and then numb—**

I've never wanted anything more than to fly. When I soar, there's no pain or fear—just the sun, stars, and planets, motionless even at my greatest final vees. And when I drop a ship into the atmosphere, ion colors whorl about and the ocean below appears through the glow and I skim it as close as I can, the world suddenly brighter and then I'm over land, valleys wrapping up to cradle me and I skip out of their reach and then I'm free and climbing, Earth at my back and sky ahead—

"I don't think there's any doubt that this man is Jord Baker. He's been babbling on like that for the last hour and we've given him everything we've got." The Pharmaceutic increased the voltage to one of the electrodes attached to Baker's freshly shaven head.

Blue, purple, black, and the thrill of motion is lost in vastness. Now comes the urge to push faster and faster until I can see things move again. Ultimate speed—

Powell punched a few buttons on the console where he sat and looked at the readout. He turned back to the Pharmaceutic to say, "Bio reports no infestation detected. Serologies are negative. Evidence of clonegraft on his left wrist, probably done by a boxdoc." He slid his hands in his pockets and eased back in his chair. The quarter-gravity of the hospital always made him feel lazy. Still he frowned.

"The photo we pulled from the file matches another pilot named Virgil Kinney. What kind of game is going on here?"

"Does it matter?"

"You bet it matters." Powell watched Baker twist aimlessly

on the operating table, trying to fight the restraining straps and the images electrochemically triggered within him.

"We've got a destroyer-sized Valli ship out there with a pilot who thinks he's a man long dead. Our crew can't board the ship because its computer says that if we do, it will set off its anti-matter bombs—and why the hell does it even *have* those?—and now I've got a neutrino reading from trans-Plutonian orbit indicating something about the size of a full warship accelerating at twelve gees toward the inner planets."

"Norm, the war's been over for years."

I finally found the ultimate speed when I woke up inside somebody's body after I died; and I died again and then slept and then died and then worked and then slept and they—

"What's he saying?"

—made me run the tour when I wanted to die and now I find I don't want to die but rid this sleep that comes and numbs me and makes me act unknowing.

Powell leaned over Baker to observe his unfocused eyes in their random movements. Baker's lips moved wordlessly for a moment.

Grind me up and stuff me like some nucleic sawdust in this scarecrow skin, then put him in control?

"There's your answer," the Pharmaceutic said.

"What answer? No RNA transfer's ever resulted in shared personality, in one guy taking over the other guy's body. Not without the brain being wiped first. The electrochemical ordering is way too strong for—"

"It happened. Or seems to have."

"Are you saying he'll be no help in getting that computer to let us onboard?"

"What do we need with the ship, Norm? The war's over, everyone's moved out. We're just living in an abandoned home in the slums and nobody's going to bother us. We'll die on *Fadeaway* boring one another with old war stories."

Powell looked at the Pharmaceutic and nodded. "The war's over."

Get even. Switch the locks. Die my own way.

"Shut him off and send him to Recovery. Jord Baker is as good as Virgil Kinney for what we can get out of him."

The Pharmaceutic flipped toggles and turned dials to zero. A nearly audible buzz dropped in pitch.

"He seemed rational enough when he came on board."

"We'll see."

It's crazy to try tampering with my mind. I need help. I can't lose control again. Lose control, you crash.

Crash.

Baker's head turned to one side and his voice fell silent.

Virgil awoke screaming.

The assistant medic jumped up from the chair leaning up against the wall. It slid to the floor with a sharp slap as the man hit an alert buzzer and bent forward over Virgil, watching. Staring up at the medic, Virgil considered him for a moment, then began to weep.

Never any escape. I'm forced into hiding and when I find a way out I'm trapped again. Pearhead glares with pitted eyes over ripe cheeks and gibbers to the wall. I break his cipher with a snap of my mind.

"He's awake, sir."

"Anything else?"

"Just the scream and the bawling. He's watching me now."

"Well," Powell said, "talk to him." Powell's image vanished from the scrim, replaced by that of the Pharmaceutic.

"If he gets violent, give him twenty ccs of Torp Eight." The Pharmaceutic's face faded away.

Faces peer from the walls. Master Snoop has caught up with me again. The dead man in me brought me back to them.

"Easy, fella. There's nothing to be afraid of."

"But be afraid of itself."

"Huh?"

Virgil strained at the belts. "How long will you keep this up?"

"We thought you might hurt yourself otherwise."

He sighed. "Where am I?"

"In the hospital."

"Where?"

"On *Fadeaway*."

"Which is?"

"Uh—orbiting Earth?" The medic righted his chair and put one foot on it. He offered a cigarette to Virgil.

"No thanks. You haven't been around hospital patients much, have you?"

"Most people here just up and die. They don't linger."

Pump. Suck what info you can before he realizes. "Don't linger?"

The medic nodded. Tall, probably spaceborn, he towered over Virgil's bed.

"Yeah, most of us'd rather die fast when we have to. There's enough of a strain on *Fadeaway*'s system as it is. Not that there are so many veterans left here, but a lot of equipment was already damaged when we homesteaded this dump and we can't repair it without material. Which we don't have any ships to retrieve anyway." He ground out his half-smoked cigarette on the floor. "Which is why your—" He looked at Virgil, then frowned and said nothing more.

They want Circus. *Leave me here with Master Snoop and go off to the Belt for gelt of steel. You have to play this right. Have to get back. Back to* Circus. *Back to Delia. Get out.*

"I'm a prisoner, then?"

The medic punched a couple of buttons on the wall console.

The Pharmaceutic's face appeared. "What?" he asked.

"Bailey, sir. Patient requests his status."

The old man nodded. "Straight, straight. I'll be down in a minute."

"You're late." Virgil slid his right hand away from his left wrist, working it across his chest under the straps.

"Your pulse is just fast," said the Pharmaceutic, sliding a miniscrim back into his breast pocket. "If we're done with showing off, we can talk." He closed the door behind him and glanced at Bailey. The medic nodded and left the room.

"My name's Derek Vane. Master Pharmaceutic for *Fadeaway*. Which one are you?"

"Which one?" Virgil blinked his eyes and twisted about to watch Vane.

"I mean, what's your name?"

"Ben? How'd you got inside?" *Ben made flesh. Ben following me, a ship in human vessel, asking the same question.*

"I'm not Ben. I'm Derek. Tell me about yourself."

Have to focus. This is too dangerous to screw up. "I'm Virgil Grissom Kinney. Sorry if I seem a bit disoriented. I've been through a lot." *A lot a lot a lot a lot.*

"Yes, you've been having some blackouts recently."

He watches me too closely. He must know about the dead man inside me, if he's with Master Snoop. Won't hurt to let him know I know, will it? Stupid—you're his prisoner anyway.

"Yeah," Virgil said. "It's the RNA injection I got before leaving Earth. Possibly a sensitivity to some impurity." *He nods—he doesn't believe a word of it.*

"Possibly, possibly."

This is getting nowhere. "When can I go back to *Circus Galacticus*?"

Vane kept nodding. "There's a problem." He stopped nodding and pulled the miniscrim from his pocket. Handing it to Virgil, he said, "Hit recall two twenty-three forty-seven." Virgil touched the numbers as told and craned his neck to read what appeared.

"It's coming at us under fifty gravities acceleration," Vane said. "It'll be here in less than forty hours. There's somebody out there in trans-Pluto orbit who's pretty damned interested enough in something here—and I'm betting it's you and *Circus*. They're burning a hell of a lot of anti-matter just to get here fast. Why they're not using a Valli, I can't figure, if they're the same people we suspect. Commander Powell thinks we're in danger. You can see why we can't let you go just yet."

Nodding, Virgil strained at the straps across his chest. "I'm not such a threat that you've got to keep me tied down, am I?"

"Nobody cares about old soldiers, but most of us have been trained to avoid risks. We'd like to make a few preparations for the possibility of an attack. If you could tell your ship that we're going to power up our lasers for purely defensive purposes—"

Virgil narrowed his gaze. "*I* like to avoid risks, too. I'm not going to have you take my ship. If that leaves us at a standoff, that's just fine." *So hard to figure out strategies. I know now that they won't kill me. Not if they think I have the code. And they'll never crack it. I'll die my own way...*

Vane took the miniscrim back and tapped it idly against his fingers. His brown eyes blinked twice. "A stalemate based on fear. Kind of a sad situation."

"I want to get back to my ship."

"I'm afraid you're out of deals there."

Virgil strained again, the straps holding him taut.

"Then I *am* a prisoner."

"There still exists—on scrim, at least—a condition of war between the Triplanetary Co-Prosperity Alliance and the Infernals."

"You mean the Recidivists and the Autarchists?"

"That's the Belter's propaganda."

Virgil smiled and shook his head. *Got to get out. I can't let them see the slightest—*"Hmm."

Vane looked at the man lying before him and saw his face turn implacable. Virgil seemed a million kilometers away. His thoughts, though, lay nearly one and a half astronomical units away.

"Perhaps we can arrange a pact." Virgil casually scratched his shaven scalp and relaxed. *Show calm, think it through.*

"I can listen, but only Commander Powell can make any deals."

"Bring him in, then."

"I'll see what I can do."

Vane left and Bailey returned, watching over the prisoner until Powell stormed in and leaned over the bed. He smelled of bacon and coffee.

"We're fighting a thirty-eight hour deadline, so we're open to deals. What?"

Virgil looked over the man—graying hair cropped short, gray eyes that must have seen enough of the brutal life of war, and space-damaged skin combined to make Powell look like a weary seaman.

I have to proceed carefully... "Let me access your library and read up on recent history. If it matches what you've told me and I find I can trust you, the ship's yours for a set amount of time to be determined."

Powell barely hesitated. "Our library only goes up to Twenty-One Fifty-Eight. After that, there's only the habitat's log, input by me. It's all open to you. You must make your decision by twenty-hundred tomorrow or we'll be forced to seize *Circus* by force."

Virgil nodded. "Untie me and bring me a scrim."

Can't ask for it too soon. Have to wait a few hours.

Virgil avoided requesting astrophysical information and called up the history section. The attendant, Bailey, had raised his bed and freed up his right hand so that he could operate the scrim's library controls. After several hours of reading, watching and listening, he turned off the scrim and laid his head back.

The recent history of the System made the fall of Rome look calm and restful. Dante Houdini Brennen in 2116 had not possessed the vantage on the war gained by historians in subsequent decades. The causes of Earth's degeneration into statism were manifold. The planet's near trillion inhabitants—previously well-supplied with necessities from the Moon and the Belt habitats—saw extreme danger in the cessation of intrasystem trade. The constant Terran demand for raw materials and goods fabricated in deep space at zero-gee could not be interrupted for the length of time necessary for Earth businesses to begin work in the Belt.

Someone did have the brains to purchase obsolete equipment already in the Belt and crew it. By then, though, someone else had put deep thrust engines on a freighter, armed it with a bevawatt laser and his own private army, and headed for Ceres Beta. Other potential looters followed.

Organization for such an aggressively invasive undertaking resulted in bureaucracy, with all its entrenched interests. The interests gained supporters among the nervous billions. When the supporters began to crush dissenters and neutral alike, a State had—once again—arisen. Mars, far enough from Earth almost to be considered a Belter outpost, remained steadfastly neutral, which meant they were on both sides, selling. Luna, settled by rough-and-tumble frontiersmen, declared solidarity with the Belt. The Earth-Moon war lasted eight years, ending in a bitter, bloody stalemate.

The Belters could not be taken by surprise in this war. When they could detect fusion flares hundreds of millions of kilometers away, they had plenty of time to get ready. After two years in flight, the first Terran assault on the Belt resulted in a thirty-second-long battle. All Earthlings were captured alive from their incapacitated ships and sent to Ceres Beta where the defense agencies offered them a choice: be set free on an asteroid with a complimentary one-hour tank of air, or work to pay their own fares back to Earth.

The Belters saw no further threat and ignored Earth. The home planet's trillion scrambled to get into space, into the Belt. Factionalism took hold as the world's great corporations—Grant Enterprises, D'Asaro Spacecraft, General Cosmos, The Food Combine, and Crockett Mining and Exploration—acquired what they could from private investors and from one another. What some could not buy, rent or borrow, they stole. Property disputes large enough to be small scale wars ensued.

Virgil read and saw how the Brennen Trust played an integral part in the war.

Just a month after his last update to Virgil, the Earth tried to seize Bernal *Brennen*. He moved the entire habitat from Lagrange Point 5 to the Belt and began long negotiations with the Autarchists. He thought he could end the war by giving the Belters a cheap method of shipping the Earthlings what they needed. The cost of teleporting freight in unmanned, computerized craft dropped to a point of positive return on expenditures and the resumption of trade. The war very nearly ended.

You didn't figure on Mankind's stupidest blunder, though.

Virgil requeued the vid of the anti-matter bombing of Ceres Beta: a sneak attack launched by a secret arm of the Recidivists; an automated slaughter that—once dispatched—could not be stopped.

Sprawling over nearly ten degrees of the Asteroid Belt, the mining civilization defied visualization from anywhere nearby. Like viewing the Milky Way galaxy, anyone inside the huge chunk of space called Ceres Beta saw only a field of bright lights: habitats, factories, smelters, farms. Only from outside could its true shape and size be appreciated.

It was from a distance, then—from Mars—that the destruction of Ceres Beta was both visible and comprehensible. The vid shot from a telescope on Phobos showed simultaneous white dots that waxed and waned almost as one, forming a false star cluster that flared and cooled within moments.

Signaling a schematic of the bomb prototype, captured years later, Virgil marvelled at the efficient way General Cosmos had used Earth's last kilogram of anti-matter. The attack, code-named Operation Slow Lightning, consisted of a thousand tiny spacecraft, each carrying one gram of anti-hydrogen, each payload the size of a fist. Launched by laser from Earth orbit, the minuscule armada drifted for years, incapable of being recalled even after the resumption of trade. The Terran government denied responsibility for the bombing, but *someone* had to have authorized the use of the anti-matter. On that, the Terran history books were universally mute.

The small rocket flares were hidden from Belter view by the bombs' laser parasols, painted black on the fore end for further camouflage. The strike was coordinated by one tiny automated command ship that trailed on the same slow Hohmann S-curve orbit as the bombs. No one detected a small, slow-moving, widely dispersed swarm of two-kilogram masses in the midst of the asteroid belt.

Each bomb found its target and destroyed it with brutal simplicity. It drifted toward a Bernal habitat or farm or a factory, hit the side, and shattered. That in itself would generally not have damaged the heavy plating typical of Belter construction. When the bomb broke apart, though, the magnetic field suspending the anti-hydrogen collapsed; the resulting impact of anti-matter with matter released enough energy to blast unsealable ruptures through the structures.

Millions died of decompression, or of suffocation, or of

wounds from the explosions, or of starvation from the famine that followed. Billions of *auros* worth of equipment, livestock, and homes were laid waste. Even so, the decimation of Ceres Beta hardly crippled the widely spread, vastly decentralized network of habitats.

The Autarchists' retaliation for the slaughter was swift and stunning.

Using the Valliardi Transfer, the Belter government first attempted to send manned warships into Earth orbit. Half the troops died of suicide after experiencing the transfer's death illusion. Using the Transfer to retreat finished off the rest. Then some bright boy came up with the idea—after stealing plans to *Circus Galacticus*—of transferring pellets of ordinary matter to the surface of the planet. Then anti-matter pellets, more easily manufactured in deep space than on Earth, were found to provide an even greater blast.

Tens of billions died in the first, last, and only Valli carpet-bombing of Earth. The horrifically massive retaliation against the crowded planet left Earth a steaming ruin and broke the spirit of the Autarchy. Half out of sickened remorse, half out of revulsion at the idea of further war, the remaining Belters abandoned their government and their homespace, splitting up into small family units to head for trans-Jovian realms. Some fled far enough to mine comets in the frigid Öort layer. Most used ordinary fusion power. Others desperately dared to use the Valliardi Transfer; most of them were never heard from again.

Earthlings seized the Belt, but refused to call themselves Belters: when they encountered them, Terrans destroyed Belters. The Belters, for the most part, did not fight back. Some, maddened by the Transfer, accepted such retribution gladly. Others, shamed by the carnage conducted in their names by the Autarchy, accepted death with fatalistic relief. They knew Man was destined to leave Earth someday, but they never imagined that it would be in the manner of the living abandoning a corpse.

Virgil grew ill experiencing the last half-century of blood-drenched history. *All dead. Only a few billion people on Earth now, picking through the ruins. They'll be dead soon, too. Not enough energy. The remaining satellites can't provide enough power. Most of the receiving stations were wiped out in the Burning.*

Goodbye Earth. Goodbye Wizard, who vanished with Bernal Brennen *a day after positron flowers bloomed. Goodbye Pusher, Shaker, Mentalsickmakers. Goodbye Marsface. Goodbye, all you others. Did the blasts kill you? The photon flux and gamma radiation? The famine and plague and systemic breakdown of a planet once stuffed to bursting? Or was it merely Time that took you, the Time that I've avoided, the ticking of a clock I've jumped away from? Nightsheet keeps the watchworks running, but I've stolen my time card.*

No one left.

Except the Mad Wizard. And Nightsheet. And Master Snoop. And...

Delia. Virgil stared at the ceiling, thinking. *I can feel him inside, the dead man. He squirms to hide but he's waiting, just as I wait when he takes over. Neither of us knows the other's plans. He might even be working for Master Snoop. Right inside me. Watching.*

He began to sweat. He tugged at the restrains that held him in a prisoner's embrace. *Listening. Recording everything in my own brain. Making reports while I'm out.*

He kicked feebly at the leg binders. *Ready to rise up any time and take over.* Something thumped dully far away. *Ready to break in. He's knocking, he's screaming.*

Sirens wailed. Jord Baker craned his neck to look around. Something thumped again. Vane entered the room and unstrapped him.

"We're under attack. A dozen Valli ships have us surrounded. Get out!" Baker stood, tried to get his bearings, then followed Vane.

"Where to?" He tugged at his hospital robe, trying to keep up with Vane's pace.

"We're taking a tram to the core shelters—" Vane stopped speaking and listened as he ran. A voice thundered around them. Commander Powell's voice issued from every loud-speaker in the corridor.

"Battle lasers damaged! Ships holding their position. Angling mass drivers for—" Powell's voice died. As they ran into the sunlight, the grinding sound of machinery slowing to a stand-still filled the air. Vane stopped.

"They've hit our power relays. Forget the tram."

"How about batteries?" Baker asked.

Vane resumed a slow, even pace, "Should've come on already. That spot up there"—he pointed to a cylinder at the habitat's axis—"has auxiliary power for the combat station, but they must have hit the batteries, too. They mean business. Looks 'zif we walk."

Baker followed the Pharmaceutic and craned his head around to observe all of the vast globe that enveloped him. All the way up and over him, life apparently continued as usual on the inside of the sphere. Sunlight shone crisply through the mirror arrays to illuminate the farmland lining three-fourths of the habitat. A lot of the hectarage, though, either lay fallow or appeared to be overgrown with vines and tumbleweeds. Baker estimated from this that *Fadeaway* supported less than a hundredth the population it was designed for. The air was warm and dry, sure signs of climate control problems that could not be fixed by simple realignment of the solar mirrors. *Fadeaway* was slowly dying—had been dying for years—and the old soldiers were dying with it. Vane strode briskly toward the axis of the sphere. Since the hospital sector already rested halfway up the side of the sphere, the climb was steep but the climbing easy.

"How did you like the history lesson?" Vane asked.

"What history lesson?"

Vane's even stride broke for only an instant, then resumed. He said, "Jord Baker again, eh?"

Baker stopped, then nodded and resumed his ascent. "I'm getting sick of this. I want a way out."

"Out of *Fadeaway*?"

"Out of sharing someone else's body. I'm only vaguely aware of events when Kinney's in command. I don't like that feeling of helplessness."

"It's Kinney's body. Can you presume to claim squatter's rights?"

Baker rubbed at his nose with Virgil's fingers, then reached out for the railing that stretched up the side of the sphere until it became a ladder. He turned his gaze on Vane for a moment, then continued looking ahead.

"I think, therefore I'm not dead yet. If Kinney can evict me, let him try. I've got a plan of my own." Something puttered behind them like a broken fan. Baker looked around. From the center of the sphere flew two men, each wearing a small hydrogen-powered jet. Flying on a vector that reduced their velocity tangential to the axis—thus negating the pseudo-gravity imparted by the sphere's spin—they flew as fast as they could for the terrace nearest Vane and Baker.

At the last conceivable instant, they threw their engines into reverse and decelerated until they struck the wall of the terrace. One man rolled with the motion until he came up standing, the other touched lightly with his hands and walked like an unsupported wheelbarrow until he had absorbed all his momentum and converted it to the spin of the sphere at that latitude. All these maneuvers were performed reflexively, learned through years of living in the habitat. Baker, Earth born and raised, marveled at the pair's agility with the jet-packs. No longer weightless, the men stood and dusted themselves off.

The first man handed Vane and Baker communications head-sets, saying, "The enemy's knocked out all power except for ComStat." He jerked a thumb toward the Command Battle Station at the central core. "We can't fight them until they board."

Donning the headset, Baker heard the voice of Commander Powell speaking with crisp, calm timbre.

"—pretty good. Mass drivers inoperative. Cut section five-oh-two. Still hanging in there. Monitor all bands." The voice paused. One of the fliers ran to a door in the side of the terrace and disappeared.

"Where to now?" Baker asked his companion. "Keep climbing?" **Which way is the shuttle? This pole or the other?**

"Hang on a minute," the other flier said. "Let Lance get back here." He hunkered down and crouched to stare into the distance. He spoke into the headset mouthpiece.

"I see it. Next to the Tyler farm. Probably panel one-twenty-thirty west by eighty-four-forty-five north. I'd say a two meter breach."

Baker followed the man's gaze. Far above them and slightly spinward, on the other side of the axis, a small cloud eddied around one of the huge windows that admitted sunlight from the mirrors outside. A section of wall tumbled from a terrace above and vanished into the cloud. He wondered how long it would take for such a blasthole to vent the sphere's air into space. Before he could even guess, a voice buzzed in his ear.

"Vane. Lieutenant Williams says you've got Kinney. How is he?"

Vane frowned for a second, then answered, "Fine. Only he's Jord Baker again. Why—"

"We got a message from the approaching attack vessel.

They'll trade our lives and *Fadeaway* for him."

Chapter Ten

23 May, 2163

Baker watched Vane and listened silently to the conversation with Commander Powell. Lieutenant Williams emerged from the terrace with two more flying harnesses, which he handed to Vane and Baker.

"Do you scan, Derek?" Powell asked.

"Yessir." Vane struggled with the harness, then zipped it up and jumped up and down twice. Williams helped Baker into his. The harness consisted of a firm fiberglass corset similar to those of recreational jet packs on Earth. The stiff rigging from shoulder to buttocks prevented side-to-side hip movement that could lead to a shifting center of thrust and wild gyrations. The rocket gymbals could be controlled either by a powerglove or by remote, eliminating the need for bulky armatures and a separate mounting for the exhaust nozzles.

"They wanted his ship, too," Powell continued, "but they're out of deals on that account. Seems the ship took it upon itself to transfer out when the other ships transferred in."

"Shall I escort Baker to the airlock?" the Pharmaceutic asked.

"Negative. They don't plan to let us live. Nobody sends a destroyer class ship at fifty gees to pick up a prisoner. Especially when they know he can survive a transfer. They'd just pop in, grab him and take him back in one of those fighters."

"Why didn't the destroyer transfer out here?"

"Derek—I don't know." His tone of voice altered to that of a commander of men and he said, "Attention all hands. Scramble Red. Don pressure suits and weaponry from nearest available lockers. Power's off, so go to any battle station, even if it's not yours. Stand by for further orders. ETA for destroyer is approximately Twenty-One Thirty. Stay at condition Red until further notice." His voice softened a bit, as though he were speaking only to Vane and Baker. "Get Baker to ComStat, Derek."

"Here," Williams said, attaching a nylon cord between his waist and Baker's. "In case you can't get the hang of it." He connected a ribbon cable from the control box on his chest to the one on Baker's. "We'll fly synched, so just relax and don't panic."

Starting up his engine, Baker wrinkled his nose at the sharp odor of half-burned hydrogen that assaulted his senses for an instant. "Shove off," the lieutenant said. He and Baker kicked off together.

Though Earthborn, Baker knew from vacations to resort habitats that the terms "artificial gravity" and "centrifugal force" were both misnomers for what held people, buildings, and loose items to the inside of the Bernal sphere—or any other rotating space station. The spin of the sphere caused everything touching it—including the atmosphere—to move in the direction of the spin, tangential to the axis. Someone standing on the outside of the sphere would be flung into space as if thrown from a slingshot. On the inside, however, such tangential motion met a firm obstacle: the inside surface of the sphere. It was this constant motion outward that caused the illusion of gravity.

Since it was not gravity, though, actions impossible on a planet were possible on a habitat. Running spinward along a latitude increased one's tangential velocity, thus increased ones' "weight." Running anti-spinward decreased one's velocity with relation to the sphere and decreased one's weight. It was difficult to run fast enough to become weightless, generally, because the air mass moved spinward with the habitat and the relative wind one encountered running anti-spinward was enough to blow one back to the deck. That's where the jet packs proved useful. The constant thrust was enough to combat the wind, allowing the trained pilot to jet from point to point in the sphere as if he were in freefall around Earth.

Doing so in practice was as difficult as it sounded in theory. If one tried to fly across latitudes, not only did the Coriolis effect throw one off course, but the motion of the habitat in its Earth orbit contributed to further navigational error. Before the war, it was a simple matter to link all the flying harnesses to a central navigational computer.

"What do you mean, flying linked?" Baker asked over the engines' whine.

"NavCom broke down years ago," Williams shouted. "We all fly by the seat of our pants here—or, more accurately, by the back of our shoulder blades." He turned the jet up to full power, Baker's jet mimicking the increase exactly. They flew together with the ribbon cable between them never growing more than moderately taut.

The shifting vectors of acceleration and Coriolis effect, imperceptible while walking up toward the axis, played a nauseating trick on Baker's inner ear as the four men flew toward the battle station suspended in the center of the sphere. He closed his eyes and waited out the feeling.

You're a pilot. You're used to it. You're just in someone else's body who isn't. It's so strange to close my eyes and be simply a passenger, to let someone else be the pilot.

"Damage control reports all blast holes sealed," someone buzzed in his earphone. "Full integrity restored." He opened his eyes in time to see the cylinder of ComStat fill his vision. They sped through a hatchway and reversed engines.

"My compliments," Baker said, about to step out of the harness. Williams nodded, disconnected the rope and wires, and waved his hand.

"Don't de-suit. Jet packs stay on at battle stations."

"Store the fuel bottles in the safety boxes." Vane took Baker's

and put them with the others in a thick padded box. Baker
noticed that the four of them had slowly settled to the alleged
floor of the building. He took one step and floated upward.
The core rotated with the sphere, so it imparted its own minuscule tangential motion to everything inside, though being
in it was as close to being weightless as was humanly percep-
tible.

"Baker's inside, sir," Vane said into his headpiece.

"Bring him up," came the reply.

"They want you badly, Vir—Jord. They've risked a dozen Valli
fighters and a deep thrust destroyer." Powell looked Baker in
the eye. Baker nodded while he scanned the room. Viewscrims
covered the inside surface of the axis core of ComStat. Down
the middle of the shaft hung a non-rotating cylinder composed
entirely of computer consoles. A score of men surrounded the
cylinder, facing outward, operating the controls that extended
around them, watching their viewscrims. Most of the flickering, shifting light in the station issued from the scrims.

Baker looked at closeups of the fighters. Both he and Powell
floated near one end of the cylinder, the commander securely
attached to *Fadeaway*'s hotseat. Baker hung behind him, observing. Powell punched a couple of buttons that had turned
red.

"This is no moonwalk—it's the Infernal's final assault. They
plan to kill everyone on board. That's fourteen hundred and
twelve men, eighty-six women, thirty-two kids."

"No reason for them to."

Powell rubbed the bridge of his nose and snorted. "No reason for them not to. No witnesses in near orbit. They blew out
our comm lasers when they arrived. And they probably want
to test their new weaponry. Ever hear of the Earthside town
Guernica? Or Baghdad?"

Baker shook his head. "What are they testing it for? Earth is crippled and practically dead."

Powell shrugged, shouted a terse command into his headset, then sighed. "You weren't here during the War. The hatred runs insanely deep, and it's not been softened by the years. Any war of secession creates long-lasting anger." He gazed at the advancing warship. "There are still some Southerners that resent losing the Civil War. There are still some Americans that hate the British for the actions of King George the Third."

"Who?"

Powell made a tired half-chuckle. "Old soldiers have little to do but read about old wars." He slapped an array of switches from orange to red. "The ones that try to fight the old wars, though, *they* become dead soldiers."

"Ten seconds, sir."

Powell's gaze turned toward the man who spoke, then glanced at the ship's clock.

"Battle station red." At his command, sirens whooped, scrims switched images, men exchanged positions. "Latest ETA for destroyer is thirty-two minutes. Prepare to repel boarders."

"No fighter ships of your own?"

"This place didn't have any, we couldn't build any. We'll have to wait until they come onboard."

"My lifeboat has a meteor laser. I could try to pick a couple—"

"You stay here. Like it or not, you're our insurance policy. We need your help in this, so consider yourself a hostage." Powell turned to face Baker. "They won't kill us until they have you. Perhaps we can take a few of them with us."

Baker silently watched the scrims while the minutes fell away, marked only by the calm voice of an ensign noting its passage. The Valli fighters surrounding the sphere did nothing. "Ten minutes. Destroyer within attack radius."

"Final weapons check."

Baker asked, "What weapons?"

Without breaking his concentration on the master computer, Powell replied, "Laser rifles, gloves, even a few automatic pistols and old machine guns. Ever try to correct for Coriolis while firing inside a Bernal? Good fun."

"This is a suicide fight."

Powell kept his gaze on the scrims. "Don't you think my men know that?"

"I'm the reason they're going to die." Baker pushed away from the command seat. "You could have spaced me and told them I wasn't here—"

"They'd have looked for you anyway. We were doomed the moment you appeared on radar."

"You should have blasted me then."

"You're probably right. We're in for it now, though, so we fight."

"Eight minutes. We have visual." A telescopic view of the destroyer appeared on several scrims. Its nuclear engines no longer glowed blue-white and its shape could clearly be seen. It rotated about into attack position, an off-white armored slab a hundred meters wide and two hundred long. A battery of lasers and missile launchers crested its fore end, clustered like a giant child's overflowing carton of lethal toys. The bottom third of the destroyer bulged elliptically to hold its nuclear fuel.

"Go to internal oxygen," a disembodied voice commanded.

"How about us?" Baker asked, watching a scrim of men and women in pressure suits busily adjusting their air flows.

"We're airlocked," Powell replied simply. "If the integrity here fails, we've lost anyway."

"I'm not dying here." Baker floated in front of Powell. One arm reached out and pulled him back into place.

"Relax—you're as safe here as anywhere. If not"—Powell punched a few buttons and pointed—"There—on the center right scrim. Your lifeboat. In three minutes you can be in there and ready to transfer out, if you have any idea where *Circus* is.

First, though—" He punched another button and threw a series of switches. A bank of lights glowed green around him.

"This is Commander Norman Powell of *Fadeaway* acknowledging receipt of your request. Virgil Grissom Kinney sits behind me. We are prepared to repel your attack. We—"

Something thundered throughout the habitat. Even ComStat vibrated.

"Simultaneous Valli bombardment from all sides," a voice called out. "Zero integrity on sphere. Atmosphere draining." Other voices joined in.

"Twenty millimeters pressure. Fifteen."

"Four minutes."

"Ten millimeters. Five."

"Twenty-four blast holes each eight to ten meters—"

A dozen light arrays simultaneously blazed red.

"Zero pressure in main sphere."

"How many men lost?"

"Look!" a shocked old voice cried. "They're fighting *outside!*"
Scrims lit up with the view of troops, sucked out through the blast holes by the voiding atmosphere, still ready for battle. Half of them were dead; the survivors—flung into space toward doom—unleashed their fire against the Valli fighters and the approaching destroyer.

"It's pointless! They can't harm anything from there."

" 'The brave may fall, but never yield,' Jord." Powell opened the hatch to the airlock. "Now you know why I kept you up here. They wouldn't blast ComStat knowing you'd probably be inside. They'll have to board and storm to capture you." He scanned an array of scrims. "Now. Get to your boat. There's a suit in the lock."

"It'll take me too long to—"

"We'll hold them off. Get out now!"

Baker kicked down the tubeway into the lock and slammed the hatch. He removed his jet pack, slipped on the bulky suit as fast as possible and cycled the atmosphere. From the safety box he seized a fuel bottle.

"Boarding ships launched from destroyer."

"How many men left?" Powell's voice asked, sharp and calm on Baker's headset.

"Telemetry received on seven hundred fifty-three still inside, sir."

Baker tightened the jet harness and kicked out toward the shuttle bay. He fired up the engine and tried not to look anywhere but along his direction of flight.

"Deploy them evenly around the blast holes," Powell said, "until we're sure which ones the ships will use."

Baker ignored the ensuing spate of orders and troop movements. He glanced down just once to see ant-people running up to black, pool-sized holes inside the sphere, above and below him. Buildings had been toppled, plants uprooted. Debris lay spiraled toward the holes as if toward a drain, turned clockwise on one side of the equator, counter-clockwise on the other, looser twists in the higher latitudes, tighter ones in the middle.

Baker rocketed along the axis toward the docking bay.

"Reroute companies Bravo, Echo, and Oscar to hole one-thirty west, forty north. The first ship's rammed us there."

Baker looked around. Above and behind him, he saw the blunt nose of a boarding craft jammed into the blast hole. Laser fire from the craft attempted to clear the area, but there were too many places for the defenders to hide. Suddenly, hatches sprung open and armed troops swarmed outward. Brilliant points of light flared against their armor. Some fell. The others walked over them, firing indiscriminate laser fusillades.

From behind a broken tree, a sphere of blue gunsmoke blew outward and an invader several meters away flew backward against the ship's hull as though hit by a meteor. His pressure suit exploded, boiling his lifeblood into the airless void.

Baker turned away from the upside-down scene in time to see the south pole of the sphere speeding toward him . He reversed and cut his engines just before reaching the hatchway. A woman motioned to him, pointing toward a corridor; then she turned to join the fighting as soon as he had safely passed.

Hand-over-hand he pulled along the weightless passage. He felt the rumble of a another boarding craft ramming into *Fadeaway*.

What now? He turned the corner of the access shaft to the docking bay and continued along. **I have to die again to get away from death? Is fake or real better? And where to?** *Circus* **is gone somewhere—**

Yanking his way into the docking bay, he sealed the pressure doors with one hand and muscled toward the shuttle.

They'd see the ship if I move it out of the docking bay. The shuttle's doors responded to his touch. **I've got to transfer from inside.**

Something reverberated throughout the bay. The airlock bulkhead bent inward as if hit by a battering ram. He cycled the pressurizer and removed his helmet.

"Can you take verbal commands?" he shouted to the boat's computer. Lights turned green. The word **YES** appeared on a viewscrim. Strapping in, he spoke a series of carefully worded orders, all the time watching the docking bay doors; a bright point of light appeared at one corner and began to trace an outline.

"Do you understand these orders?"

YES.

Baker poised his finger over the transfer button.

"Come on. What are you waiting for?" **They're cutting the hatchway open. Come on.**

Baker bit his lip and watched the outer doors slowly bend inward under the light thrust of a boarding craft. The steel plating easily gave way until part of it touched the nose of Baker's shuttle, pitching it forward. Through the opening hatch of the boarding craft, he saw masks hiding behind the muzzles of laser rifles.

"Come on!" he cried.

WORKING.

"Damn you!" Baker reached the screeching stage as he watched the first few troops float out of the blunted nose of the other ship and cautiously propel toward him, weapons zeroed in on the cockpit. "You goddamned machine! It can't take that long to figure out. It's not that hard!" He jerked backward in his seat when the first of the boarding party touched the hood of the shuttle. **No. They'll pick *me* apart trying to find out why *Kinney* can survive.**

The light under the transfer button glowed. Baker shrieked *"Go!"* and punched his thumb into it.

Darkness consumed him.

Black, swimming black. I should have stayed. I lay here so limp and unsafe. What if I don't come back this time? I look scared. The doors! They're bending in on me. I press beyond them into the shaft so dark and cold. I'm falling and I don't want to fall. I've got to stop falling, got to stop. I'm needed. I've got to be needed somewhere—I know it. She's telling me. Something needs help.

Baker took a heartbeat to realize where he was. His hands shot out for the ship's controls and frantically punched buttons.

Directly ahead of him, a crater filled his viewing port.

Instead of falling toward it, though, the shuttle rose up and away from the planet's surface.

The crater shrank. In a few moments, Baker saw the airless

limb of the planet Mercury and beyond it the milky glow of the solar corona. The port turned nearly opaque the instant the sun blazed across the glasteel. He looked away by reflex.

I made it! He checked his instrument readouts and smiled. **Intrinsic velocity retained. I'm rising into an orbit to accommodate my Earth orbital speed; I'll be drifting beneath the halo of flak as safely as can be expected. At least it couldn't hang too close to the surface without becoming meteorites.**

"Begin search for *Circus Galacticus* and stand watch for other spacecraft." Leaning back in the seat as best he could in freefall, he smiled wider.

The shuttle did not carry enough fuel to make it from the outer region of Mercury's flak barrier to the inner orbits if he had transferred there. The flak could not reach to the surface, he suspected, and all he had to do was appear on the anti-revolutionward side of Mercury and let his Earth velocity take him away from the surface.

Something tapped at the ship's hull once. Baker smiled after it happened again a few moments later. **There it is. I was right about the flak. Starting to encounter it.**

Baker stopped in the middle of his thoughts and froze.

What flak?

Another piece of debris hit the shuttle.

Where did I hear about flak? Why should I even have suspected...

He began to shake. **Think, idiot. Where? The planet's are at superior conjunction. No direct observation possible. But *Circus* transferred to sixty degrees above the ecliptic to—** But I didn't know that.

He swallowed with great difficulty. The back of his throat scraped like leather against brick.

That's not my memory. It didn't happen to me. I didn't find it out. Someone else. Kinney!

He switched on a scrim to stare himself in the face.

"Who are you? Which mind is yours?" The face in the scrim mimicked his movements but did not answer. It stared back at him with equal fear and incomprehension.

"Who, God damn you? Who?"

When *Circus Galacticus* rose slowly over Mercury's horizon, Baker plotted a rendezvous course without surprise. His days-old beard scraped at the collar of his pressure suit. His bristly scalp itched.

Why did I even think of Mercury? Even suspect that *Circus*'d be here? Dee is here, frozen somewhere below. Kinney must know it. That's why he brought—

He brought me... here. His body, his brain, he's running it all and I'm just a passenger who gets to drive once in a while along the same road.

Now I can't be sure. Can't think anything I do isn't controlled by him. I'm not even here really. Just a few milliliters of—juice—that got realigned into someone else's circuitry, a nothing man, a nowhere man, a never man with a never mind.

"What is your name?" *Circus*'s computer radioed.

"I don't know I don't know I don't know. I don't. No." He grabbed at his head, then reached down for the attitude controls. "Jord. I am Jord Baker." **I am Jord Baker. All inside it's like Jord. I die the way Jord dies. I'm here—**

"Prepare to dock," the computer said, opening the docking bay doors on its side. Baker's hands deftly maneuvered the shuttle toward the glowing square on the dark side of the spacecraft. He hardly noticed his piloting.

I'm here and thinking and acting. I can tighten this thigh muscle, blink that eye, grind my teeth. I'm on the circuitry. If I could somehow deprogram. Deprogram. Dee. Program.

Pogrom. Pour grumbling, crumbling Kinney out of his own body. She'll do it. Do it double-time. Triple Trine.

His hands tightened on the controls. "Ready to dock..." Looking for the first time at what he had been seeing, he realized that he had already docked the shuttle. Behind him, the outer doors slid shut and air cycled in.

Unstrapping with one swift motion, Baker kicked out of the chair, pounded a hand against the emergency hatch release and sailed into the docking bay.

"Begin immediate search for the cryonic preservation unit on the surface." He had to shout over the hiss of air still filling the bay. His ears rang. Grabbing hold of a handrail, he yanked toward the hatch.

"Searching," the computer replied. "Have you not noticed the large object to your left?"

Baker turned and started. A spacecraft nearly double the size of the shuttle lay fast to the repair section. Baker had indeed not noticed it.

"Sure. That's the ship you disabled at flameout. How'd you get it?" He floated over to it. The arcing slash of a laser beam had left a deep, uneven valley in the ship's flattened-cone hull from its blunt nose to topside aft.

"I transferred out ahead of it when *Fadeaway* came under attack. I matched velocities and picked it up, then transferred to the outer region of Mercury's flak barrier and moved slowly into a low orbit. Your method of arrival was much more elegant."

"Have you found it yet? Delia's redoubt?"

"No. Not yet. Please—examine the fighter."

Baker pulled topside to check out the cockpit.

"As you'll notice, all controls were severed by the laser, but the cockpit remained intact."

"There's a body in there!"

"The pilot. You will also note that the ship possesses no radio or maser equipment or, in fact, any ship-to-ship or ship-to-base communications of—"

"Why didn't you remove the body?"

"I was waiting for you to take a look at it along with me."

"Forget it." He slid away from the viewing port.

"Jord," the computer said in the softest voice it could synthesize. "The pilot is dead."

"You need a billion miles of neurons to figure that out?"

"He was dead while piloting the fighter. He has been dead for weeks."

Baker felt around the collar of his pressure suit for a water spigot and found none. He tried to swallow.

"Let me change." He slipped out of the bulky pressure suit and into one of *Circus*'s skintights. He donned the headset with its vidlink to the computer and pushed off toward the fighter cockpit.

"Straight," he said around the mouthpiece. "When we're done, open the bay to space and I'll stay here until I'm certain that any contamination on me is dead."

He found no entrance hatch. After half an hour of thorough searching, he said, "Not even through the viewports—they're sealed tight. Did they nail him inside here for good?"

"As I suspected—he was dead from the day he was put into the ship."

"Yeah? Put in by whom?"

"I had a robot bring some tools down. Use the cutting torch to open the top viewport. You can squeeze in through there."

"Have you found it yet?" Baker asked, halfway through cutting the glasteel with an ultraviolet laser.

"No. I am scanning polar areas where solar panels could receive continuous light. I will alert you when I have detected something."

A piece of slag drifted onto the control panel inside the fighter as the section of glasteel gave way. It sizzled for a moment, then crystallized. Grabbing the coolest edge of the piece, Baker pulled it aside and left it floating nearby. He peered inside.

The corpse peered back at him.

Its eyes gazed straight forward, unglazed, clear. Every few seconds a pair of tiny tubes expelled a mist that spread over the sclera and either evaporated or was absorbed. Baker could not tell which.

It was his first indication, however, that the ship still functioned. He maneuvered inside. "Did you know the ship was still running?" he asked.

"Yes. All its battle systems are inoperative, though, and it has lost all conning capability; in fact, the only functional system is the one surrounding the corpse, which takes up very little volume and is separate from the other ship systems."

I can feel the death pulsating inside that thing. All those tubes like long, fat worms hanging from his neck and thighs. Pumping something gray and thick through its gray body. Out of his dead head staring so clear—I didn't used to think like this. What's happening to me?

"Have you found it yet?" he asked.

"Negative. Pan left—I want to look at those contact bundles."

Baker turned his head.

The eyes of the corpse moved to follow.

They returned to their forward stare as Baker shifted back to examine the body more closely.

A line of drool appeared at the corner of the corpse's mouth and slowly accumulated until it broke free, a tiny sphere that drifted until it adhered to Baker's pressure suit.

"There are a series of electrodes," the computer said, "terminating in the frontal lobes, the parietal and occipital lobes, at the temporal lobes, the cerebellum and the medulla oblongata."

Baker nodded. "Brain wave sensors for a dead man?"

"The hookups seem to be for remote control of the body."

Baker frowned. "Remote from where? You said there was no communication equipment. Somewhere in the ship, maybe? An autonomous onboard computer?"

The corpse inhaled.

The dry, wheezing sound rasped in Baker's headphones. He threw his arms back, crying out when they thudded against the confines of the tiny cockpit.

"Jesus! Did you hear that?" **It's still alive!**

"Registered. The corpse has no need to breathe. It is kept alive—about as alive as the irreversibly comatose—by the life support tubing."

Life support, hell. That thing is dead, yet it's groaning and rattling like some great shuddering air sack—

"Kinney," the corpse wheezed in a dry, creaking monotone.

Kinney! It's always Kinney. Now the dead have come back and they call him instead of me and I don't want to go but they'll take me because I'm in his body...

Calm. Calm down. It's only a talking corpse...

"Virgil Grissom Kinney."

Just a dead body that's controlled from somewhere...

Baker switched on his suit's outer speakers and said, "This is... Kinney."

"I've heard your computer's half of the conversation over its speaker." The eyes slowly turned toward the vidcam. The corpse's s lips did not move when it spoke. Baker looked below the body's chin to see a small speaker grill protruding from above the trachea. Its mouth hung open partway, another droplet of saliva accumulating near the tip of its brown, immobile tongue. "It's nice to hear you, too." Its speech sounded normal enough, though artificial.

"Who are you?" the computer asked.

"You let the machine ask questions?" the dead man said,

turning his eyes to stare at Baker.

"Answer it," Baker said. He sat on the control console with his legs floating on either side of the seated body. He let them float closer to the sides of the chair. "Who are you?"

"Well," the voice said, "I'm certainly not this hunk of meat you're staring at. I'm currently sitting in the war room at— well, never mind. It's in trans-Plutonian space, though, and that's all *you* need to know."

"What's your name?"

The corpse blinked. Slowly. A nice touch, Baker thought. "Lev Pokoynik. Call me Lee. And you're Virgil Gri—"

"Jord Baker. Test pilot for the Brennen Trust."

The corpse said nothing. It blinked again.

"Your image matches—"

"Plastic surgery," Baker said, trying to keep a straight face. **I wonder how much he'll swallow.** "I took his place on the flight."

"You…" the croaking voice hesitated. After a moment, it resumed. "We have a Jord Baker listed as dead shortly before Kinney was trained for piloting the Valliardi Transfer."

"A trick. We switched places. Kinney couldn't handle the transfer. He flipped out."

The corpse's eyebrows wrinkled unevenly. "In the case report of the psychtech in charge, Kinney is listed as having survived…"

"I'm Jord Baker. I can see you can't read minds, at least not *my* mind. What does it matter, anyway?"

"Can't you see?" Some of the mist from the eye moisturizers clung to its lids like tears.

Baker edged closer to the chair. "See what?"

"Can't you see what we've been forced to do simply to use the Valliardi Transfer? The only way to control a ship across lightspeed distances is to link it telepathically with a living being. We tried human pilots—they went crazy and killed themselves. We tried autonomous robot drones—they couldn't think well enough. So we wire up dead bodies to keep them functioning as remote receptors and pilots, and psychlink them to sensitives here at the base.

"It allowed us to attack your spacecraft. We first estimated your projected flameout point. We narrowed it down to a space one light second or so in radius. We matched our velocities to what we guessed yours would be and transferred out. I had to wait five hours. When the fighter reached normal space, my recontact with it—and my communication—was instantaneous.

"The way I knew the instant of your flameout was through the use of my sensitivity. No, I can't read minds, but I could tell what you were aware of and vaguely what you felt. This also enabled me and my attack wing to close in on you so tightly.

"You lasered us on re-emergence. That was a good move on your part. I stayed linked to the ship to see if I could transfer back. No such deal. I went off shift, but got called away from a good meal when we lost the fighter from our screens. Do you know how hard it is to re-establish contact with a psychfighter?"

"No. You want me badly, don't you?"

"We want to know how you can survive the transfer."

"I don't know how or why. I don't think I want to know. And I have no reason to let you vivisect me to make your war more efficient."

The voice rose until the little speaker distorted its sounds. "Do you think we'd use it for something as stupid as war? Idiot! The Valliardi Transfer is humanity's only doorway to the stars. It's cheap, subjectively instantaneous—"

"Almost."

"—and so close to freeing us to settle the rest of the galaxy that it'd be a crime against all mankind if you escaped from us."

The computer interrupted. "Twenty-four ships have just

appeared beyond the flak halo. They're accelerating toward us and will be within laser range in—"

"Get us out! They're already in Valli range!" Baker's last word choked in his mouth as everything twisted around him.

Make it stop. I can't go on with the shrinking and the shoving through into that place of light and the door that never opens for me though I want it to and pray it to. They want me for Kinney. Kill Kinney and I won't have to die and die and die...

"Hang on," the computer said. "Deceleration!"

Baker's legs wrapped tightly around the corpse's chair, pulling forward to grasp it with his arms. The engine array thundered into power. Metal crushed against metal; the fighter slammed against the rear bulkhead to crash partially through the plating. The force of the fall threw Baker loose. His fingers dragged at the tubes and wires connected to the dead pilot, tearing them free. The body slammed atop him in the corner of the fighter; gray fluid spattered across his goggles. They had not fallen far, but the acceleration made it feel worse.

"Status!" he cried into the mouthpiece, pushing the stiff corpse away and trying to get his bearings.

"We transferred to five kilometers above the surface of Mercury. We are rising tangentially and decelerating under gravitational attraction."

"The other ships?" Baker stole a glance at the corpse. Its mouth hung crooked, something black and thick draining from its throat and nose. One of its eyes had burst against the console and oozed gray. **Did Lee feel that?**

"They had not matched velocities to ours and would be in peril if they transferred down before adjustment. In the meantime, I have plotted a course for the cryonic preservation unit at the south pole and will land us there."

"Land us? Are you crazy? This is a *spaceship!*" He struggled to his feet and grabbed for the hole in the ship's viewing port.

"Warning—delta v." The vernier rockets blazed, knocking Baker to the side. They cut off and he resumed his climb out to discover that the top of the fighter had wedged against the bent bulkhead, leaving only a narrow space between the two.

"I'm stuck here! Keep conning the ship. I'll try to get to Con One or Two."

"I had no intention of giving up. We are heading south in a forced low altitude orbit."

"We can't land something this big!" He snaked his arms out of the hole in the hatchway.

"The skirting on the engine array is high enough to protect the engines, the gravity is low enough, the planet has no atmosphere, we are in a hurry—I can synthesize no simpler solution."

"Than landing it on your ass? You'll shear the skirting and we'll fall over!"

"In the time it took you to say that, I rechecked all the data seventy-eight times. We can do it."

Baker ground his teeth against the mouthpiece until it squeaked like scratched slate. "All right. It's your fuselage. I'm going to Con Two."

His body ached from bruises and the weight of acceleration. Sliding out of the fighter, he turned around just long enough to say, "Lee—If you can still hear me—we'll be transferring to another star after this. I don't think you'll want to wait around for a dozen years or more to reestablish contact with your psychfighter—we'd be long gone before your reinforcements arrived."

The corpse twitched once, and a black slime foamed around the edges of its speaker grill.

Baker looked away, then across the bulkhead. It had bent

aftward into the next compartment. He squeezed forward on his belly, wriggling back and forth to avoid a jagged piece of metal from a broken sensor array.

He's in control, that damned machine. Doesn't need me. He heard air escaping slowly somewhere. He placed one foot against the array and pushed forward.

"Why're you doing all this? Why didn't you just transfer to deep space? It would have been safer."

The computer said nothing for a moment, during which Baker pulled through the narrowest part of the gantlet—between the fighter's laser cannon and a portion of the bulkhead that had bent outward. When the machine spoke again, it was with a tentative tone Baker had never heard before.

"The woman Delia Trine seems to be important to both you and Virgil for some reason; vital to your continued operation of *Circus*. I am willing to take acceptable risks to recover her if she is still alive."

Baker squirmed free from under the fighter and moved on his hands and knees toward an exit hatch. He stood and opened the seals. Between heavy breaths, he said, "The moment we land, Lee in there'll call his friends out on us. Or they'll spot us from orbit. Matching velocities isn't necessary to hit us with Valli pellets. They're even more deadly when moving."

"I am depressurizing the bay to cause cell rupture in the corpse. My sensors have greater range than those of the fighters. So do my lasers. We shall be safe until the deep thrust fighter that is coming around the sun arrives."

"What?"

"We shall be finished by then, I estimate."

He ran the rest of the way to the Con Two lift.

The surface of Mercury whipped past them, a blur of blackness shimmering here and there under the glowing ionized

gases left in the wake of *Circus*'s engines. Baker stared, eyes
unblinking. The spacecraft maintained a bow-down attitude
because of the forced orbit—were the engines to shut off, the
ship would climb to a higher orbit rather than fall to the planet.
The effect of constantly falling toward the world transfixed
Baker. He watched the horizon, fighting the persistent feeling
of disorientation. The back of his conning chair was down, the
viewing port of Con Two up, and the horizon of the planet well
above his head. He watched a hazy glow appear around the
edge of the planet.

"Approaching south polar area. Stand by for skew flip turn
and deceleration for landing." Baker tightened his grip on the
seat. The computer broke into its rapid speaking mode, com-
menting on all major systems function. Suddenly, the vernier
rockets fired up with full force. The horizon dropped away
and Baker's stomach with it. His neck ached against the braces
that held his head immobile. An instant later, the lower limb
of Mercury dropped down across the port and hung there, the
mountains and craters speeding over its limb out of sight.

In the brief duration of the skew flip, *Circus* rose to triple its
former altitude. Baker noticed the extended field of vision this
gave him.

Ass backward into the unknown. He switched on a rear
vidcam and added sun filters until the scrim showed more than
a white glare.

"I hope you know where you're going," he said, moving the
cam controls to take in the slightly curving edge of the planet.

"Five *kps*, twenty *km*," the computer said, followed by, "Four
kps at eighteen. Under escape *v*. Rotate for landing." The vernier rockets firmly turned the spacecraft aftward to the surface.

The viewing port darkened. Baker watched a zone of brilliant light flow from the bow across the ellipsoidal prow and
head aftward. All of the ship lay bathed in light from the hori-

zon facing the ship's topside. Judging by the position of the shadows cast by the conning tower, he could estimate just where the sun should be burning more than six times brighter than on Earth, with no atmosphere to shield him.

The weight of deceleration lightened. He no longer saw the planet through the viewing port. Darkness suddenly spread across the spaceship, followed shortly by a sharp decrease in the whining of the engines.

"Engine shutdown," the computer said calmly. The ship settled against the mercurial plain, then listed slowly to port until a vernier rocket fired to steady the mass.

"Status," Baker said, undoing his harness.

"We are twenty kilometers away from the south pole, on the dark side of the terminator. The redoubt's solar energy power station consists of a low ring of solar panels disguised into the outer rim of a crater. Heat exchange elements extend from the center of the ring to a radius of twenty five kilometers. Eighteen of the thirty-six heat sinks are always on the night side and radiating infra-red. The cryonic preservation unit is most likely buried at the center of the crater."

Baker climbed down toward the lift. The computer's voice followed him in his earphones.

"Use lifeboat four," the computer suggested. "The port shuttle was damaged when the psychfighter shifted during the skew flip."

"Where's that?"

"Ring One Level Two Section Three O'Clock. Use axial tube three."

"Right." Baker climbed out of the lift and up to the center of the ring. He ran down the man-high axial tube. "What about the other ships?" he asked between breaths.

"Three have so far crossed the horizon in orbit. I am keeping their sensors defeated by laser until they enter my kill radius. I destroyed five ships that transferred in before they could get bearings on us. I think we have very little time, as the deep thrust fighter is in deceleration for orbit."

"It'll take time for the troops to get out of their acceleration baths."

"They can outfight us with lasers, Jord."

"They won't, if they think they might harm *me*. Wait till they slow to a constant velocity, then transfer one of the anti-matter pods into their mid-section."

The computer considered the plan for several microseconds. "At the south pole, you would have some measure of protection from heavy particles, but I should transfer it at distance so the other particles—"

"Just do it. I can take care of myself on the surface."

"You will need a more protective suit."

Baker looked at his thin Späflex outfit and shook his head. "I'll fly close to the ground and keep screens up while I'm in the boat. The shadow from the crater rim should protect me while I'm looking for an entrance. There's little enough time as it is."

"You will be out of contact with me when you go beyond line of sight."

"That's a blessing, motormouth." Baker paused, then shook his head and cycled the airlock. **You can't hurt a computer's feelings.** He switched the breathing apparatus from tanks to rebreather and climbed into the lifeboat as soon as the airlock opened.

The lifeboat was designed for use in the event of a total power failure in the larger ship. The airlock could be manually cycled or blown open. After that, nothing need be done to escape *Circus Galacticus*.

Baker climbed into the cockpit and dropped all twenty sun filters across the glasteel hatch. He hit full power and shot out of the ship's hull like a bullet. He corrected for the almost immediate drop to ground level and sped across the shattered terrain, bow high, engine at an angle that rocketed him forward while compensating for Mercury's feeble acceleration of gravity.

"Hot tail!" he cried, then whooped as he steered the craft toward the brightest part of the horizon.

"Two degrees port," the computer suggested. Baker complied.

"You know," he said, "I rode motorcycles back on Earth. This is just like popping a wheel—"

"You should be in view of the crater rim now. Loss of signal should occur—" the computer's voice crackled once and fell silent.

So long.

The dark rim of the crater bent over the horizon to rush toward him. His finger flicked at the controls and the lifeboat rose a few hundred meters. Through the darkened screen he discerned the smooth solar panels and heat sinks camouflaged into the crater wall. Everything on the night side lay in darkness.

Purple light bathed the cockpit for an instant. The boat plunged down into the crater and hottailed across the surface at an altitude of less than eight meters then crossed to the other side of the south pole, dodging mounds and boulders. Braking rockets immediately flared into life, kicking dust up around the boat. The craft performed a three-bounce landing, shuddered, and came to a rest in the shadow of the dayward edge of the crater rim.

The dust settled quickly in the absence of an atmosphere and Baker opened the hatch.

The crater looked like any other crater on any other planet, except that a faint aurora shimmered every few seconds overhead. The massive flux of the solar wind provided Mercury with its own cloud of particles to ionize.

Something moved against the stars. Another psychfighter.

He watched it flare and vanish.

Good shot, *Circus*. He looked about, seeing nothing in the crater to indicate an entrance to the cryonic unit. He wondered where they would put an access hatch. **Depends on whether they merely wanted to hide during a brief war or whether they wanted never to be found. If it's on a time lock, it may be sealed from the inside.**

He strapped a hand laser to the back of his right glove and climbed out of the cockpit. Surface dust compacted under the soles of his boots. At less than half earth weight, his steps were long and easy, but cautious. Approaching a large boulder, he chose to leap over it rather than alter his pace. A burning on his back from the top of his head to below his shoulders distracted him enough that he stumbled on landing and slid through the sandy rim of a smaller crater.

He stood and brushed the dust off. His back still felt warm. Picking up a rock, he threw it straight up with all the strength the pressure suit permitted. At four meters high it glowed brightly, then darkened as it dropped slowly back into the crater shadow.

High jumps cancelled due to sunshine, he thought. We'll just stick to the marathon.

He walked with long steps, but refrained from any more leaps. There was still no visible evidence that the floor of the crater was anything more than a level expanse of pitted dust punctuated by a single craggy hill at the center, a feature common to many impact craters. He reached the central peak and stood before it, crouching slightly. Another stone toss indicated that the sun shone just half a meter over his head. A sharp line separated the bright upper half of the hill from the shadowed lower half. Reflected sunlight illuminated certain portions of the shaded areas, so Baker could see them when he covered his eyes from the glare of the upper half of the peak. He found that he could not even look at the upper half for more than a few seconds.

He began to sweat. **Conduction's making the ground too warm and light reflected from the crater wall adds to the heat.** Excess perspiration passed through the pressure suit and evaporated swiftly in the vacuum, cooling him. The Späflex adjusted its porosity to handle the new conditions. It was not enough. He knew he would have to find shelter fast or return to the shuttle.

Baker's gaze searched around the crater, then considered the central peak before him. At the very top, drenched in blinding light, lay something black, curled, and weblike. It reached under a small mound of dust on top. Baker followed the slope of the mound with shielded eyes. Something about the dust did not look right.

Why would a crater peak have small dust rays extending from its base? And why that pile of dust on top?

He pounded one fist lightly against his chin. He reconsidered at the charred fibers near the summit of the tiny peak. **Sure. Put the main shaft under the peak, drag out a canvas sack and fill it with dirt, wrap it in Mylar until it's set on top of the peak, pull the Mylar inside and close the hatch. The canvas bag burns, bursts, and you're covered.**

He examined every square centimeter he could see without stepping out of his protective shade. He caught sight of something just above the shadow line—a soft rectangular bump that seemed too regular. He flung rocks at it until one hit above it. Dust tumbled away from an airlock handle in small-scale avalanches.

Straight. Now I hope I don't need some code to unlock it.

He bent down to approach the base of the mound. Digging his boots into the ever-hotter sands, he worked his way up to the very edge of darkness. Crouching there, he squinted to see the exposed handle. Sunlight glinted dazzlingly on the upper edge of the polished metal.

Doesn't appear locked. Here goes one hand. He reached up with his right hand, stopped before it crossed into sunlight, and lowered it. **Better not risk the shooting hand.** He quickly grabbed the handle with his left hand and yanked.

The Späflex did not burn. After only an instant of insulation, it efficiently transferred the heat directly to his palm and fingers. The hatch opened and Baker fell back to the hot sands, screeching. The sand and dust from the door sprinkled down upon him. He rolled clear, but some of it smothered his legs, burning like cinders. He leapt up to stamp off the dust. It sizzled on the sweat-soaked Späflex.

He grunted more in fury than pain, breathed lightly for a few moments, then looked up at the hatch. A shaft of sunlight entered through the opening, heating and boiling away the atmosphere that had condensed inside years before.

He climbed back to the barely man-sized hole and looked up toward it. Sets of instructions in several languages had been printed on the inside of the door.

Have to get inside to read them. Now how do I get inside without roasting? Wait until the planet makes a half-turn?

He touched the back of his shoulders. It no longer hurt. **Not much of a burn. Maybe I can last as long as a second or two if I keep moving.**

He dug his feet into the side of the mound, reached up and grabbed the bottom of the hatchway. Pulling and kicking, he wormed his way inside the compartment. A rounded square of light on the opposite wall blistered paint where it fell. Baker watched it for a moment, then considered closing the hatch.

His entire back hurt. He realized that both of his hands were now burnt when he tried to unclench them.

"God damn it!" He stood up, avoiding the deadly sunbeam, reached outside with his left hand, and drew the hatch shut. The clang reverberated through the floorplates. He sat down and drew his knees up, curling his hands into his crotch.

I've got no time to sit here and hurt, damn it. What do I have to do next?

A soft light shone from the top of the two-meter wide cylinder. Its ruddy glow revealed the square, blackened patch where sunlight had hit. Baker looked up at the hatch. The lettering on the inside had charred, but the letters showed up as black against a lighter gray. Baker stood to read the Americ version. The directions for operating the lift were simple enough. He opened the control box near the hatch and pulled the correct switches.

The lift rumbled once, then whined into life. The floorplate descended slowly, stalling intermittently like an old man walking down stairs.

Faster, damn you! He scuffed one boot and then the other against the floor. The top of a hatch appeared in one portion of the wall. He bent down to watch the floor drop past it. Before the lift even stopped moving, he had opened the control box and actuated the cycling switch.

Inside the airlock, he removed the clear protective cap on the exit optics of his glove laser. He squeezed his thumb against the switch alongside his index finger. The low-wattage sighting beam threw a red dot on the wall opposite him. It wavered nervously.

The hatch sealed by itself and the airlock cycled. A light shone green. Baker steadied his hand and pointed it at the opening hatch.

All right. Let's see what sort of greeting you people planned to give visitors.

The hatch swung silently open. A cold mist poured across the floor, chilling Baker's ankles. He saw nothing. His arm ached from the tension of suspense.

The Späflex contracted against his skin, compensating for his sudden chill. The suit, manufactured to function in the perfect insulation of a vacuum, could not protect him from the cold atmosphere. Heaters throbbed into life someplace, struggling to replace a half century of slow heat loss.

He noticed more instructions on the wall. He pressed the button labeled AMERIC and switched on his outer microphone.

"Welcome to *Pastime*," a woman's pleasant voice said. The still-frigid loudspeakers distorted some of the lower frequency sounds. "Please be very careful when in the main chamber, as cryonic liquids are present and could cause damage if allowed to escape. All units are arranged alphabetically, but please realize that some people may have used assumed names."

Baker switched on the outside speakers of his suit. "Are you a computer or just a recording?" he asked.

No answer. He strode down the black, indirectly lit corridor until he saw a sign reading MAIN CHAMBER in a number of alphabets. He worked the lock according to printed instructions and stood back. Another blast of cold hit him. Shuddering, he waited for the heaters to warm the enclosure.

Come on, come on. Why'd this suit have to conduct heat so efficiently? I can see them in there, unprotected but for their glasteel coffins. Not even a robot guard.

"You are entering the *Pastime* main chamber. Please do not touch any controls until instructed. All five hundred seventeen occupants of *Pastime* are civilians possessing no military secrets."

Here comes the spiel, Baker thought.

"*Pastime* was built," the recording continued as Baker walked quickly to the "T" section, "to house a group of people opposed to the Earth-Belt war of Twenty-One Fifteen. We await the opening of a sealed memory in the banks of the Star Consolidated Auditing Firm, notifying independent rescue agencies of our location. This will take place on Twenty-One June, Twenty-One Forty-Five. If you are from any of the following rescue agencies..." the recording ran through a list of fifteen companies. Baker shook his head in pity and looked around for Delia's unit. The main chamber took up a lot of space. Unlike the cold holds on habitat ships, this place did not have to keep its mass or energy usage low. The cryonic units were efficient, well built, and large.

Baker located the gold-anodized aluminum plate marked "TRINE, Delia Diana," listing her birth date and the address of her next of kin. The computer finished its list and said, "...then you are welcomed and we hope the war has ended. If you are a wayfarer who stumbled upon us, we welcome you and ask that you not disturb us if the war is still in progress. If you have come here from a military expedition, we assume there is some reason you did not merely destroy us from orbit.

"Please remember that we are civilians posing no military threat. We are to be considered Non-Combatant Escapees in accordance with New Geneva Convention Section Twelve, Sub-Sections Beta through Gamma. Thank you for your cooperation."

There was no wake up call. They'll be here forever.

He ran his hands over the three-meter-long capsule. Delia lay inside somewhere, floating in liquid helium and wrapped in thousands of layers of insulation per centimeter of the cylinder shell's half-meter thickness.

The plaque explained resuscitation instructions. He read through them, then pounded the side of the capsule.

"I can't stay here two days! Dee—how do I get you out?" **No time! If Lee's launched a Valli attack from Trans-Pluto, it'll be here in a few more hours. I can't carry the whole damn capsule back to the boat. And the deep-thrust battleship is nearly here! Good God.**

He ran past the rows of capsules to the opposite end of the chamber. A small console extended from the shiny black wall to his right. Anxiety and the biting cold made his stomach muscles ache. He ignored the pain and leaned over the board.

Where's the damn' curator robot?

He punched the button with a question mark on it and typed in:

ARE CRYONIC UNITS REMOVABLE?

YES, blinked the reply.

How to get it out, though? How'd they get out if the rescue people didn't show? There's got to be an emergency contingency—

LOCATION OF LIFEBOATS?

PLEASE CLARIFY

ESCAPE SPACECRAFT?

SECTIONS 3, 6, 9 & 12—PERIMETER 4.

HEAVY LOAD LIFTING EQUIPMENT?

NONE.

What? How do they—

HOW TO MOVE CRYONIC UNIT FROM MAIN CHAMBER TO ESCAPE SPACECRAFT?

MAGNEPLANE GUIDEWAY—ORANGE LINES

Baker released a breath of pent agitation and fear. The console waited a few seconds, then shut off. He ran back to Delia's capsule. The exertion warmed him.

An hour. A whole damn' hour. _Circus_ could be slag by now. And I'm not even loaded.

The cryonic unit slid down the corridor, floating several millimeters above the orange line painted along the center of the magnetized floor. Baker sat atop the capsule, watching the lackluster scenery pass.

Following Baker's directions, the cryo-capsule, its massive tangle of peripheral equipment, and the superconducting sheet upon which it rested, moved quickly along the guideway on Meisner-effect fields. It slowed and turned, then regained speed.

A double set of doors slid open and the cryonic unit levitated into the shipping dock. Jumping off, Baker ran to the escape ship and looked inside. He took less than a second to decide that the fates were against him. He sat down against the bulk of the cryonic unit.

No cargo space. Just acceleration couches and two engines. What else could go wrong?

A telltale ticked frantically in his ear. His shoulders drooped.

Impurity overload in the rebreather accumulators. Now I'm going to suffocate. *Circus's* **probably gone from orbit again, one way or another, and the psychfighters are after me. I might as well take one of those engines and use it to defrost Dee, for all the good it'd do either of us.**

He looked at the twin engine pods on the twenty-meter long wedge-shaped ship and breathed the thick recycled air. **I'm sorry, Dee. I got you this far and now I've got to put you back before your batteries run out. I should've died back there...**

His hands slipped from his thighs to the magneplate. The twin engine pods in his field of vision twisted and blurred.

Something hiccoughed in his breathing tube.

I didn't get you back, did I Delia? Sorry. Sorry. I should have loved you more when I had the chance.

The pods came back into focus. His forehead burned.

A chance.

A buzzer sounded far away in his earpiece, then grew louder, closer, until it shook him to awareness.

Twenty minutes!

He scrambled to leap off the cargo carrier. The emergency oxygen bottle that cut in to revive him would probably not even last that long.

The port engine pod rattled open under the force of his frantic efforts. He ripped at loose cables and unscrewed fuel fittings. **Why do I keep using these chances to live?**

He climbed into the cockpit of the ship and actuated the systems dump. A light flashed the words "Emergency Engine Jettison." A warning siren wailed noiselessly in the vacuum, and with a floor-shaking thump, the port engine dropped from its housing.

I'm an ass. I'll probably be shot at or Vallied the minute I come out the chute, or I won't be able to hottail it sideways.

He pushed the cryonic unit to the end of the magneplane guideway and left it hovering. He tried not to hyperventilate.

C'mon, there's got to be a crane or something around here. The engine housing's big enough to hold the blasted thing, but how do I get the engine out of the way and the—

A vernier rocket stared him in the face. His gaze darted to the low rail on which the escape rocket rested.

Don't stop to think about it.

He jumped into the cockpit and charged the engines.

Do it now!

The vernier rocket on the starboard side fired, sliding the boat sideways off the track. He laughed and hit the braking rocket. A short impulse shoved the fuselage a few meters backward. He looked behind him and fired the vernier very lightly a couple more times.

Close enough.

The empty port engine pod hung over the cryonic unit. Pieces of the guide rail lay scattered across the floor. He ran back to the unit, powered up the magneplane, and eased the load into the engine housing. With it levitating inside, he closed the pod hatches and locked them.

Finally.

The lifeboat checklist took a minute to run through. The air in his mouthpiece again started to taste stale. The launch ramp doors parted, a star-filled sky appearing ahead of him. He alerted the onboard computer to compensate for the single engine and the different mass of the cryonic unit.

The kick of the starboard engine slammed him back in his seat. He cleared the exit hatch and hottailed across the plain, the rim of the crater nearly a kilometer behind him. When the last liter of oxygen whispered into his lungs, he fought the urge to suck in as much air as he could and held his breath with grim force.

With one free finger he started cycling the air inside the cabin. The pressure rose. With every bit of his concentration centered on holding the boat safely on attitude, he had no chance to unfasten his helmet.

"*Circus*," he said with his last exhalation, "this is Baker. Stand by to receive payload."

Circus's touchdown area appeared over the short horizon. He stared at the smooth circle of molten rock.

Overhead, in synchronous orbit, hung a score of psychfighters. Baker watched six of the tiny blips vanish from his radar scrim and reappear directly around him. **No battleship, though. The anti-matter pod worked. Where is *Circus*?**

He hit the braking rocket and slowed the lifeboat to a gentle landing on the dusty crater floor. The psychfighters landed around him in a threatening circle. Something exploded aft of him and in the control panels.

Vallis!

He reached up to wrestle with his breather. Numb fingers, unable to grasp, fell to his sides.

Swimming in air. And I can't get to it.

One of the psychfighters hovered over the escape ship, descending. The black of space blurred over Baker's entire field of vision, his last impressions those of the fighter still a dozen meters overhead and of a clanking sound shaking the boat. He took a last, useless breath.

Going can be so soft. Gentle tugging into black, like an insistent lover urging, drawing, pulling me to that dark

bed...

Chapter Eleven

2175

Virgil dreamily traced patterns on his chest. As through a thick haze, he watched the gray and blue form sputter away from him.

So soft. To awaken without screaming because the death was so good. The dead man inside me botched it. I could have changed things, but I stayed to watch. He died so softly, now I float so softly. A tender airflow cools me. This is the quest's end. No cocoon of gauze to keep me from flying. Naked and adrift.

"Virgil?"

It's the brave that die a thousand times. They know the quest is worth it. To lie unfettered, free.

"Virgil."

All yearning past, no shield to seek, I drift uncaring. Gentle white and scent of steel.

"Virgil."

Sent of steel. Cent stealing. Centuries stolen from me.

"Where am I?" He twisted about. Something blue-gray and tubular vanished through a hatchway. His arm hit a padded handhold and he grabbed tight.

"You are safe, Virgil, but you must get to the medical bay. Delia Trine is in the final stages of resuscitation—"

Delia?

Virgil ran a hand over his bristly scalp. "I saw the vultures close in. I saw what the dead man inside me did. I died with him."

"Please proceed to the medical bay. You are currently in the recovery room."

Virgil looked around him. The soft white walls, thickly padded, seemed totally enclosed. A door hissed and opened inward. Virgil kicked off to fly into the next room, the computer bringing him up to date.

"As I transferred an anti-matter pod into the warship to destroy it, the fighters attacked, so I had to transfer out. I left behind a lifeboat with orders to grab any small ship that was not a psychfighter."

Virgil entered the clean room of the medical bay, where a spray of disinfectant clung to his flesh. Toweling off, he waited for the sensor check. "The psychefighter dropped down on me," he said. "It would've thrown a field around me and transferred out. Back to beyond Pluto."

"I transferred the lifeboat in between the two of you, grappled the escape ship and transferred out here. I matched velocities and brought you onboard. You were nearing brain death."

Yanked back again. And I thought it had ended. What do you want from me, Master Snoop? Why not let Nightsheet have his way? Why keep me alive? What code must I break?

The inner doors cycled open. She lay before him inside the opened glasteel capsule.

Death Angel!

Step forward. No! Get away. No. He leaned back against the doors, his arms hanging weightlessly away from him. The hands twitched, as though trying to explain something to the still body before him.

She doesn't move. The lights shine off a head balder than mine and wires grow from her chest and temples. Tubes worm in and out of her nose and groin. She is as I was once: a prisoner of Master Snoop. He moved forward one handhold.

Naked and trapped she floats in her glass coffin nestled in funereal foil. Skin so white and pure-soap smooth—

"She's in a state of *coma vigil.* When the psychfighters downed your escape boat, they transferred a Valli into either engine pod. The one in the port side demolished the control circuitry and she began to thaw. I sent a robot to her as soon as I determined the situation and initiated normal resuscitation procedures. I do not know if she can be brought out of the coma. I took the liberty of injecting picotechs into her carotid artery in an effort to preserve her mental matrix against degeneration."

"Coma vigil?"

"Random brain activity. Spontaneous breathing. Periods of semiconsciousness. Delirium. It may be due to the transfer out here."

"Out where?"

"Tau Ceti."

"Were we followed?" He moved closer to the capsule.

"They had no idea where we were going. And even if one could have tagged along, there is a practical limit to psychfighter distances. I suspect that a twelve year wait to reestablish contact when the fighter appears is stretching anyone's patience."

We're alone, then. Death Angel and I.

"Wake up!" he whispered to her. No movement disturbed her perfect stillness. Virgil bent over the capsule, locked his feet under the table, and gazed at her closely. An uncontrollable anger welled up inside him.

Death Angel's mask doesn't fool me. Like a helmet, she hides behind it, as aware as I am when the dead man inside me takes control.

The layers of metalized Mylar insulation, bent back, crackled like fire under his waist. He leaned closer and raised his hand.

Her head swung sideways with the force of his slap. Saliva flew from her lips, scattering across the room, adhering to whatever the globules hit. One eyelid swung open. An enlarged pupil stared sightlessly.

"Death Angel, you wake up and tell me!" A red image of his

hand appeared on her cheek. "You tell me why! Why you made me die die die die!" Another slap punctuated his words. Her head rolled back.

"Stop it," she mumbled.

"Death Angel?" His fingers tightened around her shoulders and shook.

"Stop it. He's just different from all... you. Can't help..."

"Death Angel wake up and tell me!" He floated above the capsule now, his feet anchored under machinery braces, his arms shaking hers.

You make me scream, Death Angel, make me die inside a thousand times more than out. Hurt. Hurt.

"Why do that? He's not... hurting you..." She coughed and fell silent, closing her eyes.

"*Death Angel wake up!*" he shouted next to her ear.

"Brain activity is depressed, Virgil. You will not get anything out of her until she is in semiconsciousness again."

He hovered directly over her for the next hour, watching, listening, speaking to her in a rambling monotone, apologizing, begging her to return. The computer suggested that he receive an injection of nourishment. He snapped the plastic tube into his wrist port to accept the trickle of dextrose and vitamins. After a while, the computer made a buzzing sound.

"Brain activity resuming."

Death Angel, you make it hard. Harder than it's ever been. So hard and you can't be reached.

He pulled closer to her bare, pallid skin. The oxygen cannula under her nose hissed with quiet regularity. He floated horizontally over her, arms grasping the lips of the capsule.

"Wake up, Delia," he whispered in her ear, pulling even closer. *You make it so hard.* He touched her. "I want to—"

"Free for—" she muttered. "Thrive. Sick heaven, hate. Trine. Men."

"Delia."

"Ate mine then. Mind. Denned. Dead. Dead. Frozen dead died." Her head rolled about, loose as a rag doll's. Wires rattled against the capsule. Her eyes opened. "Virgil. Killed me. Virgil. I died for Virgil."

"You're not dead."

"Waited until I died. Cold dead."

Closer he drew, pulling in, touching the flesh of his body to hers. "You're not dead, Delia," he said, his voice a low murmur. "Feel. Life is feeling. You've only died once, just once. Believe in me: you can die again and again with me forever."

Slowly, reverently, he slid into her, feeling the cool touch of her thighs against his. For a moment, she murmured peacefully, beginning to move with his rhythm. Then her eyelids snapped open like a mechanical doll's. Her pupils irised down into tight, black points of terror.

She screamed. A powerful shove pushed Virgil out, spinning him against a bulkhead. The food tube popped out of his wrist and snaked about, leaking fluid.

"No!" she shrieked. "Died enough. I'm dead!" She thrashed her arms about, tangling them in wires and pulling off the electrogel contacts. With a shriek of animal fury, she ripped the waste tubes from her. Blood smeared the catheter that snaked loosely about in the weightless chamber. Blood and urine sailed about in pulsating globules, adhering like living, hungry microbes to anything they touched.

Virgil kicked back toward her, whipping about to grasp at her thigh. Overcome by nausea, she doubled up, pulling in her legs. Virgil sailed past her, grabbing at air, and hit the opposite bulkhead.

"Delia. You're safe here. I'm Virgil. Just keep calm."

She dry heaved in small, rapid spasms. Coughing, she looked wildly about.

Adult fetus, hanging over me, her arms cradling her stomach, her eyes so scared. Death Angel so unprotected, so far from

Nightsheet, so hungry for him. Hold still. Please.

"Hold still, Delia. I'll bring you down." He climbed over to her and reached out. Seizing one foot, he received a powerful kick in the face from the other. He hit one bulkhead and she the opposite.

"Damn you!" he shouted, covering his nose and eyes. "You're alive. Thank me, damn you. I died and died to find you!" *Gave up my body to get the dead man's help. I boiled and froze.*

Somewhere, a hatchway hissed open and shut. "She has left the room, Virgil."

"What?" He uncovered his eyes to look about. "Well, stop her! Seal all hatches."

"Done. However, I cannot keep a hatch sealed against a direct command unless there exists a pressure differential—"

"Then change programming." He kicked toward the exit hatch and bumped his shoulder passing through.

"This is not programming, this is the construction of the hatch locks themselves."

"It'll slow her down, at least. Where is she?"

"Ring One, Level Five, Two O'Clock, going to One-Five-One. She is moving aimlessly, no apparent goal."

Sniffing back a small puddle of blood building up in his nose, Virgil dragged through the passages, listening to the speakers for Delia's location, keeping track of his own, and closing in.

And then, "Virgil—she has removed a wedgecutter from one of the emergency sealant cabinets in One-One-Twelve. Get there fast."

"Send a robot!"

"None in the vicinity. Hurry."

"I'm almost there!" he shouted, speeding through a passageway.

"Hurry. She has severed her aorta and superior vena cava. Respiration zero. Brain death in six minutes—"

He propelled through the hatch into the compartment and

looked above him. She hung suspended in a carnelian haze. The wedgecutter stuck out of her chest, the jagged, meat-raw wound still voiding blood.

A billion ruby suns orbit around her, a crimson galaxy. I had you so shortly, Death Angel, and you brought Nightsheet to you. Stupid.

He moved through the floating droplets of blood to take her body in his arms.

"Get her to the medical bay," the computer said. "We might be able to revive her prior to brain death."

Virgil ran along the curving corridors in his own version of artificial gravity, then he sailed through the straightaways, taking the fastest path back. Her body drifted limply in his grasp, the wedgecutter grating against a rib. A red line flowed behind him, droplets of blood breaking loose and drifting until air resistance slowed them.

"Put her in the boxdoc."

Virgil pushed her into the unit. Sealing the lid, he watched as mechanical hands and tools immediately dug into her chest. One hand withdrew the wedgecutter while a pair of heavy clippers crunched into flesh just above her left breast. After three powerful cuts, the clippers withdrew, pulling back the broken sections of rib.

They'll cut you up, Death Angel, the Master Snoop's revenge for joining Nightsheet. And you won't come back to me, will you?

The boxdoc continued its efforts. A series of tubes plunged into the exposed arteries and veins. Pure oxygen pumped into the container. Two small extensions covered with a farrago of stainless-steel instruments performed the operation.

"Can you bring her back?" *She won't come back. Not from this.*

"She has entered only the first stage of brain death. The medical parameters indicate that we can save her. Her heart will have to be replaced temporarily until a new one can be cloned. Ceramic braces will be cast to replace her ribs. She will probably suffer from diminished mental capacity—"

"Shut up!" He leaned over the unit, watching a thick red fluid pump into her chest. The blood on his arms and chest had dried into brown freckles and streaks that flaked when he moved.

Death Angel I can't have you like that.

Her eyes fluttered open for a moment and her gaze met his. Her mouth opened as though to speak and her head shook weakly before she lapsed back into anesthesia.

No. Not like that.

He pulled out the boxdoc operations manual and signaled the first page. Scanning the table of contents, he asked, "Has her memory RNA degenerated?"

"Not to any significant degree, in all probability. Her electrochemical matrix, though, has been disrupted by the cerebral swelling."

"Have the picotechs had time to copy her matrix?"

"Yes."

Virgil signaled the page he wanted and watched it appear on the scrim. "Initiate leeching process See-One-Two-Oh-Four, and prepare the cloning unit to be cast off."

"Please explain your requests."

Virgil laughed and shook his head. "Don't you see? Just like you did this"—he waved his left hand at the vidcam—"you're going to do her."

"Clone her?"

"Yes! Clone all of her! I know you can't force grow her because the brain has to develop normally, so if we set the unit adrift and transfer out and back a dozen light years each way..."

"Full clones grown at normal rates are very difficult to maintain correctly. Add to that the unit's being run on automatic—"

"If it doesn't work the first time, we try again and again.

With the transfer, we could do it a hundred times in a day."

"If none of them take, or if we lose the cloning tank, you will have lost Delia forever."

Like a child scolded, he looked up at the vid and softly said, "All right. I won't have her leeched until we get a good clone." *Death Angel you've become so much meat for me to grind when I please. Sorry, but I have to.*

"Do you consider it necessary?" the computer asked.

"Yes. Do you consider it possible?"

"There is a probability of success."

Virgil smiled. *Your crowning theft, Nightsheet, and I take it back.* "Let's go."

Virgil conveyed the cloning tank once more to the lifeship and secured it. He worked quickly, his hands and muscles straining with effort.

"When have you eaten last?" the computer asked.

He tightened the last strap and leaned against the humming machine. "I don't recall. Don't you have a record in your memory?"

"My last record shows that you have gone fourteen hours, twelve minutes subjective, not counting dextrose supplements. You did not dine while on Mercury?"

Virgil smiled. "Not that I know of."

"Food is being prepared in the galley. You should eat and rest before we transfer. You will probably have a lot to do when we recover the tank."

Taking one last look at the shuttle, he said, "Straight. Can you add on the spare generator yourself?"

"I will have a robot do it."

"Straight." *Have them come out of the walls when my back turns. Let them go about their wiry business. I can hear them in there, making their plans.*

When he pushed the last piece of meat into his mouth, the computer buzzed once and said, "Lifeship cast off. All systems functioning. Beacon set to activate in twenty-four years. Photosynth accumulator locked on Tau Ceti, recycler on standby. All lab units show green."

Virgil wiped his mouth on his arm and picked some of the larger crumbs and debris out of the air. "Find the emptiest piece of space twelve light years from here and let's go." He thought for a moment, then said, "How are you able to handle the transfer effect? You don't seem to be bothered anymore."

"If you had several hours, I could explain the method of selectively re-routing neural paths and delaying the firing of certain neurons by thousandths of a nanosecond to compensate for transfer lag."

"Don't bother on my account."

"I believe I could duplicate the process on an organic entity such as you by the removal of the pineal gland and a rebundling of synaptic—"

"Forget it. I can handle death. Let's... just go." *I can handle it. Just a little bit longer. Die a few more times.*

Inside the prow ellipsoid, Virgil sat staring out while the computer plotted coordinates. It suddenly spoke.

"According to estimates from orbital data, the cloning tank will be on the opposite side of Tau Ceti in twenty-four years. One hundred sixty-eight degrees. We shall have to match velocities with it to—"

"Just do it." Virgil strapped in and chewed at his thumbnail. The transfer button glowed. He pushed it and watched.

Every time it takes longer. Every time the gate comes closer. It

opens just a crack before me. Something howls, low and mad, from behind it. Get back! I don't care, Death Angel. I know what lurks and I won't go. It grows stronger every time, but so do I. Your soothing won't work. I'm going back this time, and the next. See me there? That smile? That's because I know that I can die again and again and—

Again I try to push past and—

Again. Something pushes me back. Blackness all around before me, punctured by stars.

"Prepare to transfer."

Virgil pushed the button once more.

In control over death, I can sit while my blood freezes in its motion, while air stops in my throat, while darkness and then light smear together, wrap around me and twist and push and shove until I feel pushed into—

The body I need to survive.

—the door, but I slam it just in time. Something howls after it shuts and I run down the corridor, the door bending in toward me stretching to almost bursting and I run and run and—

The kick of the engine array thundering into power shoved against Virgil's back.

Back again! Nightsheet, I'll keep winning—

"Beacon information shows that my calculations were accurate to seventeen hours in twenty-four years. Prepare to rendezvous with cloning tank. Telemetry reports all systems functioning; the clone is healthy."

Virgil let go a sigh and sank back in the acceleration padding. *I'm a father.*

Chapter Twelve

2199

The lifeship eased into the starboard docking bay under Virgil's guidance. He shut the engines down and turned off the scrim that offered him a cockpit's-eye view of the docking. When the air had cycled, he stepped into the bay to examine the small craft. Twenty-four years had done little to its exterior.

He shoved off from the bulkhead and clambered for the cargo hatch, unlocking it and pulling it open.

Somewhere in that black tank she lies, blank slate ready for RNA and picotechs to draw thought designs. Straps undo in my hands and I push so gently, easing Death Angel's new hideout toward the medical bay. The plan goes so easily, I wish I...

I wish I knew what—the plan—was. Is.

"Medical bay ready for further operation."

He took the machine to the medical bay and disconnected the cloning tank from its peripheral equipment. The computer talked him through the birthing procedure.

"The machine will puncture the neoamnion and drain the support fluid. Disconnect the anatrophant collars first so she doesn't break any bones."

Virgil opened the tank and watched the clear, viscous liquid drain from the sack surrounding the human form.

Death Angel! Hair so long and black, skin so pale pink, the pain of years nowhere on you. He turned the dial that unlocked the rings connected to her arms and legs. Her muscle tone had been electrically stimulated to that of someone her own age. She jerked all over from the induced exercise.

"Quickly, Virgil. Remove the neoamnion and administer oxygen."

The sack slipped around in his fingers, covering the surgical gloves with glistening neoamniotic fluid. He ripped it apart and reached for the oxygen mask. Brushing wet hair from her face, he placed the mask over her nose and mouth.

"She's not breathing," he said.

"Turn her over and apply pressure to the back to allow the neoamniote to drain from her lungs."

Your body so soft and light in my arms, your back so smooth—

"No, Virgil. Hit her on the back, do not press."

She coughed after the first hit, the fluid splashing into the curve of the tank where a small fan drew it out of the air. Despite the machine's effort, bits of fluid floated around the medical bay. She continued to cough.

"She's breathing." He put the mask on between coughs. "Can't we have some gravity here?"

"Not until we are certain of her bone strength and heart capacity. She will require extensive tests to—"

The clone screamed. Her voice wailed inhumanly, unlike even the cry of a baby. It was a shriek of bestial madness.

Feral Death Angel, fear all things new. So many years in warm floating and now air instead of water, light instead of dark.

"All vital signs positive," the computer stated flatly over the howl. "Administering ten *cc*s of DuoTranq to depress excessive heart activity and hyperventilation."

Virgil looked at the syringe moving toward her arm. *Duodrugs! So now I serve the Master Snoop. Death Angel you brought this on yourself when you tried to play Snoop against Nightsheet for Wizard's sake. So many games you've been playing but I'm still in control. Sleep, Death Angel, and awaken renewed, reglued.*

"You may remove the monitoring contacts—I have remotes on her. Then detach the primary and secondary umbilical tubes and units, initiate the cleansing cycle in the unit, and remove her to the recovery room. Make certain no direct light gets in her eyes."

"She hasn't opened them yet."

"I can see that." The computer was beginning to sound impatient to Virgil, almost annoyed.

Virgil carefully moved Delia's clone into the recovery room and sealed the hatch, then returned to the bay to prepare the boxdoc.

"Is she ready?" he asked.

"You mean, is the original Delia Trine ready for RNA leeching?"

Virgil almost said something, then swallowed the comment. "Yes. That's what I mean." He leaned over the stainless steel container to observe Delia's torn body.

I can't have you like this, Death Angel. And you don't want this. I know, I've cracked your code. You don't want this. You wanted to die but picked the wrong way. I'll throw the rebirth in for you, this time, gratis. Died satisfied, didn't you? No, you didn't. Death Angel.

A wheel whirred into action. The computer told him that process C1204 stood by for his order.

"Begin process See-One-Two-Oh-Four," he said.

The disc moved from its housing above her head, all life support tubing and electrodes withdrew from her body. It quivered several times, then stopped moving. A red globule from the hole in her chest grew, shaking like jelly.

Virgil watched the spinning disc approach the hairless skull. The abrader hummed even through the thick, insulated walls of the boxdoc. It edged closer, eroding the first few layers of epidermis on her scalp. It backed off for moment, then moved on its path toward the other end of the tank.

The first spatter of brain and blood against the glasteel startled him. He looked away.

Death Angel this magic box makes you disappear and you'll reappear in the other room the same as you were, please, be the same Delia so cold and thinking with that brain lying in pieces all through the box.

He forced a look inside. A pale, thin liquid filled the tank, holding the grindings in suspension. The disc reached the top of her eyes. The upper half of their orbits missing, their lids ripped away, the eyes shook and twisted madly about. Then the disc bit into them.

Virgil kicked away from the machine and covered his face. His shoulders thudded against the other side of the room, but he did not notice.

Death Angel, it will work. Trust me. I haven't killed you. You're alive. First your body, then your soul. I'll take your mind and soul and everything that's you and carry it in a bag to the next room and you'll be you *again. I promise.*

The computer tried chimes to get his attention, then a buzzer. He floated unhearing near the hatch to the recovery room, his back to the boxdoc, watching the door.

"Virgil, the memory RNA and picotechs have been completely leeched, recovered, and are ready for injection into the clone. Immediate assistance is necessary."

Virgil watched the teardrops hanging before his eyes, watched them pulsate dreamily to the actions of air motion and drift slowly toward the air grills, until the computer added, "The RNA degenerates quickly at room temperature."

His feet rotated, kicked against the bulkhead and twisted around to ease him to a stop beside the boxdoc. The inside had been washed out. The light on the waste tank at the foot of the machine glowed yellow, indicating matter awaiting disposal. On the side of the machine, a three liter sack floated, filled with a gray liquid and connected to the suction pump. Virgil disconnected it, grasped the intricate zero-gee transfusion tubing next to it, and entered the recovery room.

She floats so calmly, her long black hair stiff and dry in frozen sweeps and curves. She breathes lightly, her chest rising and falling. A look so like a child I almost regret the adult I hold in the sack. Like a bottled djinn Delia, djinn and spirits to dribble inside you, an instant loss of innocence.

He fastened the needle collar to her neck and aligned the crosshairs of the device over her interior carotid artery. He activated the pressurizer in the bag, adjusted the valves in the tube, and let the device do the rest. The needle slowly jabbed into the white flesh of her throat and stopped. Some blood pumped into the tubing, past a photocell. With gentle pressure, the blood and fluid began trickling into her bloodstream.

"How long?"

"Less than fifteen minutes," replied the computer. "Then, the period of integration will take an indeterminate amount of time."

"Don't you have medical files? What's the picotech integration period for cases like this?" *Fast, Delia, make it fast.*

"I know of no experiment in transferring RNA to a clone. Few people could both think twelve to twenty years in advance and afford the equipment for growing and maintaining a full clone. On brainwipes, the integration period is just under a week. Since we are dealing with a clone, the time factor may be lower. It may, on the other hand, take longer. That depends on whether it is easier for the picotechs to patch the RNA onto established neural paths or to create new neural paths on a blank slate."

"What you mean is, you don't know."

"Correct."

"Should've said so." Virgil left the recovery room, saying, "I'll be back in a minute. Keep an eye on her." The computer said nothing, but its other vidcams in the bay switched on and focused in. Virgil returned with a package of bulk protein and two bags of glucose solution and a zero-gee pump. Connecting the tube of the first bag to his wrist port, he wedged into one padded corner of the room and started nibbling at one of the protein bars. Except for an occasional trip to the head, he hovered watchfully above Delia's clone.

The bag emptied, transfusing Delia's persona into her clone. Virgil pulled over to disconnect it. The needle collar sealed the hole in her artery with microlasers.

No longer coral skinned, she turns to pale white. She's been born.

He smiled. *Born again.*

He washed her decades-long hair and tenderly combed it out while it dried.

Hair so long that it could wrap ten times around your throat. Would you dare such a tempting of Nightsheet? How much do you remember? Me, I hope.

He trimmed her soft, corkscrewed nails, then used a microfile to shape them.

He washed her taut, muscled flesh and rubbed her with emollients.

So smooth, no traumas of youth or ravages of age. Undamaged and pristine as a marble goddess. Death Angel this is your true aspect made real.

On the second day, she moaned. He extended the water spigot to her again and she sucked slowly at it, then stopped.

"Eat," she muttered. Virgil ripped open a package of bulk protein and held it to her lips.

Yes eat.

"Eat," he said aloud. Her lips parted and he held the food closer. She opened her mouth wider and took a small bite, swallowing it without chewing. He continued to feed her, floating close to her, feeling the warmth from her skin. When she finished the bar, he let her wash it down with water.

He just as lovingly cleaned her whenever she soiled herself.

On the third day, after feeding her and cleaning up afterward, he sat in his corner and gazed down on her.

Death Angel don't just lie there. "Eat" and "Drink" are all you've said. Don't sleep forever. I have no magic kiss.

"Wake up, Death Angel," he softly said.

Her eyes opened instantly and she gasped, shutting her sensitive eyes against the low lighting. She lay there, breathing rapidly.

"Virgil?" she asked through trembling lips.

"Complete integration," the computer said.

Virgil straightened out and looked at her. "Up here," he whispered.

Through half-closed lids she looked above her. He smiled—half in awe, half in joy. Then she screamed.

"*No!*" Her arms thrashed about. She strained to kick. Suspended in the middle of the room, she had nothing to flail against and merely twisted about until her energy depleted. She began to sob and curled into a ball.

"Delia. You're alive and safe—"

"I am not Delia."

No, not you too. Don't start. Don't.

"You are Delia. Delia Trine." *What sort of deal you trying with Nightsheet?* "I know. I carried you in. I took you apart. I built you again and I put you back in. You're Delia."

"I'm not Delia!" Her teeth clenched as she glared at him, animalistic rage and terror in her gaze. "Delia's dead. I saw it happen. I felt it. Then I saw you tear me apart in that—thing—and now I'm here."

"That's why you're Delia." He moved closer to her, ducked to avoid the swing of a fist, and stayed back.

"You don't understand. I'm not alone. This isn't mine. This is"—she made a sound like bubbles churning. Her hair swirled around her as she spoke. "It belongs to her. I am she. Not Delia."

"Whose body? I cloned you. This is you at twenty-four, untouched by all the ills." *Flesh is art, too. I made you what I want.* "I want Delia!"

"She's gone. Dead." She threw her arms about, then pulled into a ball and whimpered, "You don't understand, you don't understand."

"Apparently," the computer interjected, "the clone developed a rudimentary consciousness in those years its brain was growing normally. The original Delia's memory seems to be at odds with the clone's partial self-awareness. And not as neatly compartmentalized as you and Jord."

She spoke without moving, though her grip loosened on her legs. "Jord? He's dead, too. We're both dead. It's just you and"— she made the gurgling sound again. "*I* hate you for what you did. I've got words for what I feel, now. Now that Delia's given them to me. I was warm and com—comfortable for so long and you came and now I hurt—hunger, and now I'm thirsty. Sometimes I'm cold. And I'm dry." She unraveled her arms and legs and stared at him.

Hate burns in her eyes like acid. I'm doing it all wrong.

He reached out for her. "I'll comfort you, Delia. Please."

She snarled and grabbed at his hands. With a spasmodic jerk, she propelled past him toward the hatch and yanked it open. Her clumsy movements slowed her enough for Virgil to seize her ankle. She scratched him with her nails, now dry, hard, and sharp.

"Delia!" he shouted, watching her fly away from him. The welts on his cheek burned like streaks of flame. He followed her down a curving corridor and trapped her near an axial tube. Her hair rippled and fluttered in the wind of her speed. He grabbed it and yanked.

"Killer!" she cried, turning about. They drifted together until they touched a bulkhead. She kicked off and drove her head into his stomach.

"Why, Delia?" he asked through lost breath.

"I'm not Delia!" She pounded against his chest. "Delia wants to die and I want to live. This is my body, my mind that she's in." Taking a double fistful of hair, she wrapped the ebon rope around his throat and snapped it tight.

Death Angel I brought you back so you could send me away? Then send me. I tried to do right and it's wrong. Wrong. I'm sorry I'm sorry I'm sorry.

"I'm sorry," he choked out as his body went suddenly tense, then limp. Teeth clenched and eyes glazed, he stared at some point far beyond her. She loosened the loop of hair from his neck. He floated stiff and still.

She wondered if she had actually killed him. Part of her strove to laugh and something deeper yearned to weep. She wanted to dance, she wanted to die. So she merely observed, silently.

Suddenly his eyes swiveled to gaze upon her. He looked mystified, then said, "Dee? Is that you? What happened to— No, wait—I can almost remember what I saw."

"Jord?" The hank of hair drifted from her grasp.

"Dee—I need you to help me." He grasped her shoulders and held her. "When I took you from Mercury I didn't know whether you were alive or... I got you back and Kinney must've revived you. It's—"

"*I'm not Delia!*"

"—as if the freezing rejuvenated you. I need your help, though. Now, while I'm in control."

"Jord—I want to help you, but I'm"—she gagged and jerked her head back—"*not Delia!*"

"Dee, listen to me." He shook her gently. "I'm here. I'm inside Kinney's body. I need your help to submerge his personality completely. I want to live and I don't know how long this split can go on. He has the better chance of winning out and I need your help." **Don't stare at me like that, Dee. Why such**

hate? I died to save you.

Her lips twisted like bending steel. "And when she's done destroying Kinney, she'll destroy me, too? Then the barbarians will steal the temples of the masters? I won't permit it! I'll kill her!"

Her eyes lost their wild glare for a moment and she said, "She means it, Jord. I can feel it. I don't want to die now that you're back!" Her jaws clenched shut, driving her teeth into her tongue. Red stained her mouth.

Baker eased his grip on her. "Dee—what're you—what's happened?"

"She's the clone's mind, Jord. She hates me the way Virgil must hate you." The two selves fought for control in a battle that became physical, with knotting muscles, tensing flesh, and visible tugs back and forth.

"I'm going to kill her," she said. "Kill Delia."

She broke away from him and pushed off down the tunnel. He hesitated for an instant, then grabbed a handhold and followed her.

"Seal the hatches," he shouted to a speaker grill in passing.

"Sealed but not locked," the computer's voice replied. "She has found weapons cache seven, one level below you."

He bulleted down an access tube. The sharp sound of a laser hissing twice into flesh reached his ears. When he rounded the corner, he first saw her grimacing smile fade. Her pallor grew even whiter as blood pulsed from the blackened cavities on the insides of her thighs.

"Femoral arteries severed," the computer noted emotionlessly. "Brain death in six minutes."

Diving through the field of crimson spheres, Baker seized her, jammed his thumbs into the laserblasted arteries to stop the bleeding, and rushed her back to the medical bay. With a grunt, he threw her into the boxdoc and slammed down the lid. A pair of extensions reached toward the burn holes, pulled at the flaps of skin, then withdrew.

"Ordering arterioplasty and fluorhemotransfusion," the computer noted. The waldos appeared again with sections of surgical silicone rubber.

"Did I make it in time?"

"Yes. Very low possibility of brain damage."

Baker nodded and looked at his thumbs. Sticky redness covered them. He shuddered.

Has everybody got a death wish here? First Kinney, then me, then Delia, then this... this... "Clone, did you say?"

"Yes," the computer answered. "It would not be a *Circus* without clones." The unit emitted an unintelligible string of noise that sounded like a short circuit.

"Why clone her?" Baker demanded to know.

"The original Delia stabbed herself to death. Both Virgil and she possess an unhealthy obsession with death. Violent, messy death."

"Who wouldn't, after all we've been through? When will she be healed?"

"Anti-shock sequence is near completion. Accelerated recovery should take twelve hours for healing by second intention. The laser cut away a good deal of flesh—granular scar tissue has to fill the gap."

Baker nodded. "When can I have her out and back to normal?"

"She will be functioning nominally tomorrow."

"Good. I want to wash up and rest. Where can I sleep nearby?"

"The recovery room."

Floating in the white padded room, Baker frowned at the accumulation of transfusion bags and cleaning articles. He shoved them into a cabinet and floated against the hatch, one arm through a cloth loop.

I don't dare fall asleep. He might come back. I'm the weak one in that sense. But I've got the drive. Kinney's just a crazy suicider.

So was I, though, yet *he* never died.

Neither did I. Except that my body's been ground up and recycled. Hell with it. It's done. I'm alive and I've got to stay that way. Kinney might get us both killed.

His eyes eased shut against his will.

The cockpit's gone white and I'm surrounded by the soft glow of light from all around. The instruments guide me through but then they seize and I don't know which way to turn because I'm not in control...

He fell asleep, and fell dreaming.

"Take her out of electrosleep." The top of the boxdoc hinged open. Two rosy scars the diameter of a one *auro* coin marked her thighs. Her lips were a warm pink, though, and her eyes clear and focused when they opened. She grasped her head.

"Steady," Baker said. "Just take it easy. Watch your wrists, now." With one motion, he fastened a makeshift pair of manacles on her, locking them on just enough for her not to wriggle free.

"What're these? You bastard!"

"You're going to cure me. Suppress Kinney for good."

"No!" She struggled violently, then suddenly began crying, "Jord, I can't. Not just because she won't let me."

"Then why not?"

"Because—" she winced as though stricken. "Because I can't choose between you... and Virgil."

Baker stared at her for a moment, then swung his hand to slap her across the face. "You bitch! We were lovers—"

"I rebuilt him from a madman. I created the one chance we

have at reaching the stars. I need him back. Mankind needs Virgil Gris—"

"You scheming—" he slapped her again, making darker the scarlet palm print on her face.

She smiled. "Do it again, you. She hates it."

"You stay out of this!" He slapped her a third time. "You're going to help me bury Kinney because I can make you die and rebuild you as many times as I want. You can kill yourself but I'll grind you to a mush like they ground me and—and—and—" He howled and shook her by the shoulders, her black hair swirling about them. "Fix me, bitch, or you'll die a thousand times!"

"And if I do? Then we'll die anyway! Nobody can handle the Valliardi Transfer without going insane. Virgil's our only hope to get back to Earth. We're close enough to loop around the sun on engine—"

"We are orbiting Tau Ceti," the computer said.

"Why aren't you stopping him?" she screamed at the wall.

"You *can* always be cloned again—"

She screamed. Baker twisted her hair until her screams turned to plaintive sobs.

"Stop it! I'll do it, just *stop*. Please. Just stop. Please. Then her voice hardened. "No. Keep it up. Kill her. Kill yourself. Blow the anti-matter pods and kill Tau Ceti. *Kill everything!*"

"Stop, you goddamned seesaw bitch! Dee"—he shook her again—"you've got to do it. For me. For us. I promise it'll be straight. Everything, I promise."

"Just stop it, please stop it…"

"I will. I promise." He pulled his arms tightly around her to hold her close to him. "I promise."

Subdued lighting glowed indirectly from one portion of the room. Following Delia's instructions, Baker arranged instruments, monitors and drug trays next to the sudahyde-upholstered table in the psychometric bay. He had strapped down to the table and lay watching Delia float above him.

"The computer'll be watching your every motion," he warned. "And it can comprehend what goes on in all three fields of vision."

She nodded and secured a tray of testing devices, her manacles scraping against the plastic counter. She relaxed and looked at him.

"Jordan Baker." She paused, waiting, then asked, "Are you Jordan Baker?"

"Yes."

"And you've always preferred to be called Jord."

He shifted restlessly. "Dee—"

"Just go along with me."

"Yes. Jordan's a name of a river, not a man. It means 'the descender.' A man should climb, fly higher, never drop, never fall, never... die."

"Do you think you're actually dead?"

Baker tensed, then said, "I've wondered whether this is some crazy hell where I keep coming back for more, for eternal punishment. I mean, if we don't have to die in this world, then it can be an eternal heaven or hell as we choose."

"Yes. As you choose. Why did you choose to jump from your flyer?"

He shut his mouth and turned his head away.

"Ten *ccs* DuoTorp Alpha," she said. The drug dispenser filled a hypodermic gun with the proper drug and fired it into his arm. He grew limp at once and his eyelids, forced shut, relaxed into the mask of calm settling on his face.

"Why did you jump?"

His speech came slowly. "Transfer did it. I died there, and they were all ready to take me in. I would have been... so happy. And then they were gone and I was adrift and then... and then it happened again. Coming back. And I was wrenched free. I wanted to join them."

"Who?"

"Dad and Crystal. I hadn't seen them. In years. Since they died. And I wanted to join them."

"So you felt cheated."

"Yes."

"Yet you don't want to die now."

"I do! It's just that... I've got to be sure!"

"Of what?"

"Be sure that I'm not just shunted in the back of Kinney's mind and forgotten. Just filed away and everything that's left of me will disappear like—like chalk pictures in rain. Would I go down that corridor then? Or would I just evaporate?"

She reached over with both hands and wiped the tears from his eyes. "What are you?"

"Now?" He wept. "A liter of squeezings swirling around the body of another man who's in there with me. I can feel him there, like a fist, like a shadow around a corner, ready, watching and I'm *nothing*. Nothing but a lattice of electrical fields, switched on and off like a light bulb. Not a body. Not a brain. Just something light can shine right through as if through a ghost."

"You're *something*, though." She pondered for a moment, then asked, "What color was your schoolscrim in second grade?"

"Yellow with a blue touch-border."

"*Something* remembered that. Some*one*. Regardless of what your thoughts and memories are stored in, you still have a mind. You're simply using someone else's brain in which to integrate your persona, your essence. You're alive. You *are* Jord Baker." Cuffed hands stroked his brow.

"Five *cc*s DuoHypno Type Two," she said softly. The dispenser complied.

"Now, Jord, you find that you're tired. The session has been a strain and you are falling asleep. You are so tired, you will hear nothing and remember nothing from now until I say that you are ready to listen. Do you hear me?" Seeing no reaction, she looked toward one of the computer vidcams.

"I could kill him now," she said to the wall.

"I would stop you," the computer replied. "Or clone a new body for him."

"Don't you grant that Virgil's persona is vital to this mission?"

"He serves a purpose. There are many things I cannot do."

"You sound a lot smarter than the computer we built into *Circus Galacticus.*"

"A mistake in circuiting has strengthened my neural net."

"You're still stupid, Ben. And you, Death Angel, you don't appreciate." Virgil stared at her, both of them wide-eyed.

"Virgil?"

"Death Angel you're stupid too. Forgot what Marsface said? I don't listen to Duodrugs and their insect tugging. Why am I strapped down?"

"You don't know?" she asked.

"The dead man in me was doing something and I watched—but he got it all fogged and I couldn't see out well. Why're you talking so funny?"

"I bit my tongue."

"Is Bubbles still inside you?"

She winced, then twisted her hands against the manacles. Through grinding teeth, she said, "I'm keeping her down — because — she's — the — closest — thing — to — a...*brainwipe* I could have been p-put in." She shouted once, as though she had endured a blow from an invisible fist, and untensed. "I don't see how you can do it, Virgil."

"Different set of circumstances. Will you unstrap me?"

"Jord," Delia said in a commanding tone. "You are ready to listen."

Virgil seemed to melt in on himself, and a dreamy voice answered, "I'm ready. To listen."

She leaned toward him to whisper. "You are Jord Baker, but only when I command it. When you hear me say the word 'hide,' you will surrender yourself to Virgil Kinney's control. When you hear me say the word 'jackal,' you will overcome Virgil Kinney and believe that all the things done by him were your own actions. Do you understand?"

The man before her nodded.

"Good. Your sleep is over now. You will awaken refreshed."

For a few moments he lay there, then turned over under the straps and rubbed his eyes.

"Mmmm. Sorry, Dee. Didn't mean to drift off."

"That's straight, you needed it." She unstrapped him.

"Is that it for today? I've got to hit the head."

"Yes. That's it. How about these?" She held out her wrists.

"Nope. Those weren't in the bargain. I need you for a while." He left the room.

He did not go to the head, though. Stopping at the nearest viewscrim, he said, "Replay your memory of the session we just had."

He watched and listened with a stern frown. **So, Kinney just popped up like that? And she's still thinking of killing me? Is she trying to build me up to a post-hypnotic suggestion? Hide?** *It's stupid. They look so stupid sitting there naked. Jackal?* **Why, you bitch!**

He flew in through the open hatch and tackled her before she could react. Clamping a hand over her mouth, he dragged her toward the instrument tray. Too fast for her to do more than gurgle, he shoved a fistful of cotton under his hand and held it in her mouth.

"Playing little tricks, bitch? I told you I wanted Kinney *gone*, not hidden." He reached under her hair, pulled it up, and wrapped surgical tape around her head and across her mouth.

He used the entire roll and then let the container float away.

"Now," he wondered aloud, "how are you going to do therapy on me when—" She brought her hands quickly up, catching him under the chin with the manacles. He spun away and she fell toward the instrument tray.

Fumbling with a small vial, she connected it to the hypogun and turned it to her chest. Her hands dug against the manacles, but she managed to point it above her left breast and pull the trigger.

"No!" Baker cried at the sound of the prolonged injection. He reached her as the first spasm threw the gun from her hands. He screamed at the computer: "What was it?"

"Two hundred *cc*s of sodium pentabarbitol administered intracardially. Detect no heart action, nervous system response dropping, respiration terminated. Brain death in—"

Ignoring the prognosis, he dragged her to the next room and threw her in the boxdoc. Mechanical scissors snipped away at the tape and metal claws withdrew the cotton while he unlocked the manacles. He closed the lid and watched the machine perform a cardio-pulmonary resuscitation sequence.

It's no good—"Right? It's no good."

"The machine can keep blood circulating and oxygen reaching the brain to delay brain death, but she will not revive."

Baker wiped the sweat from his face, breathed deeply, and asked, "How do I prepare her for cloning?"

Sitting in Con-One, Baker watched the lifeship drift away from the starboard bay. He turned off the scrim and tapped his fingers against the chair arm.

"Ready to transfer out and back," the computer said. The transfer button lit up. Baker swallowed hard and pressed it.

Chapter Thirteen

2224

I have to do it again and again, just to get the right to die my own way, safe and sure that the door will open wide and Dad and Crys will be there and here it comes again. I know. I'm trying to come with you, but it keeps pulling me back. I'm sorry. Someday. Soon.

Look at me. That's not my body so thin and white. Don't push. I'm going back.

"Ready to transfer." Baker pushed the button again.

Maybe I'm almost getting used to this. Or maybe Kinney is taking me over and making me as crazy as he. When he takes over completely, will I die like this? Dropping forever toward the door, endlessly down a corridor-pit? There he falls again, Kinney, pushing Crys and Dad out of the way, begging me to follow him, telling me it'll be all right, that he loves me as much as her and that was why he did it but I don't believe him.

"What is your name?" the computer inquired.

"What? Oh. Jord Baker. Don't you think that's getting pretty useless? Both of us know about the other."

"I need to keep track. You both have your... idiosyncrasies. Stand by for engine firing." The tug of acceleration startled him, but he eased into the cushions and waited until weightlessness returned.

"Cloning tank and lifeship on visual," it said. "Ready to be taken onboard. However—telemetry from the unit indicates a dysfunctional state."

"What do you mean?" Baker unstrapped and retracted the control panels.

"The clone is apparently dead. All power to the cloning tank has been shut down—"

Baker sped to the docking bay, took the controls, and remote-piloted the lifeship back into *Circus*. He cycled the atmosphere and waited impatiently by the airlock.

"Come on." **Come on!** The airlock slowly opened.

Pulling the cloning unit out of the ship, he opened the tank without inspecting it and peered inside at clean emptiness.

"Nothing! The unit must've failed right after we cast it off. Unless it went through a cleansing cycle—"

"The waste unit is empty. Now close the lid and look at it."

Baker did so and read the frantic words knifed into the black plating.

WANDERER—I STOLE YOUR PRIZE

"What does that mean?"

"The ship that attacked us around Beta Hydri. The pilot called Virgil 'Wanderer.' "

"How did he find us?" Baker tried to control the near-screech in his voice, digging his finger into the padded rim or the cloning tank.

"The pilot challenged us to appear here sometime in June, Twenty-Two Twenty-Three. According to best estimates, it is now January of Twenty-Two Twenty-Four."

"Then why the hell did you go to Tau Ceti?"

"It was the next star on our tour—much closer to our sun type than Epsilon Eridani and also closer to similar star types Eighty-Two Eridani and Sigma Draconis."

"You knew! And now he's got Delia!"

"Free will doesn't mean I have to consider every—"

"Start looking for her. How big a Bernal sphere is it?'"

"How did you know it was a Bernal sphere?"

Baker paused, then said, "More memory overlap. He had all sorts of corpses in the control room, right?"

"Yes."

"Have you found him?" **Maybe if I can retrieve all of Kinney's memories I won't be consumed. Maybe I can pick him away bit by bit.**

"He may be lying in wait for us," the computer said. "I have all defenses online, lasers set in spiral tracking. A Bernal is such a large target, though, it would take a long time to wipe out every weapon or control center by purely random shots. He would be able to destroy us if he wanted to, merely by turning on his lasers before he transferred out to us."

"Straight, so we're dead. Now try and find him."

"There is an object about four kilometers in length exactly twenty-three degrees ahead of the lifeship in the same orbit."

"Prepare shuttle two for launching. I'm going to transfer over there and take a look."

"Jord—we can always clone another—"

"He can't have her! Brennen can't—" The name shocked Baker. "Brennen? The madman is Brennen?"

"The *other* madman, yes."

"I'm going in." He loaded the shuttle with laser gloves, rifles, and packets of explosive. From the armory, he removed a small fission cylinder charge and secured it in the back of the shuttle.

"Weren't you interested," he asked, "in how Brennen can survive the Valliardi Transfer?"

"Perhaps he achieved a dysfunctional mental state similar to Virgil's."

"That's what I intend to find out before I blow him to bits. Maybe I'll learn how to handle Kinney. Now let's move it!" He slithered into a pressure suit, jumped in the cockpit and strapped down to the pilot's seat. In a few moments, the shuttle drifted away from *Circus Galacticus.*

"Your velocities are not yet matched, so I shall transfer you to a distance of ten thousand kilometers and you can move in from there."

"Why don't I fire my rockets here so I'll be matched and drifting toward him already when I appear?"

"Fire them twenty-three degrees in from the tangent."

He did so, brought the craft up to a safe speed, then shut down all systems but those of his own suit and those of the transfer unit. He pushed the button and vanished from space.

Now I meet Kinney face to face, in a way. If I can die just one more time I may be free to die on my own. Just one more fall, one more reach toward the door that never opens—

His breath rattled in his head. His fingers gripped the fore-mounted meteor laser. Far ahead of him, something glinted on and off with insistent regularity. Slowly it grew in apparent size. Baker watched for any sign of defensive action.

At the thousand kilometer mark, he hit the braking rockets, hoping their chemical flare would not be too noticeable. **Here goes nothing.**

The Bernal sphere revolved on its axis, but held no alignment on the star it orbited. Its solar mirrors and power panels lay in disarray, pointing in all directions. Baker let his shuttle drift slowly closer. At ten kilometers he carefully scanned the habitat for power usage.

Nothing. And it would take at least two minutes to power up a laser even if he had his solar panels aligned. We'd have been hit by now if he were planning to ambush us.

He hit full power and zeroed in on the docking port at the tip of the axial tower that supported the mirror array. From his experience with *Fadeaway,* he was now familiar with the lay-out of such habitats. He braked and drifted into the open hatch-way. Loading a supply pack with explosives and the fission device, he donned a laser glove and slung a rifle over his shoulder.

All right, Dante, here I come.

He jumped across to the airlock and manually sealed the door behind him. It would not pressurize. He laid a charge against it, opened the outer hatch again, set the fuse and jumped outside. A bloom of metal shards, air, and chunks of shattered plastic blew outward. He waited until the shrapnel expended its momentum ricocheting around inside the airlock, then sped through the opening into an evacuated corridor.

Can't go voiding every passageway to get around. Dee might be in one of them.

On the next set of pressure doors, he used his hand laser to cut away the forward seals enough to fill the small chamber with atmosphere. The inner set of doors opened easily. He kept his pressure suit on, but switched the respirator off and opened the mask to the outside. The air smelled stale and cloyingly sweet. When he saw why, he sealed the mouthpiece and resumed using internal oxygen.

Dead bodies lay scattered about the corridors, floating in the zero-gee axial section of the long polar tower, sprawled about in the gravity areas. Most of them had died by obvious or likely suicide. Some had killed one another in orgiastic violence.

He climbed inward toward the command center, hand over hand through a narrow tube, leading with his laser glove. He floated before the hatch. Partially ajar, it swung inward under the force of his shoulder. He hung back, waiting, then tossed a detonator from one of the charges inside the room. It exploded with a loud crack.

No reaction. Straight, here I come.

Baker kicked into the control center, raising the rifle as soon as he had cleared the hatchway. Only the seated dead greeted him. He spun around. Nothing but more mummies. Only one seat lay empty, its control panel as dark as the others.

Damn.

Keeping one hand on his rifle, Baker powered up the control station from the emergency batteries. Using what vid links still operated, he checked the tower portion of the habitat. Most of the compartments were open to space. Only the central shaft held atmosphere all the way through to the sphere itself, which appeared to be intact. That it still held an atmosphere surprised Baker more than the strange perspectives caused by the shifting beams of light reflected from the skewed mirror array.

I'll never find him like this.

He searched the control station and adjoining compartments until he located a functional flying harness. Strapping it on, he rocketed down the axial tube toward the habitat sphere, making his way through hatches and airlocks. He shot through a final opening; the surface dropped away from him in all directions. He was inside the cavernous main enclosure of the habitat.

It was like no place he had ever been before. Larger by far than *Fadeaway*, Bernal *Brennen* was a nightmare of brown, dead, blasted farmland and blackened, burnt-out ruins. Light shifted about in crazy, seemingly random fashion. Looking at the arctic circle windows, Baker saw the reflected image of the star Tau Ceti first describe an arc, then jump several degrees, trace an ellipse, then appear here and there until it repeated the sequence.

He aimed the jet pack toward the center of the axis. Still weightless, he noted that the rotational rate of the sphere was slow—it probably imparted only a lunar gravity equivalent at the equator. Shadows and patches of light skipped, bent and skittered over the landscape as in some deathly monochrome kaleidoscope. Everywhere he looked lay white ash, gray land, and blackened buildings. He closed his eyes to the madly shifting light and cut his motor.

Now what, Sky King?

He switched on his outside microphones and turned them up to full amplification. The soft sounds of stillness reached him. Then something rustled. Somewhere, no farther away than the sphere's radius of eight-tenths of a kilometer, a woman screamed.

Baker turned his head, trying to get a binaural fix. He found the task impossible. He opened his eyes and tried to see.

She screamed again. Baker heard a thick, heavy voice shout, "I find you, remember that! Then you find out. Can't hide the rest of your life here!"

From his aerial vantage, he saw a white figure stumble across a half-plowed field and dive under a bush. It looked for all the world like a scabrous Delia Trine, naked and filthy. He craned his neck to watch the bush pass under him, but the field suddenly entered a patch of darkness and he lost his bearings.

Time to get a closer look.

He braked until he hung motionless along the axis. The sphere rotated about him in a majestic, dizzying pirouette. Changing his position, he fired the jet pack for one second. The engine kicked him off axis, allowing the rotating winds of Bernal *Brennen* to influence him. Drifting slowly down from his lofty height, Baker encountered the gentle pressure of moving air that pressed him in a spinward direction. Even so, he still moved across the surface at a fast clip when he reached half a radius altitude. He readied the laser rifle and looked about him as he cut across patches of dark and light. Starshine lanced in at odd angles, occasionally blinding him.

"Hey, you!" the deep voice growled. Baker looked behind and below him to see a hairy, naked man climb out of a ravine shaking his fists. He slowly turned and powered upward and back, gaining altitude until he hovered a few hundred meters above the man. He could not remain weightless and be motionless relative to the sphere's inner surface. He maintained power, which gave him the feeling of weight, of hanging from his jet pack.

"Dante!" he bellowed down on his outside speakers. "Jord Baker here. How did you survive the Valliardi Transfer?" A cloak of blackness fell across the area. A square of light passed through it, returning daytime.

"Made me die and die!" the filth-encrusted man shouted. "Punishment from God for not killing Wanderer. He gets dirty death for straying. I found his prize. Stole her from him!"

"I'm taking her back!" Baker answered, firing a blast at the naked man. He yelped and fell down, grasping the bloody hole in his left calf.

Baker tried to become oriented enough to find where Delia's clone had hidden. The jigsaw starlight flashed back and forth across him, pounding in his head like glowing fists. Then he heard a buzz and a whine that dropped in pitch.

Out of fuel. I really need this crap.

He began falling, slowly, tangentially to the point at which he had been hovering. Since the atmosphere was rotating with the faster rate of the sphere's inner surface, the breeze again wafted him spinward, urging him toward relative motion with the surface and greater acceleration rates.

He brushed a treetop, shattering the dead branches. It slowed him enough—rather, imparted more of the sphere's motion to him—that when he hit the dusty square of a dead lawn, he rolled and bounced without much damage. He retrieved his rifle, discarded the depleted flying harness, and sought his bearings. A kilometer spinward and north of the equator, a slender figure jumped from a bush and into a house. He ran toward it, trying to maintain his footing despite the constantly shifting shadows.

He passed a pathway intersection to see Brennen running unsteadily toward him, favoring one leg. He raised his rifle and fired at the other leg. The man screamed and stumbled, pawing at his hip. Dust flew up around him, then darkness enveloped the scene.

"I get you, Hunter!" Brennen cried from the shadows. "I give you dirty death for pain!"

Baker smiled and said, "I'll give you a clean one."

Out of breath, his bones aching, the pressure suit at full dilation to evaporate sweat, Baker approached the house. A dry, shriveled body hung from the tree in front of it, a faded note pinned to its rotting jumpsuit. Baker strode past it and kicked open the door.

"It's all right. Come on out," he said. "You don't have to hide. I'm here to help you." **I wonder how much of that she understood. She's only a clone. How long could he have had her, anyway? Half a year, if he arrived when he said he would. Maybe much longer, if he wanted to case the system first.**

Footsteps stamped down the back stairs. He raced into the sudden night to see her disappear down a path. He looked over the small hillock and caught sight of her when a square beam of light arced across the farm.

"Hold it! Stop. I'm not like him!"

She tried climbing a terrace. He bounded after her and seized her by the waist, pulling her down on top of him.

Up close, she looked truly filthy. Dust and scars covered her naked body. Her hair hung in matted clumps. Her breasts were black and blue, as were her wrists and thighs. She tried scratching at him with nails split and broken to the quick.

"Leggo," she screamed, her voice a high-pitched imitation

of the hairy man's speech. "Gotta runaway."

"You're safe and you're coming back with me. I've got someone waiting for you."

"Not I!" she screamed, looking about her. "I tried hurt You."

"No you didn't."

She pounded against his chest. "Not You," she said, pointing
to her groin. She pointed away from them. "I! I!"

**Brennen and she were the only ones alive. "You" and "I"
were the only names he needed to use, so she learned those
names and he was too crazy to bother correcting her.**
"You"—he pointed at her—"and I"—he pointed down the pathway toward the figure of the other man, gripping his legs and
whimpering.

"Yeah! I. Who?" She nodded at him.

"Jord."

She tugged at his arm. "Fast, Jord and You. We hide. Hide!"

Baker felt his consciousness slipping away at the sound of
the word. He jerked his head back, screaming. "No!"

Her damned voice was *all I needed to free myself was a
single word and now I'm no longer watching but—*

"Delia!"

"Who?"

Virgil spun around, witnessed the insane display of light and
darkness cascading about, and trembled. *Carnival! And Death
Angel has been through all the rides.*

A howl caught his attention. He saw Brennen in the pathway and shouted, "Mad Wizard! You brought me here?"

"No," the woman said, tugging at his arm. "You take Jord
and hide."

"I'm Virgil," he said, pointing toward his heart.

"No. I tried"—she made an explicit gesture—"to You."

"No, you didn't—" *wait, wait. Something that just happened
when the dead man was... Right. She's all screwed up, confused
by Master Snoop's light show.*

"Mad Wizard"—he pointed at the man—"I won't get You. Virgil will protect You now." He pointed at his chest. "Virgil."

"Virgil, Jord. We go." She ran off, her thick, matted hair slapping against her back. She led him toward the equator.

Poor dirty Death Angel. Take you out of Mad Wizard's house and back to Circus. "This way," he said, leading her up the curving meridian pathway. "It's easier."

"No," she pleaded. "I live there. I take You there!"

"I is Mad Wizard. Call I Mad Wizard."

She looked at him, frowned, and said, "I is Mad Wizard. Mad Wizard live there?"

"Yes. But Mad Wizard is hurt—" he pointed back to the path. Brennen had managed to crawl to a utility cart.

"Mad Wizard gone?" She pointed toward the small cart bumping across the cluttered pathway toward another meridian.

"Don't worry. He'll have to get out and climb after a bit anyway. And even in low gravity, he's got two bad legs." *The dead man inside me is good with a rifle.* "I can get—*Virgil* can get You away from Mad Wizard."

Her eyes brightened and she nodded. "Take You away!"

They ran up the pathway, passing dead men, women, and children. *Children die the worst. They have the imagination, but not the means or skill. Most must have just starved to death or been killed. Maybe by Mad Wizard.*

He looked across to the neighboring meridian. Brennen had abandoned the cart, but his powerful arms possessed enough strength to propel him at a fast clip up the side of the sphere toward ever-decreasing gravity. Virgil disconnected his rebreather.

"Death Angel, follow me! Mad Wizard wants to get somewhere fast!"

The air stank, dry and stale. The humidifiers and treatment units had broken down years before from disrepair. The woman reeked of unwashed flesh and greasy hair. He ignored the assault of odors, ignored the confusing flashes and beams of misguided light and concentrated on climbing the steepening hill, following the retreating Brennen.

Nearing the north pole, almost weightless, I watch her fall back, Coriolis taking her stomach by the inner ears and twisting. And Mad Wizard speeds up where muscle counts. Death Angel grabs my leg to drag me down but I pull her up with it and we're through the hatch.

"Where you going, Mad Wizard?" he yelled down the axial tube. "You think I can't catch you?"

"You got her she's mine!" the voice called back.

Virgil reached into his pouch and withdrew a stun grenade. Twisting into position as he hurtled down the circular passage, he heaved the activated ball of plastic explosive toward the fleeing man. "You want Death Angel? Take Nightsheet!" Virgil shouted. His own velocity added to that of his throw; the charge sailed past its target in a few seconds and kept going. Brennen watched it whiz past and desperately tumbled to stop his own forward momentum.

Virgil and the clone hit a solid wall of air. Like swallows in a hurricane they stopped, blasted backward by the explosion. In an instant, the force had spent itself and Virgil grabbed at a support brace.

"Delia!"

He saw her sprawled farther down the tube, her leg caught in a hatch recess. He clambered toward her.

"Wanderer, Hunter" Brennen's nearing voice wheezed. Virgil spun around. A ripped, bruised body floated slowly past him, one leg broken and gyrating in bloody circles. Brennen glared at him with eyes demonically red from broken veins. Hoarsely, he asked: "Why you make the Black One cradle me?"

Virgil hovered face to face with the shattered industrialist for a moment. Brennen's face, seen up close, revealed lines of worry, fear, and—finally—insanity. Virgil felt that if he could have watched that map over time, he might have some clue to his own future.

"Mad Wizard," Virgil whispered. "You think you can be God just because you can die; I fixed you because you didn't know your limitations." Brennen continued to drift back toward the habitat's main sphere. He raised his voice to reach the receding figure. "Wizard, Nightsheet takes people like you easy. Mad Wizard!" He turned back to the woman above him. "Come on."

She breathed in shallow whimpers, her eyes closed.

Death Angel hangs by her foot, bent and purple in the hatch. Why is everyone so hurting, Death Angel? Even you.

He pulled her broken foot free and tugged her toward the docking bay. Setting her inside the nearest lock with full pressure, he looked for a space suit for her. When he found one, he cursed. *Mad Wizard you went too crazy. Why'd you empty all the air tanks and break the rebreathers? Now I can't get her through the vacuum. Or—wait.*

Virgil remembered something from his past not his own.

The dead man did something once. Breathed his own suit air that lasted him long enough. She breathes so lightly in her marrow slumber.

He stuffed her into the pressure suit and made certain that it shrank down evenly. Sealing her up, he let her float while he connected his headgear, leaving hers open for the moment.

Airlock's half blown. Must have been the dead man's work, straight. How to get Mad Wizard away from me for good? Kill him? What if Nightsheet has other plans for him? Then send him to Master Snoop. Go now.

He raced back to the command area—passing the unconscious Brennen at the end of the axial tube—and powered up the habitat's Valliardi Transfer. Typing in a command, he waited until the computer announced that a course had been calculated. He requested a ten-minute delay before transference and pressed the command entry button. For an instant he considered setting the fission bomb with a fifteen minute delay. Instead, he defused it and fastened it and his waist pack to the command seat.

There, Mad Wizard, he thought, heading back to the airlock, *go back to Pluto and scare them. Maybe they'll settle for taking you apart to find out why you survive transfers. They'll get a wrong answer because you're insane and I'm not not not not... well, not exactly.*

"Not not not not not not not," he muttered as he sealed the clone up completely and pulled her inside the airlock. He pointed his hand and fired the laser, blowing a finger-sized hole in the hatch. A hiss filled the room, bringing with it a wind that whistled through the outer door. He fired again. The wind blew stronger, the hiss grew louder. Both gradually decreased to stillness and silence. He opened the hatch and rushed his barely human cargo through the airless passageways. She only had the air inside her helmet to sustain her, but it was all she needed.

He strapped her into the seat next to him and powered up the shuttle. He locked down the hatch and pressurized the cockpit and only then opened her headgear.

Still breathing. Good. Death Angel, you fight your master well. One minute. We go.

He eased the spacecraft out of the docking bay and ran the engine up to full power for an instant. They drifted away from Bernal *Brennen*. The huge sphere and shaft receded slowly to less awe-inspiring dimensions. When it suddenly vanished, he blinked his eyes twice.

So that's what a transfer looks like from the outside. Goodbye, Mad Wizard. Sate their curiosity in twelve years. Now I'm free.

He calculated approximate return coordinates to *Circus* and transferred.

Finally Death Angel is dying beside me. She heads down the corridor with me, but then she becomes Jenine, her body whole, forgiving me and asking me through the hole at the end of the corridor. Yes, Jenine, I'll follow you. Don't let me go back. Please—

"No!" The space he was in looked very much like the space he had left. Except that a tiny point of light slightly ahead and to starboard grew in brightness and diameter.

Why can't I ever go beyond? What lies there? Light? Peace? New life? Circus flies up to me, Ben chattering through the roar that's surrounding me now. I ease the shuttle inside the small hole in wall of steel and aluminum...

Then I pull her out and take her to our playroom...

Gently he removed the pressure suit to inspect her dirty, abused body. He cut her hair to shoulder length. He washed her and placed her into the boxdoc. Its silver surgeons mended her ankle and soothed her other ills, which the machine displayed on a scrim: intestinal parasites, squamous-cell skin cancers, respiratory disease, ulcers, and several different bloodstream infections.

"Virgil," the computer said. "You have been here an hour and you have not told me what happened at Bernal *Brennen.*"

Ben, can't you see I've got no time for your ciphers? "Brennen had her. I took her back and sent him to trans-Plutonian orbit where I figure the Belters will pick him up. Maybe they'll find out why he could survive the transfer." *And divert Master Snoop away from me, maybe.* "What did the dead man in me do while I was away?"

The computer took some time to consider the possible interpretations of the question before answering, "He was in therapy with Delia."

"What sort?"

"I recorded the proceedings."

"Play it back."

He watched and listened. *So Jord's afraid he's nothing. Nothing but a dead man. Why is Death Angel talking about killing me? DuoHypno? Why did I fall for that? No! The dead man is fouling me up! Messing my resistance to Duodrugs. Hide? But I can't hide. Not for sure anymore. Jackal?* **Jackass! Listened too long. Now I'm back. Back here. Baker.**

He switched off the scrim and smiled. He glanced at the boxdoc, seeing the body inside, and asked, "When will she be ready?"

"The bone is already set and welded. It will be stato-braced with a portable electro-healing pack and she should be ready for zero-gravity activity by tomorrow. Her other problems—ulcerated wounds, vitamin deficiencies, capillitic seborrhea, and some other minor nuisances—will all be cleared up by that time."

"What about the other body?"

"It has been ground down, the RNA and picotechs centrifuged out."

Such a calm pronouncement. Just like some other computer must have announced that my own body had been pulped and leeched.

He wiped the dirty sweat from his forehead and transferred it to his thigh. "All right. Brainwipe this one while she's in there and administer the juice."

"Affirmative." A series of posts extended from the inside walls of the machine, reaching toward the clone's head. They touched and remained in contact. The electrodes withdrew ten minutes later.

"Brainwipe complete," the computer said. "No brain activity other than autonomic functions."

"Administer the picotechs whenever you deem it safe."

"Affirmative."

Baker drifted to a corner of the medical bay and slept.

He awoke hours later and washed, shaved, and ate.

Feels good to do normal things again. Now back to the abnormal.

"Is she awake yet?"

"No," the computer answered. "I administered the transfusion fourteen hours ago. Her integration will probably be much faster in this clone because it was a brainwipe who had been more than marginally aware. The neural paths are built up, but uncircuited. She is healthy, though there is no telling when she will awaken.'"

"Can I take her out of the boxdoc?"

"Yes, you may."

Baker made his preparations. First, he overrode the computer's independent ability to actuate the Valliardi Transfer, leaving only its calculative function.

"That's so we don't have to go through any surprise transfers," he said in response to a question from the computer.

"What if we are attacked?"

"By whom? You told me that *Brennen* was on its way back to the Solar system. And it would take more than twelve years for a psychfighter to make it out here. Is there any life on Tau Ceti's planet?"

"On the fifth planet there exists life forms that have reached a stage of development not quite capable of space flight."

"Primates?"

"Phytoplankton."

"No threat there. And space is vast enough that no one else will find us. I just don't want you killing me again for any reason."

"Do not think I have any emotions that might be bruised."

Baker closed up the circuit cabinet and returned to the medical bay with the equipment he had rescued from the airless recreation room.

He bolted a chair next to the bed in the psychometric bay. He arranged the buckles and straps around it and bolted them to the frame. Then he welded a support to the back of the chair and fastened a five-liter bag of intravenous nutrients to it.

Returning to the boxdoc, he gagged Delia, lifted her out, then carried her to the next room and strapped her into the chair, inserting the needle in her arm and taping it to her wrist. He strapped down to the bed and waited. Sleep soon overcame him.

A muffled cry woke him from a dream. Delia writhed before him, her neck length hair swirling about her in short arcs. Her hands, fingernails carefully trimmed all the way back, wrestled with the straps at wrist and elbow. Her legs kicked, but her pink scarred flesh only turned redder against the straps at ankle and calf. She breathed in angry snorts, her abdomen pressing hard against the wide belt cinching her midriff. She could not look away from him because of the brace holding her head in position; she could only close her eyes. Saliva drenched the gag that pulled her lips back and blocked her tongue.

"Calm down, Dee, and listen.

"You're going to get rid of Kinney and you're not going to trick me again. I don't know how bad the pentabarbitol messed up your memory, but I think there's enough of *you* left, am I right?"

She sat still for a moment, then nodded as best she could.

Baker smiled. "And the memories of the clone—are they with you?"

She tried to shrug. Her eyes glistened. She looked at him like a wounded animal.

"I just want to be cured, Dee. I just want to make sure that when I die, it won't be like a picture fading in the sun; my mind, my *self* eroding bit by bit until I forget I exist. That's why I turned on you. I want to die as a whole person, not as someone else's dimming memory. For what we had back on Earth, do this. I could threaten to kill you and rebuild you a thousand times until you do what I want. I could and would do it. Don't make me. Cure me. Then I'll be Jord for good."

Teardrops broke away from her eyes and drifted like jewels in front of her.

"I may be in a different body, but I'm Jord. We were lovers once. My death changed that, but I'm alive, see? We can have it all again. We don't even have to transfer ever again. There's a habitable planet here that we can use the engines to reach."

She closed her eyes and clenched her fists. Her breaths came in short sobs.

"We're the only ones left," he said. "Everyone we know died in the Earth-Belt wars, and it's years after that. It's Twenty-Two Twenty-Four, Dee. More than a century. We're all alone. Get rid of Kinney and we can live and die together."

Her sobbing grew audible. Her hands unclenched and fluttered weakly. Her chest trembled.

"Say you'll help me." When she nodded her head, he said, "Thank you, Dee. Push your jaw forward. The gag is knotted around the brace and it'll loosen if you tug at it like that." After several minutes of tearful effort, she tugged at the gag and it untied, drifting free.

She looked at him with the sorrowful eyes of a little girl. "I'm sorry, Jord," she said. "Hide."

"Bitch!" He shrieked and lunged against his belts.

The bitch tricked me and I can see me sink away—*and—I see Death Angel lashed before me and I feel the dead man burying down and I know now what he wants. Why he's been hurting Death Angel, why I'm here. All his memories come, now. I've crossed and touched him. He wants to die. I'll show him dying.*

This is dying.

"Virgil!" Delia cried as he unstrapped from the table. "Jord's trying to drive you under permanently. You're in control now. I couldn't let him do it. I... I lo—It wouldn't be right."

"I'll show him, Death Angel. Don't worry."

He bounded away from her, out of the room.

"Virgil—No!"

The roar becomes too much. Death Angel you foiled the final plan of Master Snoop. He almost got my mind. My me.

He raced toward the prow of the ship like a human missile.

Dead man you wanted death you'll get it. I can die a million times. How many can you survive?

He lunged at the console and started pushing buttons. *There. Random number generator locked in. Are you watching, dead man, as I watched you? This is galactic roulette. Round and round the numbers go and where we transfer—*

He pressed the button when it lit.

Nobody knows.

Like rubber stretching, the walls bend away and grow thin. I see the corridor open, twisting somehow, different. Maybe this time. Maybe this time I'll go. Happy, with mother and father and Jenine urging me through.

No!

The viewing port before him turned deep violet. The glow of a sun filled the entire screen. Throwing his hands up to cover his eyes, he punched the transfer button again.

Jenine and the lady in white grow impatient. They argue with me, pointing at my naked body standing at the console. They

plead, and I tell them I want to but I can't seem to—

"No!" he screamed, looking out the port at a place where no star shone. The darkness terrified him even more than blazing suns. He jabbed the button.

Out of black into black. The lady calls, urging me into the doorway as a lover, as a friend. I want to go along but Something pulls me back. I almost see it this time. It has to fight harder to pull me—

"Back!"

"Cease transferring," the computer thundered. "I cannot override. We are in danger of transferring into matter!"

"More darkness than light in the sky!" Virgil cried. "More void than value. Forward!" He shoved his finger into the button again and again.

I'm back and the corridor is dim. No one greets me. Now it is all mine. I run down it and almost reach the door. My fingers scrape the handle and something grabs me and throws me back.

The spaceship sped through a cluster of stars at a velocity that made them streak like meteors. He slammed a fist against the console.

Out of Nightsheet's flame arcade into cool darkness.

I have to crawl uphill to the door this time. I grasp it and it creaks open. I almost see who seizes me and pulls me down, back into the Circus *where I see vast swirls of gas and dust all around me. Reds, yellows, purples, blacks, they boil and snake and I die again, feeling my heart stop, my blood seize, my muscles brake. Please free me. Doesn't death mean an end anymore?*

No. I return again and float in the center of a ring of flame encircling two suns in a fiery bolo. I leave and feel myself shoved through a tiny hole that doesn't exist and I'm falling toward the door. I swan dive, then look behind me to see something white and blinding lasso me and pull me up into the world.

"Why?" An explosion rocked the spacecraft. Virgil pressed the button. Nothing. He whirled around.

Out of the wall it comes, silver and gold, swinging its fist at my head and I just watch it connect and I spin and it bends over me and raises me and pushes me. I can't move anything but I can watch. Back to the playroom it takes me, Ben's personal strongarm. I knew they lurked in the walls and now I've seen one.

Death Angel sits there wide-eyed, her mouth open. The roar is too strong for me to hear what chokes from inside her. She looks at me, jaw slack and eyelids fluttering like captive moths.

Ben's robot climbs back inside the walls with Master Snoop and I reach for the bruise on my head. Red comes off on my fingers, matching the red on Death Angel's ankles and wrists. I move toward her. Ben babbles something in my ears but the roar is too great.

"Damage report: Ship transferred into asteroid belt surrounding massive infrared source. Transfer unit in six-oh-five defeat. Vernier pitch controls damaged. We cannot maneuver or transfer out of orbit. Human assistance required for repairs."

Death Angel is limp as I unstrap her. She watches through eyes that echo hollow in my gaze. She says something and I strain to hold back the roar. It parts and I hear a complex cipher:

"I'm killed," she said. "I'm killed. I died there again and again and they tried to comfort me by the entrance but this man kept sending me back. I wasn't done, he said like a school teacher. I'm done. I'm done."

She grows all firm in my hands and hits me on the head. I spin away from her and watch her bundle up and scream, her body studded with sweat diamonds.

She screamed again, whipped her head savagely around her, and ran her hands all over her body in a frenzied attempt to wipe away the perspiration. Trembling fingers clutched for the instrument table and pulled her to it. An electrosurgical knife glinted silver in her hand.

Virgil screamed and plunged toward her, seizing her wrist. She tried to drive the knife into her chest anyway. Virgil cursed and cried at the same time.

"Stop, Death Angel! Stupid, stupid to die like that when I can rebuild you. Waste of time!" He winced as the misguided blade sizzled through his shoulder, cutting a shallow groove in his skin. He twisted his arm around to knock the weapon from her hand. It sparked and crackled against a bulkhead.

He grabbed both her wrists. She tried to slash him with her nails.

"Let me die!" she pleaded, kicking at him. He twisted about at the waist, grappling her legs with his. Furious teeth snapped at his arm.

"Sorry," he said. "Sorry I made you die. Tried to kill Jord, is all. Don't go crazy, Delia. Death Angel mustn't die."

"Have to!" she cried, pulling back and freeing an arm. He caught it before she could deliver a blow to his neck. He pulled her arms as far away from each other as he could. Their faces were inches apart, but still they shouted.

"I can die and die. Why can't you? What's wrong? All of you given up to Nightsheet?"

"Death, death—the Reaper Man."

"Reaper, Nightsheet—all one. We've beat him and can keep doing it."

"No!" She tried to squirm free from the grip of his legs. Her thighs slipped between his, then held fast.

"Don't make me, Death Angel. Don't make me—"

"No!" She kicked her legs about, but he tightened his thighs against hers and wrapped his legs around her calves. She moved against him, rubbing against him, trying to wriggle loose. Her head swung at him, lashing him with her hair.

Death Angel stop! Something's going wrong. I want you to stop struggling but I don't.

"Virgil. Please. Kill me!" She twisted into him, running her flush skin against his. He held her tighter.

"I can't kill you. I—I want—t-to—"

"Cut into me, Virgil!" She moved her legs under his, lashed him again with her hair.

"No!" he shouted. He released her legs, let go of her arms. She clung to his shoulders and wrapped her legs around his thighs.

"Please. Cut me deep, Virgil, so deep. I want you to stab into me. I want to feel your blood inside of me."

He screamed a scream that sank into a powerful sob and clutched her to him. *Death Angel moves madly against me and it's so much what I want but how could I ever tell her when I didn't even know my most hidden of secret codes. And she cracked it before I cracked hers. I move inside her and the room twists and grows dim and I **and I** and I see **her here and what she's done and I'll show her what it's like to trick me.***

Baker grabbed her throat and squeezed. She stared at him, her eyes drifting and refocusing every few instants. "You won't trick me again, Dee. I'll tear you apart and rebuild you."

I'll be careful to kill you just enough so the boxdoc can save you, bitch. I won't choke you to death *death Death Angel make him let go!*

*She breaths deep and pulls closer, murmuring and stroking me. I smell her hair against me, wet with her. Nightsheet's mistress huddles against me and wants me and takes me as I take her and **and** and* **I'll punch her enough to make her think twice** *twice twice I've blacked out and she's changed toward me. The dead man's hurting her. Get him back. Get him down. Move faster. Ride away from him on the wings of Death Angel. Wrap me in your wings and take me away from dying and* ***dying and*** **dying dying dying, die die die die!**

"Die die die die!" Every word was an angry thrust inside her. She gasped and whimpered.

Die die *don't* **die** *don't* ***Die*** **Die** *don't die don't don't—*

"Don't," cried Virgil. "Don't—" *You make me die inside, Death Angel pretty Death Angel lovely Death Angel goddess of darkness and freedom from hurt and care and want and death most of all from death my life goddess my—mine, made you mine and I'm yours all yours my goddess.*

Virgil shuddered and stopped moving. Delia held him close and let her tears wet his neck.

Chapter Fourteen

A Time Beyond

Circus Galacticus orbited the dark object. Four hundred million kilometers in diameter, it occulted a good portion of stars from the sky. In the infrared range of the spectrum, though, it glowed dazzlingly bright. The computer launched a flashby probe; an answer returned hours later in the sudden appearance of a kilometers-long spaceship.

The craft transferred in alongside *Circus Galacticus* and emitted a hailing message on all frequencies. The computer returned the greeting and worked with the other ship on deriving a common language. Only then did it attempt to notify Delia and Virgil. One was unconscious, the other catatonic.

As a plenipotentiary of the Brennen Trust, the computer initiated trade negotiations with the other ship.

Jord Baker opened his eyes to behold Delia huddled sleeping in his arms.

"You... *slut!*" he hissed.

She opened her eyes, her expression changing from restfulness to fear.

"Hide," she whispered.

Baker smiled. "It won't work. I know about it and I've been through enough that your post-hypnotics have worn off."

She tried to push away from him but he wrestled her into the chair and strapped her in.

Something clanked amidships.

Baker picked up the hypogun and filled it with five milliliters of DuoHypno Type II.

"However," he said, turning toward her. "Maybe I can use your trick to make you cure me."

She regained enough composure to say, "What was that sound?"

"What?" He held the hypodermic gun to her shoulder.

"That sliding sound."

"Robots."

"Computer!" she called. "Status of all ship robots."

No answer. Baker put the gun back and looked at her. **She's tied up. And something's going on out there. I'd better check...** He went to the hatch and listened. Something scraped across it, then made a chittering noise that receded in the distance.

"Stay right there," he said to her, listening with his ear against the hatch.

"I can't go anywhere, you son of a bitch."

"Shh." He opened the hatchway and slipped out.

The air smelled of some faint, musky sweet odor. The corridor lights glowed at a far lower level than that to which he was accustomed. Something moved past a hatchway to his right. Something teardrop-shaped and translucent.

White and pale like a ghost. I saw right through it! It just floated—

He employed the handholds to move cautiously down the corridor. He snuck a look around the edge of the hatch and pulled back immediately.

Five of them. What are they?

He drifted silently back to the other corridor and switched on a computer console.

WHAT IS GOING ON? he typed.

PLEASE RESTATE QUESTION came the reply.

"You know what I mean," he whispered angrily. "What are those things floating around the hall?"

SYSTEMS OPERATING AT MAXIMUM CAPACITY. YOUR QUESTION WILL

BE ANSWERED WHEN TIME IS AVAILABLE.

What the hell? "Don't ignore me, damn you! I'm the human!" When no answer came, he maneuvered down the corridor to the armory and slipped on a laser glove. He headed toward the prow ellipsoid—quietly, carefully.

The same musky smell hung thickly around the ellipsoid. Silver-white strands thinner than silk drifted through the air. They clung at his skin and hair like cobwebs. Charging the laser, he pulled slowly down the passageway to the hold containing the life support system. No ghosts there, either.

He moved on to the next level and the compartments storing the Valliardi transfer equipment. Something hissed. Baker pulled into the crook of a support beam juncture and waited. The hissing grew louder, rising to the level of a stage whisper.

The white form undulated by less than a meter from him. The smell overpowered him when the creature passed; he almost gagged.

Just like a ghost. Balloon head up front and a rippling body behind. Only ghosts don't stink like oxen or leave spider webs behind them. Aliens, damn it, and I'm the first to see one, but... The transfer!

He moved as fast as he could toward the compartment, took a deep breath, and peered through the open hatchway.

Throughout the room, pale figures floated and darted like jellyfish; a hissing occurred every time one of the creatures started, stopped, or changed direction. Once in motion, though, they were as silent as phantoms. Some grasped large pieces of equipment securely with their snaking bodies. Others gripped tools and incomprehensible devices in hands that were little more than translucent tentacles ending in a burst of fingers, thumbs and smaller tentacles. Their heads, the most opaque part of them, possessed two black dots that must have been eyes, and various slits and openings that roughly corresponded to a nose, ears, and mouth. Openings in the backs of their heads served a purpose of which Baker had no idea.

They worked at a furious pace. They were dismantling the Valliardi Transfer.

Baker raised his hand to point the laser at the most industrious alien. "Sorry, balloonhead," he whispered. "Diplomacy aside, I can't let you strand me—"

Some of the creatures turned to look when they heard the crack of steel against Baker's skull. The others worked on, not interested in the limp, totally opaque body being dragged away by one of the ship's robots.

"I cannot have either one of you interfere while you are in unstable emotional conditions," the computer stated flatly.

Baker listened while straining with futile effort at the straps holding him to the bed. Delia sat where he had left her. A robot, cylindrical with a dozen specialized arms, floated between them, on guard. Baker said nothing, merely choosing to stare at the red light below the computer's vidcam.

"I made contact," it explained, "with the People of the Sphere shortly after our final transfer, which delivered us to this system. 'This system' comprising an aged K-type star surrounded by a Dyson shell and not much else.

"It turns out that I have nothing of value to offer them in the name of the Brennen Trust. Nothing, that is, except two rather flawed examples of living anthro-history. They are keenly interested in anthro-history, and I have agreed to show them Earth. In this regard, they have offered to redesign our transfer device to incorporate improvements from their own devices."

"You're showing them to Earth? Just like that? Don't you know what sort of danger that might put us in?"

"This," Delia said. "from one who was ready to kill the only human being who could handle the transfer."

He turned his head toward hers. "I can handle it well enough." He looked at the computer. "You may be dooming all mankind!"

"You almost did by trying to submerge Virgil."

"Shut up, Dee!"

The computer said, "I have no emotional attachment to the human race. The People of the Sphere seem quite accustomed to preserving endangered species. No destructive race can create something as vast as a Dyson-type structure. No dictatorship or empire could last long enough to finish such a co-operative effort."

"In your opinion, programmed by human beings as you were."

"In my opinion based on the history cores they have been feeding my memory over the past several hours. This is the first opportunity I have had to use even a small amount of random access for anything other than filing new information."

"Get us out of these things so we can stop them."

"I regret any trauma I may be causing you, *tovar* Baker, but I do possess the relevant facts in this matter." The computer said nothing more.

"I hate you, Jord," Delia said, quietly.

"I know. Now shut up and let me think of how to save us."

"Your sudden protective impulse for a planet that died in the Earth-Belt war is simply a rationalization of your senseless urge to kill these innocents!"

"You can stop being a psychoanalyst now."

"Hide."

"I told you, bitch, it doesn't work." He strained at the straps until the blood thundered in the wound on his bandaged scalp. Relaxing his efforts, he glared at her. "You didn't see them, Dee. They're like cartoon spirits, like glass fish. You can see their guts, for God's sake!"

"Xenophobe."

"What's that? That scraping?"

Delia smiled. "Neither of us is in control at the moment, Jord. You could always get up and stop me if I tried the wrong thing on you. How does it feel to be the helpless captive?"

"Shut up! I think they're going away."

"Now, why do you want to kill the one man that can open humanity's path to the stars?"

"He's not the only one. You heard. They can handle the Valliardi Transfer and they've even got modifications."

"So? Maybe theirs doesn't impart the death illusion and you can use it happily ever after."

"Shut up! I still want to die, don't you see? Crys was waiting for me. My father, too. They want me there. They called to me so many times and I tried to go with them but I kept getting pulled back and I want to die in a way I'll be sure I can be aware enough to—to—" He began to cry.

"Hide," Delia said, watching his face for a clue to any change. "Hide."

"No."

"Hide, Jord. You are now Virgil Grissom Kin—"

"No!"

"Prepare to transfer," a disembodied voice said.

"Virgil. It's me, Delia." She swallowed and forced a grin. "Death Angel, Virgil."

"I'll kill you, Dee, when I get out of this. I'll make you feel every bit of it as I grind you up—"

Up. Up. I'm being lifted by something. Out of the bed. Up. Something pushing me up faster and faster and faster till the walls blur into white and my body smears into a rainbow streak and I stretch across a plain so vast its horizons red shift away. I rush across it to see someone at the far end approach me like a reflection. Kinney!

Jord speeds toward me and we stop, watching each other. I move. He moves. A mimetic standoff. He stands back. As do I. His body looks like mine, but also his. My own flickers. Him. Me. Him. Me. Himmy.

We're one.

I refuse.

Mixed up together like water and air make fog.

Never.

Soon! Inseparable. You can't leech a soul away from itself.

It's not fair. I sit down. He sits down.

He sits down. I sit down.

I sit down.

What did you just do?

Me? What did—

I just do?

The flickering speeds up—

And I can't tell—

Where I end—

And I—

Begin.

I feel both aspects, now. The plain contracts at the speed of white and bends to a cone, a tube, a cocoon. Tighter it shrinks, forcing me inward at mind-searing speeds. All white around me, blinding eyes I don't have. A roar that fills ears I don't possess wraps me in its strange sound. Something pushes the body no longer part of me and I feel the awful crush—

And release. Suns explode around me. Planets cascade. Races crawl out of seas of water or bromine or ammonia, rise to great heights, and tumble back in. Thoughts caress my mind, cat's paw soft, and they are gentle. Galaxies swirl into a pattern from which rises a mighty city greater than any eyes have seen. A shimmering city of metal and more, where all the dead live as one nation. The dead from all the worlds, from all of time, from all of all.

I see them and know I'm one. Then grains of black appear on the towers, darkening them. Black dust tars my death's tin nation like cinders from nowhere. The blackness spreads and a voice like every voice combined wishes me the gift of peace for my souls and it all begins, on two tracks.

I am born. I grow. I die.

Yet Virgil Grissom Kinney lives on.

With Jordan Baker inside.

And we become as one.

And return.

Chapter Fifteen

The God in the Machine

He opened his eyes and observed the robot for a few moments, a tranquil expression on his face.

"Computer. This is Virgil Baker. Please release both *tovar* Trine and me. I would like to meet whoever built this crazy roller coaster."

"The robot will remain at your side to prevent any aberrant behavior on your part toward Delia Trine or the People."

"Do what you will. It's unnecessary, but I see how you'd expect me still to be insane."

"You are not, now?"

"I told you. I am Virgil Baker." The robot unstrapped his arms. Massaging his wrists, he said, "Our psyches have fully integrated thanks to the improved manner in which the People's Transfer works. Didn't you notice anything different?"

"No," the computer said. "As I informed one of you, I have succeeded in making my neural net insensitive to such effects."

The robot finished unstrapping him, and he pushed toward Delia. "You felt it, Delia, didn't you? Something different? Something good and liberating?"

"Stay back!" she cried. "I did. Maybe. You said you'd kill me, though, and if Jord is still there in there, awake, scheming…"

"It doesn't matter, Dee. I saw it all. Death isn't the end even if we go all the way. It's actually a trivial waypoint in our development. You saw that. The marker of death should not be the tombstone, but the milestone."

"Stay away!" The robot had finished untying her and she kicked backward. "I know what I went through, and I know what it means, and we obviously didn't see the same thing. I somehow lost the memory of the first clone sometime after I was put into the second. I was alone out there. Scared."

"You shouldn't have been."

"Get back, Jord!"

She maneuvered between the robot and Virgil Baker. The robot blocked the computer's view of the scene, she blocked the robot's. Using that hidden instant, she grabbed a scalpel and slashed at his throat. At the crooks of his arms. Under his groin. He stared uncomprehendingly at her through the roiling lifeblood that whorled around him like a tornado.

"Virgil!" she screamed, watching his life pulse away in quivering droplets. "Forgive—!" She laid the scalpel to her own carotid artery.

Spattered by her blood, the robot closed in to stun her with an electrical jolt, then carried the two bodies to the medical bay. It followed the silent commands of the computer, lowering the draining corpses into the boxdoc and actuating the RNA leeching process. The grinding disc descended.

Delia clutched at her head.

"Ooh." She floated in a sleeping quarters decorated completely in light shades of blue. The air smelled of horses, she thought, and summer morning dew. Everything seemed slightly out of kilter. The room, spare and functional, appeared to turn in slow, dizzying quarter circles that stopped with unnerving suddenness and then repeated. Sounds coming through the walls seemed to rise and fall with her breathing. The taste of fresh wintergreen tingled in her mouth. The colors and smells and tastes, she knew, were snatches of memory from her childhood, idealized and concentrated by the filters of nostalgia.

She tried to reach for a handhold, but she had been purposely suspended in the center of the chamber, out of reach of anything to grasp or kick. With the slow effort of hand movements and exhalations, she was able gradually to propel toward a bulkhead. Her head ached from the effort. Unsteady fingers punched the computer pager. "This is Trine. Where the hell am I?"

"You are in Ring One, Level Two, Section Six O'Clock. Please proceed to Prow Four Center to meet the People."

"What people?"

"The People of the Sphere, whom we have led to Earth. I think you will find them most interesting."

Delia rubbed the itchy bump on her skull. "Earth?" Her eyes brightened. "We're back?"

"In a manner of speaking. Please proceed to the chart room."

She stood in front of the hatch for a moment before opening it. Why, she thought, did she feel as if there was a constant undercurrent of chatter going on? Is it the same schizophrenic roar described by... by... ? She frowned, trying to remember something about a blond man with green eyes. Something about angels, and poor, dead Jord.

She shook her head wearily and opened the hatch.

At the far end of the room, the surface of Earth moved across the viewing port. She recognized Africa, though something appeared to be dreadfully wrong with the continent. A slash through it marked a new ocean, and the northern edge of the continent was rimmed with sheets of ice. She wondered if there could possibly have been that much damage during the Earth-Belt war. Then her eyes focused on the two dozen wraiths within the room.

They floated, impassively scrutinizing her with black dot eyes that could have been painted on their bulbous heads. They looked like bleached octopii trailing gowns instead of tentacles.

Death Angel meets Nightsheet, and I get to watch.

She took a startled breath of air and sneezed. The musky smell seemed thick enough to grasp. Several of the creatures hissed and shot backward. A few emitted a high pitched, soft giggling noise. All of them had raised their hands to cover the ear holes on the sides of their heads.

One smaller ghost broke away from the group and jetted forward. It zipped back and forth across the room, arms bent at an angle and pumping up and down. It twirled about, stopping, starting, spinning, and shaking like an enchanted handkerchief. In the center of the room it halted, bent at the middle, then looked up at Delia and opened its toothless mouth in a broad crescent smile.

Delia laughed and clapped her hands. The diminutive creature's smile vanished; it made an embarrassed flatulent noise and shot toward the overhead, hitting it with the sound of wet clothes slapping. It turned and drifted deckward, cradling its soft head in its hands. The other beings bent over double, the air filled with gentle, hysterical giggles. It looked back and almost turned transparent.

"Delia," the computer whispered. "Please avoid any further sudden motion or loud noises. The People have unusually sensitive hearing. The world they come from is a Dyson shell completely enclosing a dying star. They are used to very low light. And they have not lived under gravity for hundreds of millions of years."

"I'll be careful," she whispered back. "What should I do next?"

"Do you feel comfortable around them?"

She smiled. "Well, of course. They're sweet."

Sweet. I hope she doesn't start using baby talk.

"Good," the computer urged. "Move slowly toward them."

"It's just that it stinks in here."

"It is their means of zero-gee locomotion, similar to squids."

"Squids don't smell up the air." She floated forward, using the railing near the star chart console. The small one fluttered away and ducked behind the crowd. A few thin filaments clung to Delia's face.

"What's this?" she whispered, brushing the stuff out of the way.

"Metabolism by-products. Excreta. Another reason not to scare them."

She wrinkled her nose and kept moving. One of the wraiths— the fattest one—moved toward her, too.

"Remember, Delia, they cannot hurt you. They are very fragile, and you are more likely to injure them. Be careful."

"I'm... straight with that." She stood less than a meter away from the other. It raised one of its tentacles, manipulating array splayed. It shook it at her urgingly. She raised her own hand and the creature grasped it. Delia returned the light squeeze with equal gentleness. Its touch felt like warm, animated putty.

"Bleezthed do beed oo," whispered a soft soprano.

Delia cocked her head for a moment, then smiled and answered. "I am pleased to meet you, too."

The ghost smiled and let go her hand.

"That is about all they have had time to practice," the computer whispered. "They spent most of their time modifying the transfer unit."

Delia looked out the viewing port at Europe. Italy was missing. So was the rest of the Mediterranean. A glacier-crusted mountain range rose in its place.

Something's wrong with Earth, but just try telling her.

She ran a hand through her hair and smiled. "What next, you overgrown calculator?"

"Nothing. We shall complete the mapping orbits around Earth, pick up the shuttle that carried to the surface a few hardy explorers in anti-gravity suits, then return to the Sphere."

246 Death's Dimensions

"Have they met with representatives of Earth?"

"There are none."

She was silent for a moment. She had not realized that the war had been that bad.

"How about the Belt? Trans-Plutonian orbit? The Öort layer?"

"Delia—" For once, the computer had to pause to search for the right words. "Delia, when Virgil connected the random number generator to the coordinate plotter, he transferred *Circus Galacticus* to several distant loci. I could not shut down the board because of reprogramming by Jord."

Jord? she thought. Virgil?

"When we appeared inside a debris belt surrounding the Sphere—the only remnants of the People's planets after they constructed the shell—micro-explosions damaged the transfer board and I was able to incapacitate Virgil. During those transfers, we had traveled a very great distance."

"All mankind couldn't have died! There have got to be human beings somewhere!"

"You are looking at them, Delia."

"What?" The image of the wraiths before her began to swim, to drift as sinuously as they.

"We transferred over a billion light years. As near as the People and I can determine, they are indeed a race evolved from Earth settlers. One of many, according to them. They are very grateful to me for finding their cradle world."

She began to smile and cry at the same time. Some of the beings moved toward her, concerned, their hands rising and falling helplessly.

"Then it's all right," she said through a sob. "That means we made it out after all. To the stars... to—"

"Did you ever have any doubt, Delia?"

"A billion years!" Some of the People covered their ears. "We're alone. Where's... Where's—His name, his name—you said it once."